Paul Harding was born in Middlesbrough. He studied History at Liverpool and Oxford Universities and obtained a doctorate at Oxford for his thesis on Edward II and Queen Isabella. He is now Head-master of a school in North-East London and lives with his wife and family near Epping Forest.

The House of Crows

Paul Harding

headline

First published in 1995
by HEADLINE BOOK PUBLISHING

First published in paperback in 1996
by HEADLINE BOOK PUBLISHING

10 9 8 7

ISBN 0 7472 4918 0

Printed and bound in Great Britain by
Mackays of Chatham plc, Chatham, Kent

HEADLINE BOOK PUBLISHING
A division of Hodder Headline PLC
338 Euston Road
London NW1 3BH

To Father John Armitage,
also a good priest working in the East End of London.
With every good wish.

PROLOGUE

No one will ever forget the night the demon came to Southwark. Spring was making itself felt, even in the derelict alleyways and filthy runnels of Southwark where it squatted on the south side of the Thames. The rains had washed the shit-strewn cobbles and the clouds had begun to break as daylight died on that fresh spring day. Apprentices and traders packed away their stalls. The high-sided dung-carts rattled through the streets as sweaty-faced labourers worked to clear the mess and refuse from the open, swollen sewers. The men worked cheerfully, remembering the pennies they had been promised. Not even a bloated corpse of a cat or a dog put them off the prospect of a bowl of soup and a blackjack of ale, once their labours were done.

Pike the ditcher, parishioner of St Erconwald's in Southwark, was also out. He slipped by the church and into the Piebald tavern where the Dogman, the Weasel, the Fox and the Hare were waiting for him. They sat on upturned casks, around a table pushed into a shadowy corner, their unshaven faces hidden by the deep cowls pulled well over their heads.

'You are late!' Dogman snarled.

Pike swallowed nervously.

'He who comes late,' Weasel piped up, 'always pays the tax!'

Pike groaned to himself: he called Tiptoe the potboy across and ordered five blackjacks of ale. Near the casks at the far end of the tavern, Joscelyn the one-armed taverner watched them all carefully. Pike closed his eyes and scratched his tousled beard. Did Joscelyn suspect what he was up to, Pike wondered? In which case Brother Athelstan, his parish priest, would be taking him aside next Sunday to give him his usual sermon. Pike's face softened. As always, Athelstan, dressed in his black and white Dominican robes, with his olive-skinned face and gentle eyes full of concern, would lecture Pike about the dangers of treason and the horrors of the hangman's rope.

'Well,' Dogman snarled, 'how goes it, friend?'

Pike broke from his reverie. He leaned across the table, determined to show these representatives of the Great Community of the Realm that he was not frightened.

'When Adam delved and Eve span, who was then the gentleman?' Pike chanted.

The four rebel leaders, identities hidden under their strange names, nodded in unison. Nevertheless, they watched Pike intently for any sign of unease or lessening of fervour in the support of their great cause. Tiptoe brought across the blackjacks. Pike handed over one of his precious coins and, once the boy had left, the ditcher raised his tankard.

'To the Great Cause!' he murmured.

The other four acknowledged his salute and sipped at the tangy-flavoured drink.

'Well?' Hare asked. 'How goes it in Southwark?'

'The pot bubbles,' Pike declared darkly. 'Our young King Richard is only a child, his uncle, John of Gaunt, although only regent, acts like an emperor. Taxes are heavy, discontent swirls like dirt in the water; even the merchants protest.' He slammed his tankard down. 'A Parliament has been convened at Westminster,' Pike continued excitedly. 'John of Gaunt is demanding more money but the Commons refuse. They might impeach certain ministers.'

'Pshaw!' Narrow-eyed Weasel smirked and sipped from his tankard. 'What do the fat ones expect? Clemency and pardon from a man like Gaunt?'

'So, when will you come?' Pike asked.

'Times and dates are not for you,' Hare retorted. 'But, at a given sign when Jack Straw our priest sends out the burning cross, then we will come.'

'Men from Essex, Kent, Suffolk, even as far north as the Trent,' Dogman exclaimed, 'will fall on London as fast as lightning. Like fire in the stubble, we will burn and cleanse this city from Southwark in the south to Cripplegate in the north.'

'Aye,' Weasel added. 'Purify it with fire and sword. There'll be no kings or princes, no great councils or Parliaments. The lords of the soil will be destroyed and the meek will inherit the earth.'

Dogman leaned across the table and seized Pike's jerkin. 'And the men of Southwark?' he asked.

'We will be good and true,' Pike replied. 'We will seize London Bridge and the gatehouse at both ends. We'll be there when you march on the Tower.'

Dogman watched him closely. Perhaps he noticed Pike's gaze shift a little or his lower lip tremble.

'Are you still with us, Pike?' he demanded softly.

'Yes, it's just . . .'

'Just what?' Fox leaned closer, grasping Pike's hand and squeezing it tightly.

3

'Will everyone die?' Pike blurted out hoarsely. 'Will no mercy be shown?'

'None whatsoever,' Fox replied, shielding his face with his tankard. 'The lords, the bishops, the priests. Why, Pike, do you know of a man worth saving?'

'Brother Athelstan,' Pike hissed, dragging Dogman's hand from his jerkin. 'Parish priest of St Erconwald's,' he continued excitedly. He looked over his shoulder fearfully but Joscelyn had now gone. 'Athelstan's a good man,' Pike whispered. 'Gentle and kind. He loves his parishioners, turns no man away.'

'He's a shaven pate,' Weasel replied. 'A friar. Those who are not with us,' he intoned, 'are against us. Those who do not collect with us, scatter us abroad.' He studied the determined set of Pike's mouth. 'However, mercy shall be shown to those who show mercy.'

'Such as?' Pike asked.

'He will die quicker than the rest.'

The rebel leader finished his drink and slammed his tankard down on the table. 'We shall leave,' Dogman said, getting to his feet. 'In a month's time, Pike, we shall return. We will want to know how many men you can muster; how many bows, how many pikes.' He grinned at the pun on the ditcher's name.

The rest of the group filed out. Pike did not bother to see them go. He was just about to relax and bawl for another tankard when he felt his shoulder gripped: Dogman pushed his narrow, lean face up against his; so close that Pike flinched at the man's sour breath.

'You will not,' he whispered, pushing a dirty cloth into Pike's lap, 'be hearing from Wolfsbane!'

Pike gulped at Dogman's reference to their representative in

4

Cripplegate Ward. 'Why? What happened?' he stammered.

'He turned traitor and talked too much.' Dogman squeezed Pike's shoulder.

Pike sat frozen. When at last he glanced over his shoulder, the rebel leaders had left. He slowly undid the dirt-stained cloth and stared in horror at what it contained: a human tongue, grey and shrivelled, though its end was still bloody. Pike, still clutching the grisly burden, his stomach heaving, dashed from the tavern. Outside, he threw the rag into a sewer and, unable to control himself, knelt and vomited up everything he had drunk. An hour later, a more chastened Pike made his drunken way along the narrow alleyways. He had gone back into the Piebald and downed another quart before the terrors had subsided. Yet the ale had not made him any more courageous, and Pike was deeply regretting not following Brother Athelstan's advice. He reached the end of the alleyway and, swaying from side to side, staggered towards the steps of St Erconwald's Church.

The ditcher stopped: the door was locked and he could see no light. He looked across at the priest's house but that, too, was cloaked in darkness. Pike tapped the side of his red, bloated nose. 'I know where you are,' he muttered.

Staggering back, Pike looked up at the top of the tower. Against the dark blue, starlit sky he saw the glow of flames and a dark shape moving. 'You're watching your bloody stars!' Pike muttered.

The ditcher blinked wearily and sat down on the steps of the church. 'I wish I was with you,' he grumbled. 'Well away from this nonsense.'

Pike cupped his face in his hands, musing disconsolately on his situation. London was now a seething bed of unrest. Taxes were heavy, food in short supply, the French were burning and harrying towns all along the coastline. Worse, out in the open countryside the peasant leaders, representatives of what they called the Great Community of the Realm, plotted a savage rebellion which would sweep away Church and State. Pike sighed. Sometimes it sounded exciting, but would it happen? And, if it did, would his second State be any better than the first? And what about Brother Athelstan? Would he die? Would he be hanged outside his church door as the rebel leaders had vowed all such priests would be? And if the rebellion failed, what would happen then? Pike, swaying drunkenly, got to his feet. Brother Athelstan was correct. Every gallows in London would be heavy with their rotten human fruit. There would be gibbets from here to Dover and the regent would spare no one.

'Are you well, Pike?'

The ditcher spun round and groaned. Watkin the dung-collector, squat and fat as a toad, his broad red face made even brighter by the ale he had drunk, swaggered across, swinging his spade like a knight would his sword.

'Good evening, Watkin.' Pike blinked and tried to keep his voice steady.

Watkin was leader of the parish council, a post Pike deeply coveted. He was unable to seize it, not because of Watkin, who was a born fool, but because of Watkin's redoubtable wife who had a tongue as sharp as any flail. The dung-collector stopped before him, resting on his spade.

'You've been drinking.'

'That makes two of us,' Pike retorted.

'Our wives will moan,' Watkin added slyly, 'but not so loudly if we tell them we have been on parish business.'

Pike smiled conspiratorially and both men staggered along

6

the alleyway, each rehearsing their stories to soften the anger of their respective spouses. Half-way down they were joined by Bladdersniff the beadle, who was as deep in his cups as they were. There was nothing for it but to slake their thirst at a small ale-shop before continuing their journey. By the time they had finished, all three could hardly stand, so they linked arms and stumbled back to the church. As they confided to each other in loud whispers, they could sleep in the death-house there and make fresh excuses the next morning.

By the time they reached St Erconwald's, Athelstan had apparently left his tower. All three stole into the cemetery, making their way around the mounds and weather-beaten crosses to the death-house in the far corner. Pike, finger to his lips, told the other two to wait while he fumbled with the bolt.

'Oh, Lord, save us!' he whispered. 'It's open already.'

He staggered in, took out his tinder and lit the dark yellow tallow candle which stood on its brass holder in the middle of the table. No sooner had he done this when he heard a sound in the far corner. Grasping the candle and whirling round, Pike stared in horror at the dark shape squatting on top of the parish coffin. The shape moved closer. Pike saw the glittering eyes, the terrible bared teeth and that dark, blue-red face in a halo of black, spiky hair.

'Oh, Lord, save us!' Pike shrieked. 'A demon from hell!'

He staggered back against the table. The demon followed, lashing out with its paw, gouging Pike's cheek, just as the ditcher dropped the candle and fell into a dead swoon to the floor.

On the following morning, in the Gargoyle tavern near the palace of Westminster, Henry Swynford, knight, one of the representatives from the king's shire of Shrewsbury to the present Parliament sitting at Westminster, sat on the edge of his bed and stared into the darkness. Few would have recognised the pompous knight with his leonine, silver hair, arrogant face and swaggering ways. Sir Henry was a knight born and bred. He had fought with the Black Prince in France and Navarre and was regarded in Shrewsbury as a person of importance: a warrior, a merchant, a man of the world, steeped in its workings. He had seen the glories of the Black Prince and carried the golden leopards of England across the Spanish border. Sir Henry constantly reminded the aldermen of all this as they gathered in Shrewsbury's shire hall to discuss the sorry state of affairs: the regent's pressing demands for taxes and the Parliament summoned in the king's name at Westminster. Sir Henry had boasted how he and his friends would only grant money and agree to fresh taxes if the regent listened to their demands for radical reforms.

'We need a fresh fleet,' Sir Henry had trumpeted. 'The removal of certain ministers, economies by the regent and the Court, as well as a fresh Parliament summoned every year.'

His speech had been greeted by roars of approval: Sir Henry and his friends from Shrewsbury and the surrounding countryside had received the elected vote. They had swept into London, taking the best chambers in the Gargoyle (hired so cheaply by one of their stewards) and sat together at night to plot and whisper how matters would proceed. Now all that had changed. In the room next door lay Sir Oliver Bouchon, a fellow representative. His water-soaked corpse had been dragged from the Thames, dead as a fish, not a mark on his body. Everyone said it was an accident, but Sir Henry knew different. Sir Oliver had come to him the previous afternoon just outside

St Faith's Chapel. He'd plucked Sir Henry by the sleeve, led him into a shadowy alcove and pushed the candle, the arrowhead and the scrap of parchment bearing one word, 'Remember' into Sir Henry's hands.

At first Sir Henry had been puzzled though alarmed by the change in Sir Oliver's demeanour: agitated and pasty-faced, he seemed unable to control the trembling of his hands.

'What is it?' Sir Henry had whispered. 'What does this all mean? An arrowhead, a candle and the word "Remember"?'

'Have you forgotten?' Bouchon had snarled. 'Are you so puffed up with pride, Henry, your soul so made of iron that no ghosts from the past can enter your mind? Think, man!' He had almost shouted. 'Think of Shropshire years ago, in the dead of night: a candle, an arrowhead and the word "Remember"!'

Sir Henry had gone cold. 'Impossible!' he'd whispered. 'That was years ago. Who would tell?'

'Somebody did,' Bouchon retorted. 'I found these in my chamber when I returned early this afternoon.'

And, snatching them back, Sir Oliver hurried away before Sir Henry could stop him. At first Sir Henry had dismissed it but, this morning, a dreadful creature, the Fisher of Men, accompanied by the king's coroner in the city, that fat-faced fool Sir John Cranston, had brought Bouchon's water-soaked corpse back here. The coroner had set up court in the great taproom below, drained three tankards at Sir Henry's expense, declared Sir Oliver had probably died from an accident and left the corpse in his care. Sir Henry had paid others to wash and clean the body. Tomorrow morning he would hire a carter and an escort to take it back to Sir Oliver's family in Shrewsbury.

Sir Henry considered himself a hard man: over the years, other comrades in arms had died on the bloody battlefields of

France and Northern Spain. But this was different. Sir Henry glanced at the table, and the source of his fear: the candle, the arrowhead and the scrap of parchment bearing the word 'Remember' had now been sent to him. He had found them on his return from Parliament and neither the landlord nor any of his servants could explain how they had got there. Sir Henry reflected on the past. He remembered the words of a preacher: 'Unpardoned sins are our demons,' the priest had declared. 'They pursue us, soft-footed, dogging our every footstep and, when we least expect, close their trap.'

Was that happening now, Sir Henry thought? Should he go out and warn the others? He seized the wine cup from the floor and drained it. He would pay his respects to Sir Oliver first. The priest must have finished his orisons by now. Sir Henry clasped his swordbelt around him, opened the door and went into the gallery. The door to Sir Oliver's room was half open, the glow of the candlelight seemed to beckon him on. He went in. Sir Oliver lay in his coffin but there was no sign of the priest. Sir Henry turned and saw a dark shape lying on the bed.

'Lazy bastard!' Sir Henry muttered.

He went across to the coffin and stared down. His heart skipped a beat: three bloody red crosses had been carved; one on the corpse's forehead and one on either cheek.

'The marks!' he muttered. 'What?'

He started, but too late. The assassin's noose was round his neck. Sir Henry struggled but the garrotte string was tight and, even as he died, choking and gasping, Sir Henry heard those dreadful words.

'Oh day of wrath, oh day of mourning, heaven and earth in ashes burning. See what fear man's bosom rendereth . . .'

Sir Henry's dying brain thought of another scene, so many

10

years ago; corpses kicking and spluttering from the outstretched arms of an elm tree, bearing the red crosses on their foreheads and cheeks whilst dark-cowled horsemen chanted the same lines.

CHAPTER 1

It was Execution Day on the large, bare expanse of Smithfield. Usually the place was busy with various markets selling horses, cattle and sheep; the area around Smithfield Pond would be thronged with stalls and booths offering leather, meat and dairy produce. The crowds always flocked there to see the freaks and performing animals, whilst the puppet-masters, fortune-tellers and ballad-mongers from all over London, the quacks, the gingerbread women, the sellers of toy drums and St Bartholomew babies would do a roaring trade. Men and women of every kind came to Smithfield: nobles and courtiers in their silks and taffetas, merchants in their beaver hats, the red-headed whores from Cock Lane. Their children would frighten themselves, and each other, by staring into the glassy eyes of the severed pigs' heads which were piled high on the fleshers' stalls. Nearby, in the Hand and Shears tavern, the Court of Pie Powder would deal out summary justice to those caught pickpocketing, foisting or indulging in any other form of trickery. Consequently the blood-spattered pillory posts were always busy. Wednesday, however, was Execution Day. The great six-branched gibbet would dominate the marketplace, nooses hanging; the condemned felons would be brought down from Newgate, past St Sepulchre's, stopping at the Ship tavern in Giltspur Street so that the condemned felons could have one last drink before they were turned off the ladder.

Sir John Cranston, King's Coroner in the city of London, always hated such occasions but, on that particular Wednesday, the feast of St Hilda, it was his turn to be king's witness to royal justice being carried out. He sat on his great, black-coated destrier, chain of office around his neck, his large fat face pulled into a mask of solemnity, his kindly blue eyes now cold and hard. Now and again his horse would whinny at the crowds thronging behind him but, apart from scratching his white beard or twirling the ends of his moustache, Sir John hardly moved.

'I should be home,' he moaned quietly to himself. 'Sitting in the garden with Lady Maude or watching the poppets chase Gog and Magog.'

Sir John had four great passions: first, his wife and children; secondly, a love for justice; thirdly, his great treatise on the governance of the City and finally, a deep affection for his secretarius and assistant in rooting out murder and horrible homicides, Brother Athelstan, the Dominican parish priest of St Erconwald's in Southwark.

'And your claret,' Sir John whispered to himself. 'Not to forget your London ale and sweet tasting malmsey.'

Sir John never knew in what order these passions should really be listed. In fact he loved them all together. Cranston's idea of heaven was a spacious London tavern full of sweet-smelling herbs and blossoming roses where he, Athelstan, Lady Maude and the poppets could sit, talk and drink for all eternity.

'I should be home,' Sir John growled again.

'I beg your pardon, my lord Coroner?'

14

Cranston turned and gazed at Osbert, his court clerk, whose brown berry face was wreathed in concern, his dark little eyes screwed up against the morning sunshine.

'Nothing,' Cranston muttered. 'I just wish the buggers would hurry up and get here from Newgate.'

As if in answer, the crowd at the far end of Smithfield gave a great roar and began to part, allowing through the garishly painted death-wagon, driven by the executioner and his assistant all clothed in black from head to toe. The horses they managed had their manes hogged with purple-dyed plumes nodding between their ears. In the cart stood three men, dressed in white shifts, shouting and gesturing at the crowd. On either side walked lines of soldiers from the Tower garrison, halberds over their shoulders. Behind the cart two bagpipers played a raucous tune.

Why all this mummery? Cranston thought. In his treatise on the governance of the City, he would recommend to the young king that such executions be abolished and confined to the press-yard of Newgate Prison. Cranston stood high in his stirrups: he gazed over the heads of the crowd pushing against the wooden barricades guarded by city bailiffs and beadles.

'The pickpockets and foists will be busy, Osbert,' he remarked. 'They love a crowd like this.' Sir John glared, as if his popping eyes could seek out and threaten any one of the myriad of footpads so busy slitting purses and wallets.

The execution cart drew closer; finally it entered the bare expanse in front of the scaffold. The three prisoners, their faces dirty and unshaven, were pulled down, their hands tied. The Franciscan, also standing in the cart, eased himself off, still intoning the prayers for the dying, though, from the expression on the faces of the three felons, they couldn't care a whit.

15

'Let's make it quick!' Cranston snapped, raising his hand.

The heralds on either side of him lifted their trumpets, but the mouthpieces were full of spittle and they could only squeak.

'Oh, for heaven's sake!' Cranston barked as a chorus of laughter greeted their efforts.

The heralds mumbled an apology, lifted their trumpets again. This time a shrill blast silenced the clamour of the crowd. Cranston nudged his horse forward and stopped in front of the three condemned felons.

'You are to be hanged!' Sir John declared. He nodded at Osbert to unroll the parchment.

'You, William Laxton,' the clerk proclaimed in a loud voice, 'Andrew Judd and William the Skinner have been found guilty by His Grace's judges of assize of rape, abduction, stealing hawks' eggs, stealing cattle, poaching deer, letting out a pond, buggery, desertion from the royal levies, coin-clipping, cutting purses, robbery on the king's highway, filching from the dead, conjuring, sorcery and witchcraft. For these and divers other crimes you have been sentenced to be taken to this lawful place of execution. Do you have anything to say before sentence is passed?'

'Yes. Bugger off!' one of the condemned shouted.

Cranston nodded to the executioner but the fellow just stood, eyes glaring through the eyelets of his mask.

'What's the matter, man?' Cranston barked.

'They've got no goods, no chattels,' the executioner replied. 'The law of the city is,' he continued sonorously, 'that the goods, chattels and clothes of the condemned felons belong to the hangman – but they've got bugger all!'

'I wouldn't accept that!' one of the felons shouted. 'If you're not being properly paid, let's all go home!'

16

Cranston closed his eyes. Behind him he could hear the murmur of the crowd who had sensed that something was wrong. He looked at the officer of the guard but he just shrugged, hawked and spat.

Cranston dug into his purse and, ignoring the jeers of the felons, tossed a coin at the executioner who deftly caught it in his black-gloved hand.

'And there's my assistant.'

Another coin left Cranston's purse.

'And there's the bagpipers.'

Cranston threw one more coin.

'And what about the horse's bedding and straw?'

Cranston's hand fell to the hilt of his sword.

'Now, don't get angry!' the executioner called out.

Sir John leaned down from his horse. 'Satan's tits, man! Either you hang these men now or I'll do it for you. Then I'll hang you, your assistant, and there'll still be room left for the bloody bagpipers!'

The executioner took one look at Sir John's red face and bristling white moustache and beard. 'Lord save us!' he mumbled. 'You can't blame a man for trying. I have a wife and children to support. Oh, well, come on, lads!'

The executioner and his assistants, aided by the soldiers, put the nooses round the felons' necks and pushed them up the ladder. Sir John raised his hand. Behind him, four boys started beating a tattoo on the tambours.

'God have mercy on you!' Cranston called out.

He closed his eyes, his hand dropped, the ladders turned, leaving the three felons kicking and twirling in the air. The crowd fell silent even as Cranston, his eyes still closed, turned his horse's head, muttering at Osbert to find his own way home.

17

Sir John was through the throng, almost into Aldersgate, when he heard his name being called. He stopped, pulling at the reins of his horse. 'What do you want?' he asked.

A young knight, dressed in chainmail, his coif pulled over his head, his body covered by the red, blue and gold royal tabard, pushed his horse closer and took off his gauntlet.

'Cranston, the coroner?'

'No, I'm the Archangel Gabriel!' Sir John replied.

The young man's face broke into a smile. He crinkled his eyes, giving his hard-set face a boyish look.

'I'm sorry,' Cranston growled, clasping the man's outstretched hand. 'I just hate Execution Days.'

'No man likes dying, Sir John.'

'And your name?'

'Sir Miles Coverdale. Captain of the guard of John of Gaunt, His Grace the Regent.'

'Lord John of Gaunt, Duke of Lancaster, Knight of the Garter, the king's beloved uncle.' Cranston grinned as he recited the long list of titles. 'And what do you want with me, Coverdale?'

'I don't want you, Sir John. I have enough problems at Westminster.' Coverdale pulled back his chainmail coif and wiped the sweat from his face.

Sir John noticed how the man's moustache and neatly clipped beard covered a deep, furrowed scar just below his lower lip.

'His Grace the Regent sent me,' Coverdale continued. 'He's at your house in Cheapside.'

Cranston closed his eyes and groaned. 'There was no need to send you,' he muttered. 'I'm going there direct.'

'Your Lady Maude thought different,' Coverdale replied,

18

keeping his face straight. 'She mentioned a possible assignation in the Holy Lamb of God.'

Cranston turned his horse's head and, tugging at its reins, continued his journey, secretly marvelling at Lady Maude's God-given ability to read his mind.

They went down St Martin's Lane, through the muck and offal of the Shambles, and left into Cheapside: the market was doing a roaring trade, yet the area outside Sir John's house was strangely deserted. His front door was ringed by burly serjeants wearing the royal tabard, and archers dressed in the livery of Sir John of Gaunt. As the crowd swirled by these, Cranston caught their dark looks and muttered curses.

'The regent.' He leaned over. 'Your master is not popular.'

'No man who governs is, Sir John.'

Cranston pulled a face and dismounted, his eyes surveying the crowd. 'Leif!' he roared. 'Leif, you idle bugger, where are you?'

Some of the bystanders looked round in surprise but then quickly made way for the skinny, red-haired, one-legged beggar who came hopping through with the agility of a spring frog.

'Sir John, God bless you, is it time for dinner?'

The beggar leaned on his crutch and, gaping round Sir John, stared at Sir Miles. 'You have company, Sir John?'

'Look after the horses,' Cranston snapped. 'And, when my guests leave, take mine across to the Holy Lamb of God.'

Leif hopped in excitement: if Sir John had company, that not only meant gossip which Leif could dine out on, but also, perhaps, one of Lady Maude's tasty pies and a cup of the coroner's best claret. Sir John, a deep sense of foreboding furrowing his brow, led Sir Miles through the cordon of soldiers into the house. The maids huddled in the kitchen, terrified of the men in half-armour who thronged the hallways and passageways. Sir John brushed by these, marched up the stairs, along the gallery, and threw back the door to his solar with a resounding crash. Lady Maude sat at the far end of the canopied fireplace. On either side of her, Cranston's twin sons, bald, blue-eyed, two perfect peas out of the same pod, clung to her green sarcanet dress, their eyes fixed on the gorgeously dressed stranger who now dared to slouch in their beloved father's chair. The stranger rose as Cranston came in, straightening the murrey-coloured houppelonde or tunic which fell down to long, leather, Spanish riding boots. Around his neck was an ornate, heavily jewelled collar clasped by a golden brooch carved with the double 'S' of the House of Lancaster.

Cranston drew himself together and bowed. 'My Lord, you are most welcome to our house.'

His guest's sunburnt face broke into a smile: he languidly stretched out his jewelled fingers for the coroner to clasp.

'Cranston, it's good to see you.'

Sir John stared into the light-green eyes of John of Gaunt, Duke of Lancaster, quietly marvelling at Edward III's most handsome son. He reminded Cranston of a silver cat with his light blond hair, neatly cut moustache and those eyes – never still – betraying the man's vaulting pride.

Gaunt let go of his hand. 'Whenever I see you, Sir John, I always remember my dearest brother, the Black Prince,' Gaunt smiled. 'He spoke so highly of you.'

'Your brother, God rest him, was a powerful prince, a noble warrior,' Cranston replied. 'Every day, your Grace, I remember him in my prayers. I deeply regret that he did not see his own son crowned king.'

'My dear nephew also sends his regards,' Gaunt replied

sardonically. 'He talks of you, Sir John. You and that secretarius of yours, Brother Athelstan.'

Behind him Lady Maude had risen, her small, pretty face creased in concern: she warned Sir John with her eyes and a slight shake of her head not to bait this most powerful of men.

'You wish wine, Sir John?' she called out.

'Aye, a glass of Rhenish, chilled,' Cranston replied, winking at her quickly. He knelt, stretching out his arms. 'And some marzipan for my boys.'

The two poppets staggered from their mother's skirts and ran across, bumping into each other, almost knocking the regent aside as they threw themselves at their father's embrace. Cranston kissed them quickly on their hot, sticky faces.

'Fine sons,' Gaunt smiled down at him.

'Go and play,' Cranston whispered.

'Dog not play,' Stephen stuttered. He pointed to the far end of the solar where Cranston's two wolfhounds, Gog and Magog, lurked beneath the table. Cranston grinned. The dogs were frightened of no one except Lady Maude. He could tell by their woebegone expressions that they had both received the sharp edge of her tongue, warning them to behave whilst guests were in the house. The boys left, following their mother outside whilst Cranston took his own chair, waving at Gaunt to take Lady Maude's. Blaskett, Sir John's steward, served them wine on a tray, his large, sad eyes watching his master intently. From the passageway outside, one of the poppets began to wail. Blaskett raised his eyes heavenwards, put the wine cups on a small table between Cranston and Gaunt, and silently withdrew. Cranston picked up his cup, toasted the regent and slurped noisily.

'I am a busy man, Cranston.'

'Then, my Lord, we have something in common.'

'And what great crimes confront you now?' Gaunt taunted back.

Cranston could have given him a list a mile long. The foist he was pursuing, the counterfeiters, the pimps and apple squires, the defrocked priests dabbling in sorcery . . . Still, as the poor Cranston concluded, the rogues were always with him.

'Cats,' he announced bluntly: he enjoyed seeing Gaunt almost choke on his drink.

'My lord Coroner, you jest?'

'My lord Regent, I do not. Someone is stealing cats from Cheapside.'

'And should that be the concern of the city's coroner?'

'My lord, have you ever met Fleabane?' Cranston replied. 'He's a trickster, a cunning man. If it moves, Fleabane will steal it. If he can't move it, Fleabane will try to sell it. Now and again I catch him. He's punished, but he always returns to his old way of life, regarding my hand on his collar as a part of life's rich tapestry. In other words, my lord Regent, the criminals of London will remain as long as the city does. However, there are other crimes where the innocent are truly hurt, and the theft of these cats is one of them. An old lady in Lawrence Lane has lost six, her only companions. A merchant in Wood Street, two. Now the old lady in Lawrence Lane has lost her family, the merchant in Wood Street possibly his livelihood. You see, he buys in fruit and cereals from outlying farms and stores them in his warehouses. If there is no cat, the mice and rats thrive, bringing infection and spoiling what is good.'

Gaunt put the goblet down on the table, fascinated. 'And you don't know who is stealing them?'

'No, I don't know how they are taken, by whom or where

they go. But the Fisher of Men has dragged at least four or five dead cats out of the river—' Cranston slurped at his wine goblet – 'which is some consolation. At first I suspected they were being killed for their fur, or that some flesher in the Shambles had run short of meat.' He saw the regent's face go pale. 'Aye, my lord, it's not unknown for cooks, be they working in a royal palace or a Cheapside tavern, to serve up cat pie, the meat well stewed and garnished with herbs.'

'Yes, yes, quite.' The regent lifted his cup but then thought differently. 'Sir John,' he declared, 'you will have to leave all that. You have heard of the Parliament my nephew the king has summoned at Westminster?'

'Yes, you need more taxes, whilst the Commons want reforms.'

'My lord Coroner, I am pleased by your bluntness but, yes, yes that's true. Now the Commons do not like me. They draw unfair comparisons between myself and my brother, God rest him. The war in France is not going well. Our coastal towns are attacked by French pirates. The harvest was poor and the price of bread is three times what it was this time last year. Now, I am doing what I can. Grain barges are constantly coming up the Thames, and the mayor and aldermen of the city have issued strict regulations fixing the price of bread.'

Cranston's eyes slid away. He knew about such regulations, more honoured in the breach than the observance, but he decided to keep his mouth shut.

The regent leaned forward. 'Now all was going well,' he continued. 'The Commons assembled in the chapter-house of Westminster Abbey. The speaker, Sir Peter de la Mare, is a good man.' Gaunt paused.

In other words, you've bribed him, Cranston thought, but

still kept his mouth shut. The regent ran his tongue round his lips.

'Some of the members are amicable; others, particularly those from Shrewsbury and Stafford, are proving intractable. They are a close-set group comprising, Sir Henry Swynford, Sir Oliver Bouchon, Sir Edmund Malmesbury, Sir Thomas Elontius, Sir Humphrey Aylebore, Sir Maurice Goldingham and Sir Francis Harnett—'

'And?' Cranston intervened.

'These knights are lodged at a hostelry, the Gargoyle tavern. On Monday evening Sir Oliver left his companions abruptly: next morning his body was found floating face-down near Tothill Fields, no mark on the corpse. We do not know whether he was pushed or suffered an accident. Anyway, the corpse was pulled out and taken back to the Gargoyle, where his fellow knights planned to hire a cart to carry it back to Shrewsbury. Now, to recite prayers during the death-watch, a chantry priest was hired. He entered the tavern late last night and apparently took up his post in the dead man's chamber. Later on, a servant wench passed the chamber: she saw the door ajar and went in. There was no sign of the priest. Sir Oliver still lay sheeted in his coffin, but beside him on the floor was Sir Henry Swynford, a garrotte string round his throat.'

Gaunt paused. Stretching out his hand, he played with the silver filigreed ring on one of his fingers. 'Both deaths might be murders.' He glanced up. 'Both men received a warning before they died: a candle, an arrowhead and a scrap of parchment bearing the word "Remember".' Gaunt cleared his throat. 'Each of the corpses had also been slightly mutilated, small red crosses being carved on either cheek as well as on the forehead.'

'And no one knows what all this means?' Cranston asked.

'No. Oh, there are the usual stories: both knights were loved and admired. Men of stature in their community.' Gaunt smirked. 'The truth is both men were bastards born and bred. They served in the wars in France, where they amassed booty and plunder to come back and build their manor houses and decorate the parish church. Apparently they had no enemies at all which,' he added bitterly, 'is the biggest lie of all, if anyone ever bothered to talk to their tenants.'

Gaunt put his goblet down and rose to his feet. 'Now, I don't care, Cranston, whether they are dead or alive, in heaven or in hell. But I do care about the whispers and the pointed fingers which claim that both men were murdered because they opposed the regent, as a punishment for them and a warning to the rest.' He leaned over Sir John, gripping the arms of the other man's chair, his face only a few inches from Cranston's. 'Now, my lord Coroner, get yourself down to Westminster. Take your secretarius, Brother Athelstan, with you. Discover the assassin, stop these murders and, when you are finished, you can come back to Cheapside and find out who is stealing its cats.'

'Is there anything else, my lord?' Cranston held the regent's gaze and nonchalantly sipped from his goblet.

'Yes.' Gaunt straightened up, pushing his thumbs into his swordbelt. 'Sir Miles Coverdale, captain of my guard, is responsible for the king's peace in the palace of Westminster. He will assist you.' Gaunt stepped back and sketched a mocking bow. 'My thanks to your good lady.' He walked to the door.

'My lord Regent.' Cranston didn't even bother to turn in the chair.

'Yes, my lord Coroner.'

'I was thinking of cats, my lord. Do you have any?'

Gaunt shrugged. 'What does it matter?'

25

'Nothing much.' Cranston replied over his shoulder. 'Our king is young, his father's dead. I was thinking of the proverb, "When the cat's away, the mice will play".' Sir John sipped from his cup and smiled as he heard the door slam behind him.

In the parish church of St Erconwald's of Southwark, Brother Athelstan, much against his will, was holding a full parish council near the baptismal font just inside the main door. He sat, as usual, in the high-backed sanctuary chair brought down especially for the occasion: across from him were the members of his parish council who sat on stools in a semi-circle waiting for his judgement. On the wooden lid of the baptismal font sprawled the huge, tattered tom-cat, Bonaventure, which Athelstan secretly considered his only true parishioner. Now and again Bonaventure's one good amber eye flickered open, and the cat would stare at Ranulf the rat-catcher as if he knew Ranulf's secret desire to buy him. After all, Bonaventure's prowess as a mouser and a ratter was known throughout the parish. Today, however, when Athelstan should be doing the parish accounts and letting Bonaventure hunt, he had to hold this special meeting: Watkin, Pike and the bailiff Bladdersniff had all taken the sacrament at Mass this morning then solemnly sworn how they had seen a demon crouching in the death-house.

'It was black,' Watkin trumpeted so loudly that even the hairs in his great flared nostrils seemed to bristle with anger. 'It was huge with bright eyes, hideous face, blue and red round the mouth and it moved like lightning.'

'You were drunk,' Mugwort the bell-ringer snorted. 'Pernell the Fleming woman saw the three of you: you had not one good leg amongst the six.'

26

'More like nine,' Crispin the carpenter added, but no one seemed to understand this salacious reference.

'Drunk or not,' Pike screeched, tilting his face and pointing to the great red weals across his cheeks. 'Who did that, eh?'

Athelstan pushed his hands further up the sleeves of his gown and rocked gently to and fro. He stole a look at Benedicta: he expected to find her eyes dancing with merriment and those lovely lips fighting hard not to smile, but the widow-woman looked concerned.

'What do you think, Benedicta?' Athelstan asked before Watkin's bellicose wife could intervene to take up the cudgels on her husband's behalf.

'I believe they saw something, Father.' Benedicta played with the tassel of the belt round her slim waist. 'I dressed Pike's wound: savage claw marks. Any higher,' she added, 'and he could have lost an eye.'

'You are always telling us . . .' Tab the tinker spoke up. 'You are always telling us, Father,' he repeated, 'how Satan prowls, seeking those whom he may devour.'

'Yes, Tab, but I was speaking in a spiritual sense, about that unseen world of which we are only a part.'

'But that's not true,' Watkin's wife intervened. 'In St Olave's parish, Merry Legs claimed a devil was dancing round the steeple as I would a maypole.'

'And I have heard imps whispering in the corner,' Pernell the Fleming intervened. 'Small, Father, no bigger than your fingers. I heard them scrabbling at the woodwork.'

Athelstan closed his eyes and prayed for patience.

'What did it look like?' Huddle the painter asked, and pointed to the far wall of the church where he was busily

27

sketching out, in charcoal, a marvellous vision of Christ's harrowing of hell.

'Never mind,' Athelstan intervened. He glanced quickly at Simplicatas, a young woman from Stinking Alley who had whispered after Mass how she wanted to talk to him about her missing husband. 'We have other matters to discuss.'

'But this is important.' Bladdersniff drew himself up on his stool, wrinkling his fiery red nose and blinking drink-sodden eyes. 'If you don't believe us, Father, let's go to the death-house. Let's see for ourselves.'

His colleagues did not seem quite as enthusiastic, but Athelstan saw it as a way of pacifying them all.

'Come on.' He got to his feet.

'Father, I'm frightened,' Pernell wailed.

'Don't worry.' Athelstan fingered the wooden crucifix hanging round his neck. He shooed Bonaventure off the baptismal font, unlocked and lifted the wooden lid then, taking the small enamel bowl held by Mugwort, scooped some of the holy water out.

'If there's a devil in the death-house,' he declared, 'the cross and holy water will soon make him flee.'

Led by their priest, Bonaventure stalking solemnly beside him, the parish council left the church. They crossed the cemetery, following the beaten path around the headstones and crosses to the great black-painted shed in the far corner. The door was still flung back on its hinges, a sure sign of the three men's flight the previous night. Athelstan turned and winked at Benedicta.

'Now, stay here. All of you.'

Holding the crucifix in one hand, the cup of holy water in the other, Athelstan strode across and stopped outside the death-

28

house. He looked at the earth, scuffed where Pike and his two companions had fought to get out.

I never asked them what they were doing, he thought. Probably drunk: I just hope they didn't have Cecily the courtesan with them. The only people who are supposed to lie in this graveyard are the dead. Athelstan went into the death-house and, as soon as he did, caught a fetid, pungent smell.

'For God's sake, man!' he whispered to himself.

He put the cup of holy water on the long, stained table and stared around. The smell caught the back of his throat and made him cough. Athelstan took a tinder out of his pocket and, trying to keep his hands from trembling, lit the tallow candle and held it up, filling the dark, cavernous place with dancing shadows.

'"Arise, O Lord,"' he whispered, quoting the psalms, '"and defend me from my enemies!"'

He walked carefully round the death-house. He always kept this place clean. He scrubbed the table and swept the floor every week. There was a small window high in the wall, and when a corpse lay in the room he always burnt incense, as he had only two days ago when Mathilda the seamstress had lain here awaiting burial. So what was the source of that horrible smell? Athelstan put the candle down and picked up the cup of holy water, blessing the place. 'In the name of the Father, the Son and the Holy Ghost,' but, even as he did so, his mind teemed with possibilities. He recalled a recent letter from the master general of his Order about the signs of demonic activity: violence, unexplained phenomena.

'Aye,' Athelstan whispered to himself, 'and a terrible smell which curdles the mind and frightens the soul. Nonsense!' he added.

'Father?'

Athelstan spun round. Benedicta was standing in the doorway. The widow-woman stepped into the death-house and then, covering her nose and mouth with her hand, abruptly backed out. Athelstan followed her.

'Benedicta, what is the matter?'

The widow-woman's face was pale. 'Last night, Father. I didn't want to mention this, but I was in my garden just after dusk, and under the apple tree I saw a dark, hideous shape.'

Athelstan stared into Benedicta's frightened eyes. 'Surely, woman, you don't believe all this?'

'Athelstan!'

The friar looked round. Sir John Cranston was standing at the far end of the graveyard, legs apart.

'Oh Lord save us!' Athelstan breathed. 'Having the Lord Satan in Southwark is bad enough, but Cranston as well . . .!'

CHAPTER 2

'So, you think there's a devil in Southwark?' Moleskin the boatman asked as Athelstan and Cranston stepped into his wherry, ready for the journey downriver to Westminster.

'There are a lot of bloody imps in Southwark!' Cranston retorted, taking a sip from his 'miraculous' wineskin, always full and ever present, hidden beneath his cloak. 'What's more,' Cranston smacked his lips and put the stopper back in, 'most of them are members of Brother Athelstan's parish.'

Moleskin glowered angrily from under his brows as he strained at the oars, pulling his boat across the choppy Thames. He glanced at his parish priest for comfort. Athelstan, however, had his cowl well over his head and sat staring into the bank of mist now lifting under the morning sun. Cranston nudged him playfully.

'Come on, Brother. You've hardly said a word since we left the church. Don't be downcast. Benedicta will see all is well. And, if the devil reappears, she might catch it with her pretty face and beguiling ways.'

'It's not a joking matter, Sir John.' Athelstan replied. 'Benedicta saw a shape in her garden; Pike was definitely attacked. Some terrible creature was lurking in our death-house last night.'

'But a devil, a demon?' Cranston exclaimed. 'Walk through the city, Brother. You'll see plenty of demons dressed in the finest silks, supping the best wines and smelling ever so fragrantly.'

'This is different,' Athelstan retorted. He smiled at the boatman. 'Moleskin, keep rowing. What you hear is not for discussion in the Piebald tavern. Holy Mother Church teaches.' Athelstan stirred, and pointed to the choppy waters of the Thames. 'You see, Sir John, two worlds co-exist in this river. What is on the surface and what is underneath. Both affect each other. Both are linked, yet we only see what is on the surface; beneath the Thames there is another world: wreckage, fish, plants, all forms of living things. Now, God made a visible and invisible world. When we pray we enter the invisible world.' He paused to admire a long line of swans, their slender necks arched, their wings up, swim serenely by. 'What happens, Sir John, if those intelligences and powers hostile to God and Man manifest themselves in our world? Oh, I am not talking about the hobgoblins and the warlocks, but something else.'

'But you're not just worried about that, are you?' Cranston asked.

'No.' Athelstan shook his head. 'I am worried about Pike. Joscelyn, the landlord at the Piebald, tells me about his secret meetings with men who call themselves after animals: the Weasel, the Fox . . .'

'The Great Community of the Realm?' Cranston asked.

'Aye, Sir John, the peasant community busily plotting rebellion.' He shook his head. 'It will all end in blood and Pike will hang.'

Cranston stared across the river. He could see the gleaming spire of St Paul's and the great cross surmounting the steeple, packed with famous relics as a protection against lightning.

'Pike's right,' Cranston muttered. 'Oh, he's not right to plot, but there is a vengeance coming.' He pointed to a long line of barges heading towards Queenshithe.

'Grain barges,' Moleskin volunteered.

'I know they are,' Cranston snapped, but Moleskin continued, unperturbed. 'Without them there'd be no bread in the bakeries. The Corporation is buying from across the seas.'

'Where do they go?' Athelstan asked.

'To the warehouses at East Watergate,' Moleskin replied. 'You should take Bonaventure across there, Brother. The barges are full of rats and mice.'

'When do you think it will come?' Athelstan asked. 'This planned revolt?'

'This summer, next summer,' Cranston replied.

'And what will you do, Sir John?'

'I'll put on my helmet and armour, ride down to the Tower and put myself under the king's banner. I am his coroner.' Cranston paused. 'I just pray I don't see Pike or any of your parishioners at the end of my sword.' He leaned closer. 'And what will you do, Brother? The rebels say that those who don't join them will die, and they have no love of priests.'

'I shall rise every morning, God willing,' Athelstan replied. 'I shall give Bonaventure his bowl of milk. I shall lock my church, kneel beneath the rood-screen, offer Mass and go about my own business.'

Cranston snapped his fingers in annoyance. 'And you think you'll be safe?' he snarled.

Athelstan grabbed him by his plump hand. 'Sir John,' he replied, 'I can only do what I can. Father Prior has already raised the matter. He wants members of our Order to leave the capital until the crisis has passed.'

Cranston's blue eyes blinked furiously.

'And, talking about the Tower,' Athelstan hurriedly added, eager to change the subject, 'that, too, is concerning me.'

'What do you mean?'

'It's Perline,' Moleskin interrupted.

The boatman's old face was now wrinkled in concern. Athelstan secretly admired the way he could deftly eavesdrop and yet row so expertly at the same time.

'Perline Brasenose,' Athelstan explained. 'A rattle-brained young man: his mother was a whore who raised him in the stews. He spent a year in the Earl of Warwick's retinue, then left and married a girl, Simplicatas, a member of the parish. A young man, a good fellow,' Athelstan declared, 'but a bit of a madcap, attracted to mischief as a bee to honey.'

'And?' Cranston asked.

'He has gone missing,' Athelstan declared.

'I always said he would,' Moleskin volunteered.

'Oh, shut up!' Athelstan replied. 'For God's sake, have some charity! Perline entered the royal guard at the Tower. I thought he was settling down but now he has gone missing.' Athelstan fingered the girdle round his waist. 'And, before you say it, Sir John, some men may desert their wives, but not Perline. For all his faults he loved Simplicatas, yet no one's seen hide nor hair of him. Could you just keep an eye open, and if you hear anything . . .?'

'I did see him.' Moleskin looked aggrievedly at his parish priest. 'I saw him two nights ago. He was standing on the quay-side just near the steps of St Mary Overy. I was bringing one of those knights from the Parliament across.' Moleskin stopped rowing and rested on his oars. 'That's right. Sir Francis Harnett

34

from Stokesay in Shropshire. Funny little man he was.' Moleskin drew back his oars. 'All a-quiver, sitting where you were.'

'And what would a distinguished member of Parliament want with Southwark?' Cranston sardonically asked.

Moleskin just winked whilst Athelstan glanced away. Aye, he thought, what do the rich ever want with Southwark but the pursuit of some fresh young whore from the many brothels there. He glanced at Moleskin.

'And Perline?'

'He was waiting for him on the river steps. Up goes the knight, Perline shakes him by the hand, and into the darkness they go.' Moleskin pulled a face. 'That's all I know.'

Athelstan sighed and squeezed Cranston's arm. 'Sir John, this business at Westminster?'

Cranston tapped his nose and nodded towards Moleskin, so Athelstan leaned back in the stern. The wherry, now in mid-river, rounded the bend past Whitefriars and the Temple, crossing over to the northern bank of the Thames. Moleskin, straining at the oars, guided it expertly past the dung boats, a royal man-of-war heading towards Dowgate, fishing craft and the interminable line of grain barges and other boats bringing up produce to the London markets. Even as he rowed the mist was lifting, and Athelstan glimpsed the turrets and spires of Westminster as they caught the morning sun. He closed his eyes and quietly began to recite the '*Veni Creator Spiritus*', asking for guidance in the problems which faced him in his parish, as well as those awaiting him at Westminster. In their walk down to the quayside, Sir John, apart from shouting good-natured abuse at Athelstan's parishioners, had told him a little about the regent's visit: the deaths of Sir Henry Swynford and Sir Oliver Bouchon. Athelstan realised that, once more, they

35

were pursuing a son of Cain. Most of his work with Cranston involved crimes of passion – a knifing in a tavern; a savage quarrel between a man and his wife; the death of some beggar crushed under a cart – but, now and again, something more sinister, evil, swam out of the darkness: cold-blooded murder. Athelstan sensed that at Westminster, what Sir John called the 'House of Crows', terrible and bloody murders had been carried out, and that more were yet to come.

Athelstan had reached the line, 'Life immortal, life divine', when Cranston dug him in the ribs. Athelstan opened his eyes and realised they had reached King's Steps. Moleskin was resting on his oars, staring at him curiously.

'I am sorry,' the friar muttered, and followed Sir John out of the boat, up the slippery, mildewed steps and along the pathway into one of the courtyards of the palace. All around him rose great, majestic buildings: Westminster Hall where the King's court sat, St Margaret's Church and, dominating them all, the Confessor's Abbey, its huge towers soaring up into the sky. Westminster was always busy. Pedlars, hucksters, journeymen and traders all made a living from those who flocked there: plaintiffs, defendants, lawyers, sheriffs and, more importantly, members of Parliament.

Cranston told the friar to wait by a huge stone cross and went into the abbey through a side door. He was gone some time, so Athelstan sat down on the stone steps leading up to the cross and watched the red-capped judges in their ermine-lined black gowns sweep by: the serjeants-at-law in their white hoods strutting, arm in arm, heads together, discussing the finer points of some statue or legal quibble. Athelstan smiled as a huckster barged between them, shouting at the top of his voice how he had, 'Oysters! Fresh oysters for sale!'

Two bailiffs came next, a string of prisoners in tow. Athelstan stared compassionately at the captives. All were in tatters, their faces unshaven; their boots and shoes had already been stolen by the gaolers of the Fleet or Newgate Prisons. The bailiffs stopped to refresh themselves at a water tippler's. Athelstan rose, slipped the boy a coin and, taking his bucket and ladle, went along the line of prisoners offering each a stoup of water. Thankfully, the bailiffs did not protest, and Athelstan had just handed the bucket back, murmuring his thanks, when he glimpsed a face he recognised.

'Cecily!' he shouted.

The young blonde-haired girl, dressed in a long yellow taffeta gown, looked round, startled. Athelstan noticed the black kohl around her eyes, and saw how her cheeks and lips were heavily rouged.

'Cecily!' he shouted. 'Come here!'

The young girl tripped across, face as innocent as an angel's.

'Father, what a surprise. What are you doing here?'

Athelstan fought to keep his face severe. 'More importantly, Cecily, what are you doing here?'

The young girl opened her pert little mouth.

'And don't lie,' Athelstan warned. 'I missed you at Mass this morning and we had an important parish council.' He grasped her hand and thrust one of his precious pennies between her fingers. 'Now go back,' he ordered. 'Go to King's Steps. You'll find Moleskin there. I need you, Cecily.' He leaned closer. 'There's been a demon seen near St Erconwald's.' He gripped her warm hand and tried not to flinch at the cheap perfume the girl had covered herself in. 'Now go back there and help Benedicta! Stay away from here!'

Cecily, biting her lips, nodded. Athelstan pushed her gently

37

away. 'Go straight home!' he ordered. 'I'll ask Benedicta when you arrived.'

Cecily was already running, and Athelstan gave small thanks that Cecily's curiosity about a demon would, perhaps, outweigh any reason for her to stay here. He sat back on the steps and glared around, noticing how the young women flocked here, as noisy as starlings.

'This is God's house,' he muttered. He glanced at a pair of girls flirting with an overdressed lawyer. 'Sir John's right! It is a "House of Crows".'

Athelstan recognised the attractions of such a place for people like Cecily. Men from all over England came here: free of their wives and families, they would take full advantage of their short-lived freedom to indulge their every whim. Athelstan glanced towards the abbey. Perhaps the Parliament would change things for the better. Even his parishioners had talked about it.

Pike the ditcher, however, had been as cynical as ever. 'Only the lawyers get to Parliament,' he had declared, 'and we know what liars they are!' Pike had lowered his voice. 'But when it comes, when the great Change comes, we'll hang all the lawyers!'

'Dreaming, Brother?'

Athelstan looked up sharply. Cranston was just popping the cork-stopper back into his miraculous wineskin.

'Most of the abbey is sealed off,' the coroner explained. 'The Commons are now sitting in the chapter-house and will be until well in the afternoon. So,' he helped his companion to his feet, 'let's look at the corpses. They both lie coffined in the Gargoyle tavern.'

He led Athelstan out of the abbey precincts, along quiet side streets and through the deep arched gateway into a large courtyard which fronted the Gargoyle. It was a long, spacious tavern, three storeys high, its frontage smartly painted, the plaster gleaming white between black polished beams. The roof was tiled and the elegantly boxed windows were full of leaden glass. The courtyard was a hive of activity: ostlers and grooms took horses in and out, a farrier covered in sweat hammered at an anvil. Geese and chickens thronged about the stable doors, scrabbling for bits of grain. Dogs yapped and huge, fat-bellied pigs, ears flapping, snouted at the base of a large, black-soiled midden-heap.

They entered the tavern hallway. The paving stones were scrubbed, the walls lime-washed, the air fragrant with the smell of sweet herbs and savoury cooking. The taproom was large and airy: there were vents in the ceiling between the blackened beams, and large, open windows at the far end looked out over a garden and one of the largest stewponds Athelstan had ever seen. A few customers sat about, mainly boatmen from the river though, even here, the lawyers thronged, sitting in small alcoves, manuscripts on the tables before them as they whispered pretentiously to each other.

'You wouldn't think the corpses of two murdered men lay here, would you?' Athelstan whispered at Cranston, who was smacking his lips and looking around. 'No drinking,' Athelstan warned. 'We have business with the "House of Crows", remember?'

'And what's your custom, sirs?' a tall, thickset man asked.

'None at the moment,' Cranston replied, 'except a word with the landlord.'

The man spread his hands. 'You are talking to him,' he replied. 'I am the tavern-master, Cuthbert Banyard, born and bred within the sound of Bow Bells.'

Athelstan stared at the fellow. He had a strong, arrogant face, burnt brown by the sun, with a thick bush of black hair. The eyes were deep-set, the nose curved slightly; his chin, close-shaven face and thin lips gave him a stubborn look. A man with a sharp eye to profit, Athelstan thought.

The taverner gestured at his stained cote-de-hardie which fell down to just below the knee. 'It's a fleshing day,' he explained. 'Meat has to be cut and blood spurts.'

'As it does in murder,' Cranston retorted.

Banyard drew his head back.

'I am Sir John Cranston, Coroner of the city. This is Brother Athelstan, my secretarius, parish priest of St Erconwald's in Southwark.'

Banyard smiled deferentially. 'My lord Coroner, how can I help?'

'First,' Cranston replied, ignoring Athelstan's groan, 'a blackjack of ale. Your best, mind you, not the scrapings of some open cask. And whatever smells so fragrant in your kitchen?'

'Capon cooked in mushrooms and onions.'

'One dish.' Cranston looked at Athelstan. 'No, two dishes of that, and a drink, Brother?'

'Some ale,' Athelstan replied resignedly.

Cranston swept by the landlord to a table under the window: ignoring Athelstan's warning glances, he began to point out the different herbs growing in the garden.

'Now that's motherwort,' Cranston explained. 'You can tell by its hard, brownish stalk: it makes mothers joyful and settles the womb, provokes urine, cleanses the chest of phlegm and kills worms in the belly.'

Cranston turned, rubbing his hands, as the tapster laid down two pewter dishes with delicate strips of capon covered in rich sauce followed by two pots of ale. Cranston and Athelstan took out their horn spoons. Athelstan nibbled, for he had little appetite. Sir John finished his, then attacked his companion's with equal relish. Once he had finished, Cranston beckoned over Banyard, who had been standing in an alcove watching them closely.

'Sit down, man. Where are the corpses?'

'Upstairs, each in their chamber,' the landlord replied, wiping his hands carefully on a napkin. 'It's good that you ate, my lord Coroner, before you viewed them.'

Cranston turned on his stool and leaned against the wall. 'Corpses don't upset my humours, man. Human wickedness does. Sir Henry was killed when?'

'Late last night. He went into Sir Oliver's chamber.' He pointed to a slattern, a jolly, bouncing girl with long blonde hair. She was at the far side of the tavern, busily serving a number of boatmen and laughing at their banter. 'Christina saw the door open and went in. You could have heard the screams at Whitefriars. I ran upstairs. Sir Oliver was in his coffin, Sir Henry dead as a doornail upon the floor.'

'And where were his companions, the other knights?' Athelstan asked.

'Most of them were in their chambers,' Banyard replied.

'Most of them?' Athelstan queried.

Banyard smiled deprecatingly. 'Brother, I have my hands full managing a tavern. I cannot tell you where each of my guests goes in the evening.' Banyard grinned. 'Though it would be interesting to speculate.'

'What do you mean by that?' Cranston demanded.

'My lord Coroner, it's best if you ask them.'

'And so all the knights and representatives from Shrewsbury stay here?' Athelstan asked. 'Is that customary?'

'Yes, it is,' Cranston intervened. 'Members of Parliament tend to sit according to their counties or lordships. The chancellor issues a writ, convoking a Parliament, to every sheriff in the kingdom. He then organises a meeting of the freeholders of the shire who elect their representatives.' Cranston grasped his chin. 'There have been Parliaments at Westminster for the last hundred years, and the Commons are becoming more organised.'

'You know a lot, my lord Coroner.' Banyard's admiration was obvious.

'Ahem, yes.' Cranston cleared his throat. 'I am writing a treatise.'

Athelstan closed his eyes and just hoped Cranston wouldn't wander off on some interminable lecture. The coroner must have caught his look because he grinned.

'Suffice to say I've studied the whole question of Parliaments. However, as I have said, they are becoming more organised. They have a speaker, they meet in their own chamber, and they have learnt not to grant taxes until certain demands are met.' He blew his cheeks out. 'Accordingly, many members know a Parliament is to be summoned months in advance.'

'And that is what happened here,' Banyard added. 'Weeks ago the knights sent a courier asking me to set chambers aside. We have all the representatives from Shrewsbury here.'

'Yes, yes,' Cranston snapped, 'but when did they arrive?'

'Oh, nine days ago,' Banyard replied. 'Five days before the opening of Parliament.'

'And before these deaths, nothing amiss happened?'

'Nothing.' The landlord shook his head. 'Very little, my lord

Coroner, except talking. They're all very good at talking. They'd break their fast talking and return from Westminster to sit in the taproom here and gossip until even the dogs droop with exhaustion.'

'And Bouchon's death?'

Banyard pointed across the room. 'He and his companions were over there feasting and drinking. Oh, they were all full of themselves, though I noticed Bouchon looked quiet and withdrawn. They drank deep.' Banyard pulled a face. 'But why should I object? Well, on that particular evening, the gentlemen were discussing business of a different sort, the pleasures of the flesh.'

'You mean a bawdy house?'

'Yes.' Banyard looked uncomfortable. 'Now, there's nothing of that sort here, sirs. I keep a respectable house, though I confess I turn a blind eye to whomever they bring back.'

'This bawdy house?' Cranston demanded.

'Dame Mathilda Kirtles conducts a discreet establishment,' Banyard replied. 'In Cottemore Lane, a little further down the riverside.'

'And did Sir Oliver leave with them?' Athelstan asked.

'Oh no. Towards the end of the meal, Sir Oliver rose, put his cloak on, pulled his hood up and left the tavern. The others called after him but the man was lost in his own thoughts. He was gone in the twinkling of an eye.'

'And you don't know where?'

'My lord Coroner, I was busy that night. Ask any of the servants here. I never left the tavern. We closed well after curfew. We have a licence to do so,' he added hastily.

Athelstan sipped from his blackjack and stared round the tavern. It was, he thought, a veritable palace amongst hostelries:

43

the plaster walls were freshly painted, the rushes underfoot were green and crisp and, when he pressed his sandal down, he could smell the rosemary sprinkled there. The tables were of oak and finely made. There were stools, proper benches, and even a few high-backed chairs. Glass and pewter plates stood on shelves. Above them on the mantelpiece was a colourful depiction of a gargoyle fighting a knight which curled and writhed around its opponent's sword. The food was well-cooked and, from Cranston's murmurs of pleasure, the ale was undoubtedly London's finest.

'You do a fine trade here, Master Banyard,' Athelstan commented.

'Oh, most comfortable, Brother. Most comfortable indeed.'

'Do you know most of the people who come here?'

Banyard's eyes moved quickly. 'Yes I do, Brother. And, if they are strangers, they always come back. I can tell from the cut of a man's cloth what he is: a boatman, a serjeant-at-law, a courier, a bailiff, or one of the royal officials from the Exchequer or Chancery. But, before you ask, I saw no strangers, nothing out of the ordinary.'

'And Sir Oliver's body?' Cranston asked.

'It was found downriver,' Banyard replied. 'Some fishermen found it amongst the weeds near Horseferry.'

'Oh, of course.' Cranston leaned back. 'I remember playing there as a boy.' He declared. 'The weeds grow long, lovely and thick.' He smiled over at Athelstan. 'Just near Tothill Fields.'

'How did they know it was Sir Oliver?' Athelstan asked.

'Oh, he had some documents in his wallet, water-stained but still legible, so the fishermen called a clerk. He could tell from the cut of the corpse's clothes that he was a man of importance: the body was brought back into Westminster Yard, where Sir

44

Miles Coverdale, who is responsible for guarding the precincts of the palace, recognised the corpse and sent it back here.'

'And was a physician called?' Cranston asked.

'The man was dead and smelt of fish, Sir John. But no,' Banyard added hurriedly, seeing the coroner frown. 'He was taken upstairs. In the afternoon his companions came from the chapter-house. I hired an old woman from Chancery Lane. She stripped the body and laid it out in a shift.' Banyard glanced at the timbered ceiling. 'But I'll be glad when they move it and the other to the death-house at St Dunstan's in the West.'

'Quite so,' the coroner nodded. He waved his empty tankard in front of Banyard's nose, hoping the taverner would refill it, but Banyard, used to such tricks, refused even to notice it.

'There was no mark on the corpse?' Athelstan asked.

'So the old woman said.'

'And Sir Henry?'

'Well, he seemed the most upset of Bouchon's companions. I offered to send for a chantry priest to come and conduct the death-watch. He agreed. Now Father Benedict, he's a Benedictine monk,' Banyard explained, 'and chaplain to the Commons. But he's so busy that I sent for a chantry priest from St Bride's in Fleet Street. You can go there and ask. But as for last night – well, you'd best ask the wench. Christina!'

The slattern whom Athelstan had noticed earlier came across, her milk-white face slightly coloured from the heat of the kitchen, her rich blonde hair now firmly tied back by a ribbon. A pretty, lively lass with merry blue eyes and lips which Athelstan quietly thought, God must have made for kissing. She wore a thin stained smock pulled tightly over an ample bosom, girdled at her slim waist by a red woollen cord. She grinned at Sir John and blinked nervously at Athelstan, but the

45

friar could tell by the way she answered Banyard's call how the landlord must be the love of her life.

'Sit down, girl.' Cranston pointed to a stool at the next table. 'It's good to rest from your labours. Perhaps, Master Banyard, some ale for all of us, eh?'

Banyard just sat on his stool, staring at him; eventually Cranston sighed and dipped into his purse. 'And don't worry about the cost,' he snapped.

Banyard called to one of the potboys, then turned to Christina. 'Don't be nervous, lass. This is the famous Sir Jack Cranston.' He glanced slyly at the coroner. 'And Brother Athelstan, his secretarius.'

Christina blinked prettily. 'I have heard of you, sir.'

Cranston preened like a peacock whilst Athelstan quietly prayed that the girl would keep the flattery to a minimum.

'Last night,' he asked abruptly, 'when Sir Henry was killed . . .?'

'Choked he was,' the girl replied swiftly, taking the ale from the tapster and supping at it greedily. She licked the froth from her upper lip. 'Just like a chicken. The string was tied round his neck as tightly as a cord round a purse.'

'Tell Sir John about the priest,' Banyard insisted.

'We were busy last night,' Christina replied. 'Master Banyard here was in the cellar.' She turned and smiled beatifically at the taverner. 'A priest came in.' The girl cradled the tankard then raised it to press against her flushed cheek. 'He was cloaked and cowled, the hood pulled well across his face. I was very busy. I saw the rosary beads in his hands. I asked him if he was the chantry priest. He nodded.' She shrugged. 'I told him where the chamber was but he was already going upstairs. The tap-room was thronged,' she continued. 'I never gave him a second thought. Later on, I took a tankard up to Sir Henry Swynford. He was just sitting in his room, staring into the darkness. Only one candle was lit on his table. I asked him if he was well and he muttered some reply.' Christina sipped from the tankard.

'Tell Sir John what happened next.'

'Well—'

'Excuse me,' Athelstan intervened. He'd studied the lass carefully and quietly wondered if she was a little simple: she chattered like a child without any reflection or fear.

'Did you see the priest's face?' Athelstan asked.

'Pull up your cowl, Father,' Christina replied.

Athelstan shrugged and pulled his hood up to conceal his face.

'Oh no, Father,' Christina said. 'It was like this: put your face down.'

Athelstan obeyed and Christina pulled the hood closer across his head, then lifted the front part of the mantle to cover his mouth.

'You see, Father, he looked like that.'

Athelstan pulled back the hood, and a little embarrassed, tugged the black mantle down, away from his mouth and chin. In the dark even he, dressed like that, would not be recognised by many of his parishioners. Indeed, only recently the master-general of his Order had issued an instruction to all Dominicans to be careful about their use of the hood and cowl lest people mistake them for an outlaw or footpad. 'Continue,' he told her.

'Well, a little later,' Christina chattered, 'I went up the stairs. I heard a sound from Sir Oliver's room, chanting, a prayer.' She closed her eyes. 'Something about, something . . .' Her voice faltered. 'Yes, that's it.' She opened her eyes. 'About a day of wrath.'

47

'A day of wrath?' Cranston asked.

'You recognised the voice?' Athelstan interrupted.

'No, it was deep, muffled, as if the speaker had something across his mouth. But, there again,' Christina's eyes moved quickly, and Athelstan wondered whether she was sharper than he judged, 'I thought the priest, perhaps with his head bowed, was praying.' The girl shivered. 'It was eerie. The passageway was lit by one torch and the shadows were dancing. I was frightened: I knew about the corpse and wondered about ghosts and that voice talking about wrath, God's anger and the earth burning.'

'The "*Dies Irae*"!' Athelstan exclaimed. 'O day of wrath, O day of mourning!' He stared at Cranston's bewildered face. '"O day of wrath, O day of mourning, See fulfilled the prophet's warning,"' Athelstan chanted. '"Heaven and earth in ashes burning." It's from the Mass for the dead; the priest always chants it before he recites the Gospel.' Athelstan grasped Christina's hand. 'And you are sure it wasn't Sir Henry Swynford's voice?'

'Oh no, this was different, deep, muffled.'

'What does it mean, Brother?' Cranston asked.

Athelstan rubbed his face with his hands. Despite the warmth and cheer of the taproom, he felt cold and frightened. Most assassins killed quickly and quietly.

He replied slowly. 'What it means, my lord Coroner, is that the chantry priest, and I do not think he was the one hired by our good host, was the assassin. As Sir Henry knelt before his companion's coffin, this assassin quickly garrotted him but, as he killed him, the assassin chanted those words, not in prayer but as a terrible cry of vengeance.'

CHAPTER 3

The taverner, shaking his head, led them up to the first-floor gallery. He stopped on the stairwell, his dark face framed by the mullioned glass window behind him. Athelstan smelt the fragrant pots of herbs on the small sill and, from the yard below, heard the strident crowing of a cock. For some strange reason Athelstan recalled the words of the Gospel, about Peter's betrayal of Christ before the cock crowed thrice. He steeled himself: he and Cranston were about to enter a dark, tangled maze of murder and intrigue amongst the wealthy lords of the soil. Swynford's and Bouchon's deaths were certainly no accidents, nor were they the victims of unhappy coincidence.

'Well, what are we waiting for?' Cranston snapped.

Banyard lifted a finger. 'Listen, Father.'

Athelstan strained his ears and heard the faint mumbling.

'It's Father Gregory,' the taverner explained. 'He came this morning to anoint the corpses. After that,' he continued cheerfully, 'they'll be taken down to the local corpse-dresser, an old woman on the far side of the palace. She will remove the bowels and stuff the bodies with spices. I understand Sir Edmund Malmesbury is hiring a small retinue to escort them back to Shrewsbury.'

Cranston made to go on, but Banyard put his arm across the

49

next flight of stairs. 'I think we should wait,' the taverner declared.

'And I think we shouldn't,' Cranston growled.

Up he went. Athelstan shrugged apologetically and followed. He glanced down the stairs where Christina was staring up at them, her mouth in a round 'O'.

'Don't worry, child,' Athelstan called back. 'We'll all be safe with Sir John.'

They went along the gallery and into a chamber. Even though the windows were open and the shutters thrown back, the air reeked of death and decay. The two corpses lay in their coffins on a specially erected trestle-table at the foot of the four-poster bed. The priest kneeling on a cushion crossed himself and got up hastily. Grey-skinned, grey-haired, with a long, tired face, watery eyes and slobbery mouth, Athelstan took an instant dislike to Father Gregory. He looked a born toper; Athelstan, feeling guilty at his harsh judgement, walked forward, hands extended.

'Father Gregory, we apologise for interrupting your orisons. I am Brother Athelstan from St Erconwald's, this is my lord Coroner, Sir John Cranston.'

The priest forced a weak smile and limply shook Athelstan's hand, then winced at Cranston's powerful, vice-like grip.

'God have mercy on them!' the priest wailed, his hands fluttering down at the corpses. 'Terrible deaths! Terrible deaths! Here today and gone tomorrow, eh, Brother?'

He swayed slightly on his feet, and Athelstan wondered if he had fortified himself with more than prayer.

'Why didn't you come last night?' Cranston asked, squatting down on the stool and mopping his face with the hem of his cloak.

'I was away you see. Every . . .' The man was gabbling. 'Every week I visit my mother for a day. I came back this morning and found Master Banyard's note. Terrible, terrible.' He babbled on. 'To think that a priest could garrotte a man so.'

'If you wait downstairs,' Banyard said kindly, 'Christina will give you some food, Father. My lord Coroner here needs to inspect the corpses.'

The priest threw a fearful look at Sir John, then scuttled from the room.

'And you can join him,' Cranston smiled at the taverner. 'We no longer need you here.'

Banyard pulled a face but walked out, slamming the door behind him. Wheezing and grumbling, Cranston got to his feet and stared down at the corpses.

'It happens to us all, Brother, but death is a terrible thing.'

Athelstan sketched a blessing in the air and squatted down beside the corpse on the left. A yellowing scrap of parchment at the top of the coffin proclaimed it was Sir Oliver Bouchon: a thin beanpole of a man, his harsh, seamed face made all the more dreadful by the slimy water of the Thames. The skin had turned a bluish-white, the lips were slack. Someone had pressed two coins on the eyes; Athelstan noted also the small red crosses dug into the forehead and each cheek. The corpse had been stripped of its clothes and dressed in a simple shift. Athelstan pushed this back and, swallowing hard, felt the cold, clammy flesh. Bouchon's cold corpse was covered with scars and welts which Cranston identified as sword and dagger cuts: others were the marks of tight-fitting belts or boots.

'An old soldier,' Cranston declared. 'He must have seen service abroad. Hell's teeth, I need a drink!'

'In a short while, Sir John, but please help me.'

51

Cranston obliged and they turned the corpse over. Athelstan stared at the flabby buttocks, muscular thighs and hairy legs: he felt a strange sadness. Here lay a world in itself: what hopes, what joys, what fears, what nightmares permeated this man's life? Was he loved? Did he have ideals? Would people mourn that he had died? Athelstan ran his fingers through the still wet, thick black hair at the back of the man's head.

'Ah!' he exclaimed.

'What is it, Brother?'

'Feel for yourself.'

Cranston's stubby fingers searched the back of the skull but stopped as he felt a huge, hard welt.

'Bring me a candle,' Athelstan said.

Sir John handed him one of those Father Gregory had lit, and Athelstan held this down close to the hair. The hot oil from the tallow candle sizzled and spluttered as it slipped on to the still damp hair, yet it provided enough light for Athelstan to make out the huge, angry contusion.

'If anyone says,' Athelstan declared, 'that Sir Oliver Bouchon slipped and fell into the Thames, then he's a liar or ignorant. Someone gave this poor man a powerful whack on the back of his head.'

'Why didn't anyone else notice it?'

'Because no one was looking for it, Sir John.'

Athelstan got up and handed the candle back. 'Sir Oliver here was knocked senseless and then thrown into the Thames. It's a pity the corpse is undressed; I would have liked to have established that he was knocked unconscious whilst he was walking along the river bank.'

'What makes you think that?'

Athelstan turned the corpse over and gently grasped each

hand, pointing at the dirty fingernails and the muddy marks on the palm of each hand.

'If he was knocked unconscious elsewhere,' Athelstan explained, 'I would expect to see bruises where Sir Oliver's body was either dragged along the cobbles or thrown into some cart. However, as you can see, apart from the bruise on the back of his head, there are no others. But there are the dirt marks under his nails and on the palms of his hands. Bouchon must have been near the river edge. His assailant knocked him unconscious and Sir Oliver fell face down, probably in some mud. His body was then lifted up and rolled into the river.'

'But wouldn't the water wash the stains off his hands and nails?'

Athelstan shook his head. 'It might from the clothes, even from the face.' He knelt down and examined Sir Oliver's stubby features. 'Though even here, apart from these small red crosses, there's no mark or contusion, which is strange. Whatever, to answer your question directly, Sir John, the river water would remove any superficial mud stains from the face and clothing. But tell me, my lord Coroner, have you ever seen a corpse, the victim of some brutal assault, where the hands are open and the fingers splayed?'

Sir John smiled and shook his head.

'Sir Oliver was no different,' Athelstan continued. He held his own hands up, curling the fingers. 'Next time you look at your poppets, or the Lady Maude when asleep, notice how they curl their fingers into their hands. The unconscious man is no different. After a short while, even in the river, rigor mortis sets in. The body stiffens, hence the faint dirt on the palms of his hands and beneath the nails from where he fell. What is more,' Athelstan grasped Sir Oliver's right hand, 'notice how the dirt is deeply embedded. Sir Oliver must have fallen and, for a few seconds before he lost consciousness, gripped the mud as he fell, clawing it like an animal.' Athelstan shook his head. 'Poor man. May God grant him eternal rest! Now, for Sir Henry.'

Sir John went across to the other side of Swynford's coffin. Athelstan knelt down and loosened the shift tied under the dead man's chin. The friar had to pause and close his eyes at the terrible rictus of death on the grey-haired knight's face. The mouth was still contorted in a grimace, the eyes half open, the head slightly turned so that the coins placed on the eyes had slipped away. It looked as if the corpse was about to waken and utter some terrible snarl of fury at being thrust so swiftly into the darkness. Swynford's face, too, had been disfigured by the red crosses gouged in his skin. Athelstan tilted the man's chin back. He studied the angry weal around the throat, digging deep where his Adam's apple now hung.

Athelstan loosened the shift and pulled it down, but could detect no bruise or contusion; though Sir Henry, like Sir Oliver, bore the weals and scars of a soldier's life. Then, with Sir John's help, he turned the corpse over and stared at the bruise on the small of the man's back.

'How did that occur?' he whispered.

'Kneel down, Brother.' Sir John smiled at his secretarius. 'Go on, kneel down, and I'll show you how he died.'

Athelstan knelt.

'No, no, on one knee only,' Sir John declared. 'That's how a knight prays: one leg up, one down, ever ready for action.'

Athelstan obeyed. He heard Sir John come up quietly behind him: suddenly his head went back as Sir John's belt went round his throat, biting into his neck even as he felt Sir John's knee dig into the small of his back. Athelstan spluttered, his hands flailing out, the belt was whisked away. Sir John pulled him to his feet and spun him round. He saw the alarm in the gentle Dominican's face.

'Here, Brother, have a sip from the wineskin!'

This time Athelstan did not refuse: he took a generous mouthful and thrust the wineskin back to Sir John.

'Well done, Coroner. You were so quick!'

'The mark of a professional assassin.' Sir John rewarded himself with two generous swigs. 'The garrotte is much speedier than many people think. In France I saw young archers, no more than boys, do the same to French pickets when we went out at night. A terrible death, Brother; so quick, even the strongest man finds it hard to grasp his enemy.'

Athelstan nodded. Even though he had panicked, he realised he could not have fought against Sir John, who had kept him thrust away with his knee whilst swiftly choking him with the belt. He wiped his mouth on the back of his hand and stared down at Swynford's corpse.

'That's how he died. He came in here and knelt. The assassin, pretending to be a priest, came up behind him. Sir John, how long would it take?'

'Well, Brother, if you started counting to ten, very quickly, Swynford would have been unconscious by the time you'd reached five.'

'And all the time the murderer was chanting, making a mockery of the "*Dies Irae*".' Athelstan stared round the chamber. 'Sir John, we need to examine the possessions of these dead men.'

Cranston agreed and went out of the gallery. Athelstan heard him at the top of the stairs shouting for Banyard. The friar stood between the two coffins, closed his eyes, and said his own requiem for these souls snatched so abruptly from their bodies.

Cranston came back. 'Come on, Brother, they are in the next room. The taverner has given me the key.'

Athelstan followed him out into the adjoining chamber which had apparently been Sir Henry Swynford's. The men's clothing lay in two heaps on the floor. Athelstan went through these carefully. Bouchon's was sopping wet, still marked and stained by the river, but he could find nothing amiss; even the knight's dagger was still in its sheath. Cranston, meanwhile, was sifting amongst the other possessions: going through wooden caskets covered in leather, opening saddlebags, small metal coffers, each bearing the arms of the dead men: Bouchon's, a black boar rampant against a field of azure; Swynford's, three black crows against a cloth of gold, quartered with small red crosses. There were coins and purses, knives as well as several small, calfskin-covered books sealed with leather clasps. Athelstan opened these.

'What are they, Brother?' Cranston asked.

'*The Legends of Arthur*,' he replied. 'You know, Sir John, Launcelot of the Lake. Tristram and Isolde.' He picked up another tome. 'The same here: *Sir Gawain and the Green Knight. The Search for the Grail*. It's strange . . .'

'Oh, for God's sake, Brother! King Arthur and his Round Table are popular legends. Chaucer and other poets are constantly writing about them. When I was younger, it was quite common for young, fashionable knights to hold Round Tables where they could joust and tourney.'

'I find it strange that two knights, albeit from the same shire, should enjoy the same stories. And here, look.' Athelstan sifted amongst the jewellery on the bed. 'Here are two chains bearing identical insignia.' He separated the items. 'Each carries the image of a swan with its wings raised.'

Cranston picked them up. Both medallions were identical, the swans exquisitely carved with ruffled, fluffed wings and arching necks.

'They are no gee-gaws from some market booth,' the coroner murmured. 'These were the special work of a silversmith.'

'And look,' Athelstan added, picking up two rings. 'Each of these, wrought in silver, also bears the image of a swan.' He put them close together. 'They are different sizes,' Athelstan declared. 'I saw the marks on the fingers of the corpses next door. What I am saying, Sir John, is that both Swynford and Bouchon belonged to some society or company with an interest in the legends of Arthur, and the badge of their company was a silver swan.'

'Knights of the Swan.' Cranston sat on the edge of the bed and chewed the corner of his lip. 'During the wars in France...' He smiled at Athelstan. 'Well, you know about those, Brother, you were there. But do you remember the companies? Each, raised by some lord, included knights, men-at-arms, hobelars, archers, all wearing the same livery and sporting the same device: a green dragon or a red lion rampant.'

'Aye, I remember them.' Athelstan threw the rings back on the bed. 'Colourful banners and warlike pennants. In reality just an excuse for a group of men to seize as much plunder as they could lay their hands on.'

Cranston went back to his searches. 'And, last but not least, Brother,' he declared, going across to a small table which stood underneath a large black crucifix, 'I asked Banyard where these were.'

He came back carrying arrowheads, candles and small scraps of parchment. Athelstan examined these, then studied the dirty

57

scraps of parchment with the word, 'Remember' scrawled across.

'Each of the victims had these,' Cranston explained. 'But what do they signify?' He shook his head. 'And why were those red crosses carved on the dead men's faces?'

Athelstan went and stood by the open window and stared out, watching Christina: a gaggle of noisy ducks had gathered round her, waddling from the pond which lay near the tavern wall.

'It signifies, my lord Coroner,' he said, 'that no sin, no evil act, ever disappears like a puff of smoke: it always comes back to haunt you.'

'Oh, for God's sake, monk!'

'Friar, Sir John!'

'You talk like a prophet of doom, friar,' Cranston snapped.

'Then perhaps I am one. Here we have two knights from the king's shire of Shrewsbury going about their lawful – or unlawful – business, whichever way you wish to describe it. They come to London to preach and lecture in the Commons. Like any men away from their kith and kin, they want to enjoy themselves in the fleshpots of the city: good food, strong wine, soft women. But then two of them are murdered. The first leaves a banquet in a highly agitated state, his body is later fished from the Thames. When his corpse is laid out and his companion comes in to pray, an assassin, masquerading as a priest, garrottes him whilst chanting certain verses from the Death Mass. Now, I suggest poor Bouchon was agitated because he received those signs: an arrowhead, a candle and a script telling him to "remember". Swynford received the same.' Athelstan glanced across at the coroner. 'You follow my line of thought, Sir John?'

Cranston leaned his bulk against the edge of the table and stared at his secretarius thoughtfully.

'It means, first, they were probably killed by the same assassin who holds a grudge against both of them,' Athelstan explained. 'And, whatever that may be, the arrowhead, the candle and the scraps of parchment are warning signs of their deaths. The red crosses carved on their faces by this assassin, masquerading as a priest, are also part of the grudge.'

Sir John cradled his wineskin like a mother would a baby. 'It also means, my good friar,' he declared, 'that our assassin is a careful plotter. He waited for this opportunity and executed both men with the subtlest form of trickery.' He paused. 'But what then, friar?'

'Well, our noble regent is frightened that he will take the blame; though he must take a quiet satisfaction in the fact that two of his critics have been permanently silenced. Secondly, when Sir Oliver left the tavern, none of his companions followed him though, there again . . .' Athelstan turned away from the window and leaned against the wall. '. . . Sir Oliver may have been lured by anyone to some secret assignation where he was killed. Sir Henry's death is more mysterious. His companions were in the tavern, yet this assassin turns up, disguised as a priest, and that begs two questions. Who knew a priest had been sent for? What would have happened if the false priest had turned up at the same time as Father Gregory?'

'That's no great mystery,' Cranston replied. 'Remember what Christina said: the tavern was very busy. The arrival of a priest would cause no consternation. If Father Gregory was upstairs, the assassin might have waited or even joined him. Be honest, Brother. As parish priest of St Erconwald's, if a priest turned up at your church and wanted to pray beside the coffin of one of your hapless parishioners . . .?'

'*Concedo*,' Athelstan quipped back. 'One, two priests, three or four, it does not really matter. The assassin would have waited for his opportunity or created a new one.' He tapped the scraps of parchment against his fingers. 'This is the important question to resolve. What were Sir Henry and Sir Oliver supposed to remember? What was the significance of an arrowhead and a candle? The marks on the face? And why here?'

'Which means?' Cranston snapped.

'Why kill the two knights in London? Why not at Shrewsbury, or journeying to and from Westminster?'

Cranston snorted, his white whiskers bristling. He was about to launch into speech when there was a clatter on the stairs, a knock on the door, and Sir Miles Coverdale, dressed in half-armour, swordbelt on, bustled into the room.

'Sir John, Brother Athelstan.' He stopped, sketching a rather mocking bow at the coroner and his companion.

'What's the matter, man?' Cranston shoved the wineskin underneath his cloak and stood up. 'You come charging in like a war-horse.'

Sir Miles grinned, removed his gauntlets and wiped the sweat from his forehead. 'Sir John, I am simply carrying out your orders when you came into Westminster.'

'I know what I asked,' Cranston barked.

Athelstan smiled at Coverdale's tolerant, easy-going manner. The captain seemed more amused by Sir John's peevishness than anything else. The young man stretched out his hand and grasped Athelstan's. 'Father, I have heard a lot about you. His Grace the Regent often talks about Sir John and his helpmate.'

'Secretarius!' Cranston snapped. 'Athelstan is my secretarius and parish priest at St Erconwald's. He is a Dominican friar and—'

'—And a very good preacher,' Sir Miles finished Sir John's sentence for him. 'Or so rumour has it.' He winked at Athelstan then stared at Sir John. 'My lord Coroner, the morning session of the Commons has finished early. I asked Sir Oliver and Sir Henry's companions to stay in the chapter-house. They await you there.'

The captain turned as the door opened behind him and a black cowled monk came silently as a shadow into the room.

'What the . . .?' Cranston exclaimed.

'Sir John, may I introduce Father Benedict, monk of Westminster, librarian and chaplain to the Commons.'

Cranston shuffled his feet in embarrassment and extended a podgy hand which was clasped by Father Benedict, who now pulled back his hood to reveal a thin, ascetic face, head completely shaven. Deep furrow marks etched either side of his mouth, his eyes were close-set but sharp.

'Sir John Cranston.' He glanced at Athelstan, his face transformed by a smile. 'And you, Brother.'

Athelstan came forward and exchanged the kiss of peace with him. As he did so, Father Benedict squeezed him by the shoulders.

'Welcome to our community, Brother,' the Benedictine whispered.

'*Pax Tecum*,' Athelstan whispered back.

'Why are you here, Father?' Cranston asked.

'I came to pay my respects to Sir Henry and Sir Oliver,' the Benedictine replied. 'I am chaplain to the Commons. Sir Miles told me about their deaths this morning.'

'Did you know the dead men?' Athelstan asked.

The monk seemed surprised by his question. He opened his mouth, blinked, and moved his hands sharply.

'Yes and no,' he replied. 'I know of the representatives from Shropshire. Many, many years ago, a good friend of mine, Antony, was a young monk at Lilleshall.' Father Benedict smiled wanly. 'He died last winter.'

'And?' Cranston asked.

'Sir Henry, Sir Oliver and the others used to meet in our chapter-house at Lilleshall.'

'For what purpose?'

'They were young knights,' the monk replied. 'According to Antony, their brains were stuffed with dreams of King Arthur and his knights of the Round Table. Both Sir Henry and Sir Oliver and the others used to ape such stories. Every month they would meet, with the permission of the abbot, in our house at Lilleshall, where they would feast, recite the legends of Arthur, and hold a tournament in the great meadow outside. The meetings became famous.' Father Benedict coughed and glanced away.

'And they took as their title the "Knights of the Swan"?' Athelstan said.

'Oh yes!' Father Benedict leaned down and rubbed his knee. 'Sir John, Athelstan, I beg of you, I must sit down. I have rheumatism; the abbey is not the warmest place in winter.'

Cranston pulled up a chair and the old monk sank gratefully into it.

'Do you wish something to drink?' Cranston asked hopefully.

'We were talking about the Knights of the Swan?' Athelstan interrupted, throwing Cranston a warning glance.

'Oh, if Father Antony were to be believed, they were a glorious band,' the Benedictine monk replied. 'Some of them

62

are dead now, God rest them! But there must have been twenty or twenty-four in their company. I once visited Antony at Lilleshall when the Knights of the Swan held one of their great Round Tables. They came riding up to the abbey, preceded by a squire carrying a broad scarlet banner with a beautiful white swan embroidered on it. They'd set up their pavilions in the meadow and the crowds flocked from Shrewsbury even as far as Oswestry on the Welsh border. They all came to see the colours, the gaily caparisoned destriers, the tourney. God forgive me,' he whispered, 'even I, a monk, a man of peace, loved the sight. Stirring times! The great Edward was organising his armies to fight in France and, when the news of the great victory at Crécy swept the country, the Knights of the Swan became local heroes.' He glanced at Sir John. 'Surely, my lord Coroner, there were such days in London?'

'Aye, there were.' Cranston sat on the edge of the bed, a dreamy look in his eyes. 'I was just like that,' he murmured. Then he caught Coverdale's grin. 'Don't judge a book by its cover, young man.' He tapped his broad girth. 'Once I was as sleek and trim as a greyhound, as sharp and swift as a swooping hawk.'

Athelstan put his hands up his sleeves and looked down to hide his smile.

'There used to be great tournaments on London Bridge and at Smithfield,' Cranston continued. He wagged a finger at Coverdale. 'Not like the young popinjays today, traipsing around London in their fancy hose and ridiculous shoes. The only thing they hold out in front of them are their codpieces, and those are usually stuffed with straw.'

'But Sir Miles,' Father Athelstan prompted him, 'you remember Lilleshall surely?'

63

The captain's head came up sharply. 'I was only a child,' he stuttered.

'But your father held land in Shropshire, outside Market Drayton, between there and Woodcote Hall.'

Sir Miles blushed slightly, his hand falling away from his sword. Athelstan couldn't decide whether he was just embarrassed or had something to hide.

'Was your father a Knight of the Swan?' Cranston asked.

'No, he wasn't.' Coverdale's face became hard-set, no longer youthful; his grim, pinched mouth gave him the look of a sour old man.

'I meant to give no slight,' Cranston continued softly.

'And none taken, Sir John. My father's manor was little more than a barn: he died when I was young. My mother was sickly. We had no time for junketing and tourneys. I left Shropshire as a squire. I served in Lord Montague's retinue at sea against the Spanish.' Coverdale moved his swordbelt and sat down on a stool. 'The Knights of the Swan mean nothing to me.'

'Did you know Sir Oliver or Sir Henry?' Athelstan asked.

'By name only. But, there again, I know the same could be true of knights from Norfolk or Suffolk.' He held his gaze. 'I am John of Gaunt's man in peace and war. I wear his livery, I feed in his household.'

'You had no liking for these knights?' Cranston insisted.

'I hear them like a gaggle of geese cackling in the chapterhouse.' Coverdale snapped. 'They criticise the regent for the war against France and yet will not vote a penny to help him. They talk of bad harvests, poor crops and falling profits, but they keep their tenants tied to the land by force and the use of the courts. No, I do not like them, Sir John.'

'And if you were the regent?'

'I would levy the taxes not on the peasants but on the prosperous knights and fat merchants: those who refused to pay, I'd call traitors.'

Athelstan looked at Father Benedict but the monk sat like a statue, though his eyes looked troubled, frightened by Sir Miles's threats.

'Are you there to guard the Commons?' Cranston asked, now enjoying himself. 'Or are you the regent's spy?'

Coverdale's hand fell to the pommel of his sword. Cranston, despite his girth, suddenly lurched forward with a speed which belied his bulk.

'Don't be stupid,' he murmured, standing over the young knight. 'I didn't mean to give offence but wanted merely to describe things as they are.'

'And I have answered you truthfully, Sir John,' Coverdale replied. 'I am there with men-at-arms and archers to ensure the Commons can sit in peace and security. I do not have to like what I hear but I have no personal grudge against them.'

'And you have been with the Commons from the start?' Athelstan intervened quickly.

'Yes. The chapter-house and its approaches have been sealed off. I and my men guard them. Before the session began I was also responsible for hiring barges to take the representatives upriver to see the king's menageries in the Tower.' Coverdale now relaxed. 'They were like children,' he added. 'Many of them had never seen a lion or a panther or the great brown bear which the regent has brought there.' He glanced at Cranston. 'And, yes, Sir John, I guard their soft flesh and listen to their chatter. Some of them should be more careful with their mouths: what they say I report back to the regent.

65

Just as you will, after this business is all finished.'

'Did you have any conversation with Sir Oliver Bouchon or Sir Henry Swynford? Or any of their party?' Athelstan asked.

'None,' Coverdale replied.

'And is this the first time you have ever been to the Gargoyle tavern?'

'Of course. My task is to keep the cloisters secure whilst the Commons are in session. I have as little to do with Sir Oliver and his ilk as possible.'

'And you, Father Benedict?' Cranston asked.

The monk pulled a wry expression. 'I offer Mass in the abbey at the beginning of each day. I am also available for those who wish to be shriven.' He smiled sourly. 'And, before you ask, Sir John, that is not taxing work. Many of the Commons have drunk deeply the night before, not to mention their other pleasures.'

'I find it strange,' Athelstan commented, 'that whilst the Commons meeting is in full session in the chapter-house at Westminster, two knights from Shropshire are brutally murdered.'

'What's so strange?' Coverdale interrupted harshly.

'That the captain of the guard comes from Shropshire, whilst the chaplain had a close friend who also served in Lilleshall Abbey, not far from Shrewsbury and in the same county.'

'There's nothing strange in that,' the Benedictine answered quickly. 'When you go to the chapter-house, Brother, you'll find it guarded by a company of Cheshire archers. Sir Miles was born in Shropshire, but so were many in my Lord of Gaunt's retinue. As you know, the regent holds lands there and highly favours men from those parts. As for myself, if you ask

Father Abbot, he will tell you that I am not the only monk who has connections with our community at Lilleshall. I am a trained librarian and archivist; I have similar ties with our houses in Norfolk, Yorkshire and Somerset. More importantly, when Father Abbot asked for a volunteer to serve as chaplain to the Commons, I was the only one: I offered my services because the chapter-house is near the library and under my jurisdiction.'

Athelstan stared at him coolly. 'Did you speak to either of the dead men?'

'No.' The monk's eyes shifted too quickly. He licked his lips and swallowed hard.

You are lying, Athelstan thought: you have got something to hide. Why should an old monk, ill with rheumatism and arthritis, come to a tavern to say prayers over corpses of two men he hardly knew? Such prayers would be equally effective in some oratory or chantry chapel in the abbey.

Father Benedict glanced at Sir Miles. 'Time is passing,' he murmured. 'I still have my duties here.'

Cranston got to his feet and slurped noisily from his wineskin then beamed around. 'Ah, that's better. Father Benedict, it was a pleasure meeting you, though I regret the circumstances.' The coroner would've liked to add that never had he heard of two murder victims receiving the attention of so many priests but, like Athelstan, he realised lies had been told. There would be other opportunities to probe further.

Sir Miles also rose, swinging his great military cloak round his shoulders.

'We'd best hurry,' Cranston muttered. 'Come, Brother.'

And, making their farewells, they and the captain left the monk and went downstairs to the taproom.

'Give our thanks to Master Banyard,' Athelstan whispered

67

to Christina as Cranston and Coverdale swept out of the door before him.

The young girl smiled but Athelstan glimpsed the fear in her eyes. He grasped her hand. 'What's the matter, child?'

'Nothing, Father. It's just that terrible voice. Will he come back?'

Athelstan shook his head. 'I doubt it. But, if you remember anything else, send a message to Sir John at the Guildhall.'

The girl promised she would, and Athelstan hurried off after his companions. They walked down the narrow alleyways and into the grounds of Westminster Abbey. As they did so, the man waiting just inside the gate, under the shadow of a great oak tree, watched them go: the friar, the soldier and the ponderously girthed coroner.

'O Day of Wrath, O Day of Mourning,' the watcher whispered. 'See Fulfilled the Prophet's Warning!'

CHAPTER 4

As Athelstan and Cranston left the Gargoyle tavern, Ranulf the rat-catcher made his way to a large, deserted house which stood on the corner of Reeking Alley in Southwark. The rat-catcher closed the door, locking it carefully with the key the merchant had given him. He placed his two cages on the floor and sat down with his back to the door. He mopped his face with a rag tied to the broad leather belt from which hung all the implements of his trade: small cages, chisels, hammers and a large leather bag for the rodents he caught and killed.

'Ah, that's better!' Ranulf murmured. He pulled back the black-tarred hood from his pale pink features. 'I am happy,' he declared, his voice echoing eerily through the empty house. Ranulf stared up the long dusty staircase and, half closing his eyes, listened with pleasure to the scrabbling and the squeaking from behind the wainscoting and under the floorboards. Such sounds were always music to Ranulf's ears.

'Rats!' The merchant who had recently bought the house had roared, 'The whole place is infested with them: black, brown and varieties I have never heard or seen before!' The merchant had poked Ranulf's tarry jacket. 'Ten pounds sterling! I'll pay you ten pounds sterling to clear the place of rats. Three now, three when you have done it, and the balance after

69

my steward has inspected your work.'

'Ten pounds!' Ranulf chortled.

He opened his eyes. Although a widower, Ranulf had a large brood of children, all of whom dressed and looked like their father, but all with appetites and a penchant for growing which constantly worried him. Nevertheless, the warm weather had been good to Ranulf. Rats were back in London, whilst the disappearance of cats from Cheapside had meant their numbers had multiplied. The rat-catcher had been in great demand, and his mound of silver and gold, so carefully stowed away with a goldsmith just off Lothbury, was growing quite steadily. Out of the corner of his eye, Ranulf saw a small black furry shape race across the floorboards. Ranulf smiled beatifically.

'Others might curse you,' he whispered into the darkness, 'but, every morning in church, Ranulf thanks God for rats.'

He put his finger to his lips. Would there be rats in heaven? And, if there were, would he be allowed to catch them? But how could there be rats in heaven? Brother Athelstan had told him that it was a beautiful place and rats only existed where there was muck and dirt. Ranulf had pondered deeply on this. He had even raised it at the last meeting of the Guild of Rat-catchers when they had met in the Piebald tavern. None of his colleagues could give an answer.

'You'll have to ask Brother Athelstan,' Bardolph, who was skilled in catching bats in church belfries, had declared.

Ranulf pursed his lips and nodded. The guild were to have their special Mass at St Erconwald's soon: they would ask Brother Athelstan, he always had an answer; though Ranulf sometimes wondered if the little friar was teasing him with his gentle, sardonic replies. Another black shape raced across the floorboards further down the gloomy passageway. Ranulf stared

70

at the two ferrets he had brought: Ferrox, his favourite, and its younger brother, Audax. He picked up Ferrox's cage and stared at the little beady eyes and quivering snout.

'Don't worry,' he murmured. 'Hunting will soon begin: as soon as Daddy catches his breath.'

If a ferret could smile, Ranulf was sure Ferrox did. The ratcatcher put the cage down and stared at the dust motes dancing in the sunlight pouring through a small window in the stairwell above him.

'If I could only buy Bonaventure,' he murmured.

Ranulf had a vision of the united power of Bonaventure, Ferrox and Audax: an unholy trinity to loose upon the rat population of Southwark. Athelstan had been most unwilling.

'Bonaventure might kill your ferret,' the friar had warned.

Ranulf had violently disagreed. 'No, Brother, they always unite against rats. Rats be their common enemy. Anyway, there's not a cat alive which could catch old Ferrox.'

'In which case,' Athelstan had replied, 'remember the tenth commandment, Ranulf. Thou shalt not lust after thy neighbour's goods, nor his cattle, nor, in this instance, his cat.'

Ranulf smiled. He would remember that next time Bardolph asked to borrow Ferrox. His face became grave. He had come back from across the river: he had heard about more cats being stolen from the streets, and how the great Sir John 'Horsecruncher' Cranston was now pursuing the felons responsible.

'Old Big Arse will catch them,' Ranulf whispered. 'But Brother Athelstan should be careful about Bonaventure. Our little friar does love that tom-cat.'

Hadn't Athelstan once said Bonaventure was the only parishioner the friar was sure of getting into heaven? And then made a joke about his pet being a true 'Catholic'. Ranulf stared

71

down at Ferrox who was now beginning to show great interest in the squeaking and scrabbling behind the wainscoting.

'A lot of strange things are happening, Ferrox my son,' Ranulf whispered. 'Perline Brasenose, our young soldier, has also disappeared, and a demon has been seen outside St Erconwald's.'

Ranulf loosened the clasp at the top of his jacket and dabbed the sweat with his fingers. Were the two connected, he wondered? Or even all three mysteries? Perline was a scapegrace, a roaring boy. Had he deserted from the Tower garrison and turned to thieving cats? But where would he sell them? To the tanners for their skins? Or the fleshers for their meat? Ranulf shook his head: that would be dangerous. The traders would buy them only to turn poor Perline over to Cranston just for the reward. Or was Perline pretending to be a demon? He had acted a similar role in the parish play last Lammas Day? Ranulf congratulated himself on his perspicacity and stirred himself. Ferrox and Audax began to squeak, circling their cages, pushing their snouts through the bars. Yes, their time had come!

Ranulf got to his feet. He was about to pick up the cages when he heard the sound on the floor above him. Ranulf remembered the demon and his blood ran cold. He walked quickly into a small chamber on his right and became more aware of how dark and dank it was; the cobwebs in the corner seemed like nets spread to catch him. There was a terrible smell and the old house was creaking and groaning around him. The light was poor, shadows danced, and Ranulf wondered whether he was truly alone.

'Nonsense!' he whispered.

He saw a small hole in the far corner; going across he undid the clasp of the cage, grasped Ferrox's thin, muscular body

72

and, in a blink of an eye, the ferret disappeared down the hole. Ranulf walked back into the passageway and despatched Audax in a similar fashion.

'Now the dance begins,' Ranulf muttered, quoting his favourite phrase.

He sat down, undid the small bundle he carried, and ate the bread and cheese his eldest daughter had wrapped for him in a linen cloth. The rat-catcher tried to close his ears to all sounds, except for that of his two ferrets now engaged in a busy, bloody massacre under the floorboards. Time and again Ferrox and Audax reappeared, carrying in their sharp teeth the corpse of some hapless rat. They dropped these at their master's feet before disappearing again.

Ranulf felt a warm glow of satisfaction and bit deeply into the bread and cheese. But suddenly he heard a different sound. No rat or ferret could make the footfall he heard in the gallery above. Someone was moving there, slithering along the floorboards. Ranulf, a piece of cheese in his hand, rose and walked to the bottom of the stairs. He peered up into the gloom and almost choked on the cheese: on the top of the stairs was the demon of St Erconwald's! Large, dark and furry, teeth bared, its face so terrifying that Ranulf forgot about his ferrets and fled for his life.

Cranston and Athelstan followed Sir Miles Coverdale through the Jericho Parlour of Westminster Abbey, across Deans Yard and along the south cloister towards the chapter-house. Every so often they passed Cheshire archers resplendent in their green livery and white hart emblem. These were professional soldiers from the garrisons at the Tower or Baynard's Castle; hair cropped, faces dark and lean. All carried longbows and a quiver of twenty yew arrows, as well as sword and dagger. Men-at-arms wearing the red, blue and gold royal livery also stood on guard at every door and on every corner.

'Why so many soldiers?' Cranston asked as they entered the cloisters.

'His Grace the Regent is determined that the Commons be allowed to sit unmolested,' Coverdale replied. 'No one enters the cloisters or chapter-house who is not either a member of Parliament or one of the royal clerks commissioned to assist them in their discussions.'

'Don't the Commons ever object?' Cranston declared. 'Some might claim the soldiers overawe them.'

'Aye, some addle-brains might say that, but there are no soldiers in the chapter-house, Sir John, whilst the good knights and burgesses are free to come and go as they wish.'

They entered the eastern cloister where some monks, taking full advantage of the spring sunshine, now sat at their desks, copying or illuminating manuscripts. In the centre garth, soldiers played checkerboard games whilst a few conversed with the monks.

'The brothers certainly welcome our presence,' Coverdale declared.

'It's the same in any enclosed community,' Athelstan replied. 'Always eager for fresh faces, or to indulge in gossip about the great ones of the land.'

They entered the vestibule to the chapter-house. A line of archers stood in front of the closed double doors. Whilst one of them unlocked these, Athelstan stood back and admired the gloriously carved stone triptych above the doorway, showing Christ in Judgement.

'I thought the session was finished,' Cranston declared.

'It is, but the doors are always locked,' Coverdale replied. 'The representatives have only to knock and they'll be allowed in or out. Each of them possesses a special seal or pass.' He smiled grimly. 'Our regent is thorough.'

Cranston did not disagree. They entered the outer vestibule and went along a marble corridor lined by Purbeck marble columns. Just before they came to a second set of doors, Athelstan stopped, noticing flights of stairs to his left and, on his right, another staircase going down into the darkness.

'Where do these lead?' he asked.

'The steps going up lead to St Faith's Chapel,' Coverdale replied. 'The others will take you down to the Pyx chamber.'

Athelstan was about to ask about the latter, but Coverdale was already snapping his fingers at the guards to open the next set of doors. These were unlocked and swung back and they entered the chapter-house itself. It was deserted except for one balding, dark-faced, fussy little man who stood at the lectern. He came hurrying towards them, hands flailing the air.

'You are late! You are late!' he cried at Coverdale. 'The honourable representatives from Shropshire could wait no longer. They have gone to one of the cookshops in the abbey yard.' He drew his head back, reminding Cranston of a noisy, busy sparrow. 'You can't keep such men waiting,' he bleated.

'Nor can you the king's coroner,' Cranston intervened. 'Who are you, anyway?'

'Sir Peter de la Mare, Speaker of the Commons. Sir Miles, what is happening?'

Coverdale introduced Cranston and Athelstan, and de la Mare became more obsequious. 'Well, wait here,' he rattled on. 'And I'll see what I can do, I'll see what I can do.' And off he waddled.

75

Athelstan stared round the chapter-house. 'God in heaven!' he exclaimed. 'Look, Sir John, what a beautiful place!'

The chamber was octagonal in shape and ringed by great windows that increased the impression of light and illuminated the glory of the great arched roof. This was supported by a single squat column, before which stood a huge wooden lectern.

'Where do the representatives sit?' Athelstan asked.

Cranston pointed to the three tiers of steps which ran round the room.

'Over there,' he replied. 'The chapter-house can hold hundreds.'

Athelstan nodded even as he gazed at the beautiful tympanum above the doorway depicting Christ in glory. The Saviour was clothed in a beautiful crimson cloak, and round his head glowed a golden nimbus against a bright blue sky. On either side, white robed angels, each with three sets of wings, bowed their heads in adoration. In the windows and along the walls beneath them were more scenes from the Bible: the Four Horsemen of the Apocalypse: the Great Beast in conflict with Michael the Archangel, St John being miraculously preserved in a cauldron of boiling oil; whilst other pictures showed the saved simpering in righteousness whilst the damned writhed in screaming torment.

'All this must have been built by angels,' Athelstan murmured. 'Just look, Sir John! I must bring Huddle here. If he could only study scenes like these! The representatives are most fortunate to meet in a place like this.'

'Little good it does them,' Coverdale broke in harshly. 'They squat around the walls, shouting and yelling.'

'Surely they do more than that?' Athelstan replied.

'Well, the Speaker keeps order,' Coverdale said. 'He sits in

76

the centre just beneath the window. He directs whom he chooses to speak from the lectern. Whilst over there –' he pointed to a small table containing scrolls of parchment – 'sit the clerks and lawyers.'

Athelstan nodded. He walked slowly round, admiring the different scenes painted on the walls, now and again standing back, marvelling at the artist's skill. He paused at the sound of footsteps in the vestibule; the door was flung open and a group of men swept into the chapter-house.

'Cranston.' The leader was a thickset, narrow-faced man, his iron-grey hair shaved high above his ears. He stood, just within the doorway, hands on his hips, legs apart.

'Over here,' Cranston cooed back. 'And who, sir, are you?'

'Sir Edmund Malmesbury, representative of the Commons from Shropshire. We waited for you.' Malmesbury glanced disdainfully at Coverdale. 'But we are busy men. We need to eat and drink.'

'Aye, so you do,' Cranston wheezed as he got to his feet. And, thumbs stuck in his belt, he waddled over. He stopped only a few inches from Malmesbury.

'We were late, Sir Edmund.' He smiled. 'But let me introduce myself: Sir John Cranston, King's Officer and Coroner of the city of London; Brother Athelstan, my clerk; Coverdale you know.' Cranston peered round Malmesbury. 'And these are your companions?'

The rest of the group came forward: red-haired, bristling-bearded Sir Thomas Elontius, with his fierce popping eyes; Sir Humphrey Aylebore, his head bald as an egg, fat and podgy, his shaven face weak and rather slobbery; Sir Maurice Goldingham, small and neat in appearance, his oily black hair coiffed like that of a page's; and finally, Sir Francis Harnett, small and blond-haired with close-set eyes. Sir Francis's brown, clean-shaven face reminded Athelstan of a kestrel and, remembering Moleskin's story about Perline Brasenose meeting the knight on the river steps at Southwark, the friar wondered what such a man would want with the likes of his headstrong young parishioner.

Cranston stood back, bowed, and gestured at the steps. 'My noble sirs, take your ease, we have only a few questions.'

The five knights of the shire swaggered across and sat on the ledges. They did so slowly, arrogantly, chattering and whispering amongst themselves.

Peacocks! Athelstan thought, with all the arrogance of Lucifer. The knights looked what they were: successful, hardened warriors; merchants, men of great importance in their own shire as well as here in London. They were all dressed in expensive houppelondes or gowns, red and gold, scarlet or green, all edged and trimmed with ermine along the fringes of hem and cuff. Costly belts clasped their bulging waists above multi-coloured hose and ornamented shoes. Men of middle age but with all the fripperies of court gallants. Silver bells were stitched on their sleeves. The shirts underneath their gowns were of costly cambric; jewelled clasps and silver rings decorated fleshy fingers and wrists. None of them were armed, except for dress-daggers pushed into embroidered scabbards.

Malmesbury was their leader, bellicose and aggressive. For a while he whispered quietly to Sir Humphrey Aylebore, whose fat face broke into a malicious smile as he quickly glared at Sir Miles Coverdale. Athelstan sensed there was no love lost between these powerful men and Sir John of Gaunt's officer. Elontius began to whistle under his breath. Goldingham, who must have drunk deeply, leaned back, eyes half closed, whilst

Harnett appeared more interested in the paintings on the walls.

Athelstan stood by the lectern and wondered how Sir John would deal with these men, so different from the footpads, felons and foists of London's Cheapside. The friar quietly prayed that the coroner would keep his temper, and hoped that he had not drunk too much from the miraculous wineskin. Above them, the abbey bells began to toll; calling the monks to Divine Office, their chimes rang through the hollow cloisters. Cranston cocked his head to one side, as if more interested in their sound than the malice of Malmesbury and his companions. The bells stopped clanging, the knights still kept whispering amongst themselves, whilst Cranston began to admire the ring of office on his finger. At last the whispering stopped, but still Cranston did not lift his head. Athelstan gripped the edge of the lectern as the silence grew more oppressive.

'Very good, my lord Coroner.' Malmesbury sprang to his feet. 'You have summoned us here.' He slapped a pair of leather gloves against his thigh. 'If you have no questions, we'll go. Let me remind you, Coroner, we are not under your jurisdiction: members of the Commons cannot be arrested because of stupid civic regulations.' He glanced down at his companions who murmured approval.

'A very pretty speech.' Cranston got to his feet and came over to stand beside Athelstan. He pointed to the door. 'All of you may go, if you wish. Sir Edmund is perfectly correct. I have no jurisdiction here. However, let me remind you of a few legal niceties. First, two of your companions, members of the Commons, have been foully murdered. This is an attack upon the authority of the Crown. I talk not about the regent but of Richard, King of England, whose officer I am. The lawyers of the Chancery may also argue that an attack upon my authority

79

is an attack upon the Crown. However,' Cranston smiled, 'that would be decided by the king's justices: it could take a long time and require your return from Shropshire to London. Secondly, you are protected as long as the Commons sit. Once this Parliament is dismissed, and it will be dismissed whatever happens, I shall swear out warrants for your arrest on suspicion of murder.'

'This is preposterous!' Goldingham spluttered, half rising to his feet. 'You accuse us of the murder of two of our companions?'

'I said suspicion, based on the very sound legal point that you refused to answer the questions of the king's officer.'

'But we had nothing to do with their deaths,' Thomas Elontius shouted, his face puce-coloured, his eyes popping so much that Athelstan thought they would fall out of his head.

Cranston smiled. 'Very good,' he purred. 'In which case you will not object to answering a few simple questions.'

Goldingham slouched back on the steps. 'Get on with it,' he muttered.

'Good, on Monday last—' Cranston began.

'Tarry a while.' Harnett pointed at Coverdale. 'Must he stay?'

'Yes, he must. If he goes,' Cranston replied, 'so do I. Sir Miles, do relax. Sit down. This will not take long.'

Cranston paused to dab his face with the edge of his cloak, glanced across at Athelstan and winked. The friar stepped forward. Pushing his hands up the sleeves of his habit, he walked towards the knights. They watched him curiously.

'My lords,' Athelstan began, 'on Monday night Sir Oliver Bouchon left a supper party which you all attended at the Gargoyle tavern. According to witnesses, Bouchon was distressed and subdued. He did not return and his body was later recovered amongst the river reeds near Tothill Fields.'

'So?' Malmesbury asked. He watched Athelstan like Bonaventure would a mouse.

'Why was Sir Oliver so upset?'

The knights just stared back.

'Did he tell you where he was going?'

Again silence.

'Did he tell you about receiving the arrowhead, the candle and the scrap of parchment with the word "Remember" scrawled on it?'

'He told us nothing,' Malmesbury replied. 'Isn't that true, my lords?' He mimicked Athelstan's words and grinned at his companions.

'We have talked about this amongst ourselves.' Elontius scratched his red, bristling beard: close up, he looked not so fierce, and Athelstan caught a softness in the man's popping eyes.

'Brother, we do not mean to insult you, or Sir John,' he continued. 'But we know nothing of Sir Oliver's death, God rest him. Yes, he was quiet; yes, he left the tavern; and that's the last any of us ever saw of him.'

'So you know nothing which might explain his death? Why should someone send the arrowhead and other articles to him? And why would anyone want to kill him?'

This time a chorus of denials greeted his questions. Athelstan looked down at the tiled floor and moved the tip of his sandal across the fleur-de-lys painted there.

'And later that evening, my lords?' He raised his head. 'You left for other entertainment?'

'That's right,' Goldingham mimicked. 'We left for, er, other

81

entertainment at Dame Mathilda's nunnery in Cottemore Lane.'

Harnett began to snigger. Elontius looked a little embarrassed. Aylebore smirked but Malmesbury kept watching Athelstan intently: as he did so, the friar began to wonder where he had seen Sir Edmund before.

'So you went to a brothel?' Cranston came over. 'That's what Dame Mathilda runs: a molly-house for men away from their wives.' Cranston now stood over the knights, legs apart, his blue eyes glaring icily at them. He shook his head and wagged a finger at them. 'This is not a matter for laughter. What happens, my lords, if these deaths are not resolved and I have to come to Shrewsbury to ask these questions before you and your wives?'

'That would be rather difficult,' Goldingham spluttered. 'Mine's dead.'

'Then, sir, she is most fortunate.'

Goldingham's hand flew to his dagger.

'Why don't you draw?' Cranston taunted. 'Or, better still, Sir Maurice, smack me in the face with your gloves. I can still mount a charger and tilt a lance. My aim is true and my hand as steady as when I fought for the Black Prince.'

Malmesbury turned and gripped Goldingham's shoulder. 'Sir John, we apologise. And to you too, Brother Athelstan. I will answer for the rest and they can contradict me if they wish. Sir Oliver left the tavern that night and did not return. None of us knew what he was worried about. True, we tried to cheer him up, but he was in a deep melancholy. After supper, our good landlord took us to Dame Mathilda's house in Cottemore Lane. We all stayed there till the early hours, then came back –' he forced a smile – 'much the worse for drink. Naturally, we were all shocked by Sir Oliver's death but, there again, London is full of footpads. And,' his words were veiled in sarcasm, 'we understand such attacks are common.'

Athelstan stared along the row of faces. You are lying, he thought. You've all sat together and prepared this story: if Sir John and I questioned you individually, you'd just sing the same song.

'The same is true of Swynford's death.' Harnett spoke up.

Athelstan caught the tremor in the man's voice, the quick flicker in his eyes. He decided to seize an opportunity to ask Sir Francis what business he had along the river.

'Yes, yes.' Cranston walked back to the lectern. He peered over his shoulder at Coverdale. The young captain lounged on the steps, such hatred in his eyes that Cranston wondered whether he had acted wisely in asking Gaunt's henchman to remain.

'I suppose,' Athelstan declared wearily, 'that Swynford's death also came as a surprise and distressing shock to you all; that you know nothing about why an arrowhead, a candle and a scrap of parchment were sent to him; and that last night, when he was murdered, you were all busy in your own affairs?'

'Yes, that's true,' Malmesbury replied. 'We were tired after the night before, distressed about Sir Oliver's death, so we stayed at the Gargoyle.'

'And you have witnesses to that?'

'I was with Sir Edmund,' Elontius replied. 'In his chamber, rolling dice and talking about events.'

'And you, Sir Humphrey?'

Aylebore pulled a face. 'I retired early. I paid my respects to Sir Oliver's corpse. For a while I sat talking to the landlord and Goldingham here. I left the taproom and went to my own

83

chamber. The first I knew anything was wrong was when the landlord raised the alarm. Isn't that correct, Goldingham?'

Sir Maurice ran a hand through his neatly coiffed hair.

'It's true and the landlord will stand guarantor for me. For a while I talked to him about the wine trade and the attacks by French pirates on our cogs from Bordeaux. He left and I flirted with the lovely Christina.'

'And one of you saw the priest arrive?'

'I did.' Goldingham spoke up. 'The tavern was rather busy, the taproom filled. I was trying to seize Christina's hand when the door opened. I saw a figure in a cloak and cowl.' Goldingham shrugged. 'He swept into the room, Christina said something to him and he went up the stairs. After that,' he yawned, 'I really can't remember. I went up to prepare for bed until I heard the landlord shouting.'

'Did anyone see the priest leave?' Athelstan asked.

'How could we?' Malmesbury retorted. 'I was with Sir Thomas. Aylebore was in bed, Goldingham in his chamber. The first we knew of Swynford's death was the landlord screaming like a maid.'

'Which leaves you, Sir Francis.' Athelstan smiled at Harnett. 'Where were you last night?'

'I was . . .' The close-set eyes blinked. 'I was in my chamber all the time.'

'And on the previous evening?' Athelstan asked.

Harnett opened his mouth to lie, but the silence of his companions betrayed him.

'I left Dame Mathilda's early,' he confessed. 'I went down to King's steps and hired a barge.'

'For where? Sir Francis, please tell me the truth.'

'I went to the stews in Southwark, to the bath-house there.'

He gazed round, flushed, as his companions hid their sniggers behind their hands.

'So, you were not tired from the evening's exertions?' Athelstan remarked drily. 'Sir Francis, I am parish priest of St Erconwald's: the bath-houses on the riverside are notorious brothels.'

'So?' Harnett's face came up, his lips pursed. 'I went there for refreshments, Brother, as probably do a great many of your parishioners.'

'And then you came back,' Athelstan continued, ignoring the insult.

'Yes, I came back.' Harnett shrugged. 'What more can I say?'

What more indeed, Athelstan thought? He smiled to hide his despair: these men were lying, even laughing at him. Yet there was little he or Sir John could do to bring them to book. He glanced over his shoulder. Cranston had now moved to sit beside Coverdale. Athelstan coughed noisily because the coroner was now leaning slightly forward, eyes drooping. Oh, don't fall asleep, Athelstan prayed. Please, Sir John! He felt they were treading a narrow, dangerous path; the slightest slip and these powerful knights would break into mocking laughter. They would declare they had nothing more to say and sweep out to continue their pleasures and other pastimes.

'And Sir Henry Swynford,' Athelstan almost shouted as he turned and walked back towards the knights. He hoped Sir John would stir himself. 'And Sir Henry,' he repeated just as loudly, 'gave no indication that he had received the same artefacts as Sir Oliver Bouchon?'

'No, he didn't,' Aylebore grumbled, 'and I'm getting tired of this, Brother.'

'And so none of you knows of any reason why he should have been murdered?'

'If there was, we'd tell you,' Malmesbury retorted.

'What were Sir Oliver and Sir Henry supposed to remember?' Athelstan asked.

'If *we* knew,' Sir Edmund sarcastically replied, 'you'd know.'

'You were all friends?'

'More companions and neighbours,' Aylebore replied.

'But you were all Knights of the Swan?' Athelstan asked.

For the first time he saw the mask slip: Malmesbury flinched whilst his companions stirred restlessly.

'That was many years ago,' Malmesbury muttered. 'The foolishness of youth, Brother Athelstan. Times goes on. People change and so do we.'

'So the noble Fraternity of the Knights of the Swan no longer exists?' Athelstan asked.

'It just died.'

'When the friendship between you did?' Athelstan asked.

'Friar,' Sir Humphrey Aylebore warned, 'you are becoming impertinent.'

'Brother Athelstan,' Sir Thomas Elontius intervened kindly, 'we all live in the same shire. We fought in the same battles. We marry into each others' families. We meet for the tournament or the hunt. We laugh at weddings and mourn at funerals. We have our disagreements, but nothing to provoke murder between us.'

You are like Sir John, Athelstan thought, glancing at Elontius; despite your red hair and bristling beard, you are a kind man.

Sir Thomas held his gaze. 'We know nothing, Brother,' he whispered hoarsely, 'of why these two good knights should be so foully slain.'

86

'And the red crosses etched on the faces of the two corpses?'

'Nothing,' Malmesbury rasped.

'In which case,' Cranston declared, wheezing as he got up from the steps and ambling across the chapter-house floor, 'my secretarius will write down what you have told us. You are innocents in this matter. You know nothing that could assist us. You are willing to swear as much on oath?'

'Show us a book of the Gospels,' Goldingham taunted, 'and I'll take my oath.'

'In which case . . .' Cranston looked over his shoulder at Coverdale.

'*Festina lente*,' Sir Maurice Goldingham spoke up. 'Hasten slowly, my lord Coroner.' He spread his podgy hands. 'We have sat here and answered your questions, but the fact remains that two of our companions lie foully slain. You and your friar have come here and, by your questions, insinuated that their assassin could be one or all of us. Yet,' Goldingham got to his feet shrugging off Malmesbury's warning hand, 'these men were killed in London, in your jurisdiction, my lord Coroner. Both men, like us, spoke out strongly against the regent and his demands for fresh taxes.' Goldingham pressed a podgy finger into Cranston's chest. 'Now people are beginning to whisper that they might have been killed by those who do not like such outspokenness.' He pressed his finger even harder but Cranston did not flinch.

'These men were our friends,' Goldingham continued hoarsely. 'Their blood cries to heaven for vengeance. You have been sent by the regent so I tell you this: if these deaths are not resolved and the assassin caught, I personally will stand at that lectern and tell the Commons that their murderers walk free because certain officers of the king are too incompetent to catch

87

them, and that those same officers should be replaced.'

Cranston grasped the knight's podgy finger and squeezed it until Goldingham winced. 'I have heard you, Sir Maurice,' he whispered, 'and I call you a fool. I swear two things myself. First, I shall trap this murderer and watch him hang, his body cut down, quartered and disembowelled.' The coroner raised his voice. 'Secondly, the deaths of these men are shrouded in mystery, but you are all fools if you believe that they will be the last to die.'

CHAPTER 5

'Thank God we are out of there!'

Cranston and Athelstan stood in the forecourt before the great doorway of the abbey. They had left the knights in the chapter-house, Cranston not waiting for any reaction to his warning. He had just spun on his heel and strode out, with Athelstan and Coverdale following behind. The captain of Gaunt's guard had been grinning from ear to ear at the way Cranston had dealt with those powerful men. After they had passed through the cordon of soldiers, he was impatient to enjoy the representatives' discomfort, and could hardly wait to whisper his goodbyes to Athelstan.

'Did I do right?' Cranston breathed in noisily.

He took out his wineskin, toasted the statue of the Virgin standing on a plinth next to the abbey door, and took generous swigs.

'They threatened you, Sir John, and there was no need for that. However, Goldingham might be correct. We have no proof that Bouchon's and Swynford's killer is one of those knights.'

'Bollocks!' Cranston cursed. 'They were telling a pack of lies. They sat there like choirboys or mummers in a play reciting lines.'

'But that does not mean they are trying to hide anything about the murders,' Athelstan insisted. He linked his arm through Sir John's and guided him away. 'You have met such men before, Sir John. You know their ways,' he added flatteringly. 'They grew up together, served as pages and squires in the same households. They are linked by blood and marriage. They go to war, share the spoils and, in peace time, stand shoulder to shoulder.'

'Don't speak in riddles, Friar!'

'Come, Sir John, there is no riddle. You have just taken one swig too many of that wineskin. No, don't glare at me. You're father of the poppets, and glaring at me from under those bushy white eyebrows is only pretence. What I am saying,' Athelstan continued, 'is that of course those men have got a great deal to hide, but they may have nothing to do with the murders.'

'So how do we find out?'

Athelstan poked the wineskin beneath Sir John's cloak. '*In vino veritas*, Sir John. In wine there's truth.'

'You mean Banyard?'

'Of course. Show me a landlord who says he doesn't eavesdrop on his customers' conversations and I'll show you a liar.'

They made their way out of the abbey. They had to take a circuitous route through narrow, foulsome alleyways to the Gargoyle, since a burning house had closed off the more direct path.

'Isn't it strange?' Cranston murmured. 'We have just left the abbey where kings are crowned and parliaments are held, a sacred and venerable place; yet every rogue in the city seems to gather round it.'

Athelstan had to agree. He saw two characters, one with a patch over his eye, both with their hoods pulled up, following a pretty whore who was tripping along past the stalls. Both men were greedily watching the embroidered purse which swung from her gaudy girdle. At the corner of the alleyway three dummerers were holding up placards claiming they were deaf-mutes, had been since birth, and would passers-by please spare them a farthing?

'Liars!' Cranston snorted with disbelief.

'But they are genuine,' Athelstan exclaimed.

'Watch this,' Cranston muttered.

He crossed the street, jumping over the overflowing sewer in the centre, and waited till a small crowd had gathered round, ready to give coins. Cranston drew his dagger, sidled close behind one of the dummerers and, as he passed, nicked the man's bottom with his dagger point. The fellow dropped his sign and screeched like a bird.

'Who did that? Who did that?'

The spectators looked on in stupefaction.

'A miracle,' Cranston declared, holding up his dagger. 'The man can speak.' He advanced threateningly on the other two. 'And perhaps I can perform the same for you.'

All three men grabbed their small bowls of coins and fled like hares up an alleyway. The word must have spread: as Cranston swept by, different characters, all begging for alms, disappeared into the shadows. Their places were soon taken outside doorways, or in the empty spaces between houses, by a legion of other vagabonds: ballad-mongers, hucksters, relic-sellers, as well as the ubiquitous pardoners eager to sell indulgence and penances to pilgrims flocking to the tomb of Edward the Confessor. At times the alleyways became packed, the noise so intense that Cranston and Athelstan had to struggle to get through.

'Why is it that religion attracts so many rogues and fools?' Cranston bawled. 'Surely the good Lord objects?'

Athelstan felt like reminding him that, during his lifetime, Christ had attracted both saints and sinners. However, the clamour was so loud he decided to leave his advice for another time. At last they turned a corner and found themselves under the tavern sign of the Gargoyle. Athelstan stared up at the devil's head depicted there. Truly frightful, painted in a greyish-green against a scarlet background. The demon's straggling hair, horrid eyes and roaring mouth as it attacked a knight in full armour, reminded the friar of his own troubles at St Erconwald's. They entered the taproom: Banyard was standing up by the wine tuns holding forth to a group of boatmen about the rising price of ale and beer. He broke off and smiled at Athelstan and Cranston.

'Well, my lord Coroner, what can I do for you? Some refreshment?'

'Yes,' Athelstan replied hastily. 'And if I can hire a writing-tray?'

'Feed the body first,' Cranston growled.

'Some charlet?' Banyard offered. 'Pork mixed with egg,' he explained. 'And the bread will be fresh.'

Cranston and Athelstan agreed, and the landlord showed them to a table away from the rest. He brought them blackjacks of ale, then sent a boy across with a writing-tray, containing a quill, a small pot of ink, a scrap of parchment and some sealing wax.

'What's the matter?' Cranston asked.

Athelstan seized the quill and began to write quickly, his

hand racing across the page. He stopped and recalled those scraps of parchment sent to the dead knights.

'Well, it wasn't done here.'

'What wasn't?'

'The parchment and ink are different,' Athelstan explained. 'I just wondered if the warnings had been written here.' He narrowed his eyes. 'If we could only find what those two dead men were supposed to remember. Anyway,' he dipped the tip of the quill into the inkpot and continued his scribbling. 'I am writing to Father Prior,' he explained. 'I have to tell him about our demon in Southwark.'

'What help can he give?' Cranston asked.

'He has the cunning of a serpent and the innocence of a dove.'

'You mean just like yourself?'

'Sir John, you flatter . . . But, seriously, in a recent letter from our superior, all Dominican priests were warned to study demonic possession more accurately, and have such phenomena investigated.' Athelstan finished writing, put his pen down and asked the potboy for a candle to melt the wax.

'You see, Sir John,' he continued when he'd done this, 'Pike the ditcher can see all sorts of demons when he's drunk, but Benedicta is level-headed. You may scoff, but something foul lurked in our death-house that night. I have to be sure. Why, Sir John,' he blew the candle out, 'don't you believe in Satan and all his powers?'

'Yes, I bloody well do.' Cranston sipped from his tankard. 'And a lot of his friends live in Cheapside. However, you surely don't believe that demons come up from hell to cavort along Southwark's alleyways? I can think of more suitable, plumper prey across the river.'

93

'Whatever it is,' Athelstan picked up the letter as Banyard approached with their meal, 'I must report to Father Anselm and seek his advice.'

Once the landlord had placed the steaming platters of food before them, Athelstan handed him the letter.

'Would you ensure this is taken to Blackfriars?' he asked. He took a penny out of his purse. 'I'll pay for the boy.'

'Nonsense!' Banyard replied. 'There's no need to pay, Father.'

'In which case,' Cranston put his horn spoon down, smacking his lips, 'one good turn deserves another. Send the lad running, Master Banyard, and come back here. Be our guest.'

Banyard accepted. He returned from the kitchen and sat down, a tankard of frothy ale in his huge fist. Cranston took a silver coin out of his purse and slid this towards him.

'We would like your advice, Master Banyard.'

The landlord sipped from his ale, but his eyes never left the silver coin.

'About what?' he asked, wiping his mouth on the back of his hand.

'Don't let's be children.' Cranston lowered his voice and pushed the silver coin towards Banyard. 'Upstairs, sir, you have two corpses, both former customers: that cannot be good for trade.'

'Death is a sudden visitor, Sir John. The Gargoyle has housed many a corpse.' The taverner stared up at the smoke-blackened roof beams. 'It has stood here for many a year. Customers die in their sleep or in a fight. We have also taken in many a corpse fished from the river.'

'But this is different,' Athelstan persisted.

Banyard put his tankard down; he stretched out his

hand and the silver coin disappeared.

'I have told you what I know and what I have seen,' he whispered. 'However, our noble representatives are not the band of brothers they appear to be. On the night Bouchon was killed, there was considerable discord over a number of matters.' He pulled a face. 'Local matters: the buying up of grain as well as the fixing of prices on the Shrewsbury markets.'

'And?' Cranston asked.

'The discussion grew heated,' Banyard continued. 'They argued about a ship they'd hired to import grain from Hainault. Apparently this was done on Malmesbury's advice, but the ship hadn't fared well and was seized by French pirates in the Narrow Seas. Goldingham, the small dark one who walks like a woman and has a tongue like a viper, declared Malmesbury should reimburse them. Sir Edmund, red in the face, said he would not.'

'And?'

'Well, this led to other matters. They talked of a goblet which had disappeared. I heard the name "Arthur" mentioned.' Banyard sipped from his tankard. 'I was going in and out of the room, but when I returned the conversation had changed. Sir Henry Swynford was saying how they should not oppose the regent so vehemently. He talked of unrest in the shires and the growing attacks upon isolated farmhouses and manors, be it in Kent or along the Welsh march.' Banyard stopped speaking, cradling his tankard. 'Then Sir Francis Harnett said something very strange.' Banyard closed his eyes. 'Yes, that's right: he said the old ways were the best ways. Malmesbury leaned across the table and grasped his wrist. "Don't be stupid!" he hissed. "Stick to your beasteries!"'

'What do you think he meant by that?' Athelstan asked.

95

'Oh, Sir Francis Harnett is apparently interested in all forms of exotic beasts. When he returned from the Tower, he babbled like a child about the elephants, apes, and even a white bear kept in the royal menagerie.'

'No,' Athelstan smiled. 'I meant about the old ways being the best ways.'

Banyard raised his eyebrows. 'Father, I am a taverner, not some magician at a fair.'

'And Sir Oliver Bouchon? He was quiet?'

'He was silent throughout, never touched his food.' Banyard got to his feet. 'That's all I know; now my customers wait.'

'You could have told us this before.'

'Sir John, I sell wine, good food and gossip. All three demand payment.'

'And will you take us down to Dame Mathilda's in Cottemore Lane?' Cranston demanded.

Banyard smirked. 'You need solace, Sir John?'

'No, no!' Cranston replied hastily. 'The Lady Maude, God forfend her, would be horrified to know that I had visited such a place. I simply need to discover whether all our good knights spent Monday evening there.'

Banyard made a face, playing with the empty tankard in his hands. 'Sir John, they all came back here after midnight, much the worse for wear.' He shrugged. 'When you are ready, I'll take you.' He got up and walked back into the buttery.

'Well.' Cranston pushed the plate away. 'All we've established is what we know already. The good knights are liars. There is rivalry amongst them.' He licked his lips. 'I wonder what this cup of Arthur means, or Harnett's claim that the old ways were the best ways?'

'Those knights,' Athelstan replied, 'know the significance

96

of the arrowhead, the candle and the word "REMEMBER". They were killed because of some secret sin committed many years ago. But that begs another question.'

Athelstan cleaned his horn spoon and put it back in his wallet. 'If these knights are being pursued by the furies from their past, why don't they panic? Why don't they flee back to Shropshire?' He glanced at Cranston and leaned across the table. 'I mean, Sir John, if you, I and others travelled to Shrewsbury, and let us say we'd committed some secret sin, and suddenly members of our party began to be murdered. What would you do?'

Cranston lowered his tankard. 'Though I hate to admit it, I'd leave Shrewsbury as quickly as an arrow from a bow.'

'So, why don't these knights?' Athelstan asked. 'Two of their companions are dead, yet . . .'

Cranston stared across the tavern. 'Oh, well put, little friar.' He murmured. 'To flee London, put as much distance between themselves and Westminster would be the natural thing to do.' He blew his cheeks out and ran his fingers along the bristling moustaches. 'Of course, there's still time for them to do that, yet the men we met in the chapter-house seemed quite determined to stay.' He leaned over and nipped Athelstan's wrist. 'You pose questions, Friar. Do you have any answers?'

'Well, first,' Athelstan replied slowly, 'they can't flee immediately. It would look as if they were guilty and wished to hide something. Secondly, they are representatives of the shire. They are duty-bound to stay in Westminster until this Parliament is finished. But,' Athelstan paused, 'they could always claim sickness or some urgent business at home.' Athelstan continued slowly. 'It's possible there might be two other explanations. First, not all the knights we met this morning might have some secret sin to hide. Secondly, perhaps there's a greater fear which compels them to stay.' He pushed away the plate and writing-tray. 'But come, Sir John, the day is drawing on.' He smiled. 'And we still have to visit Dame Mathilda and her ladies of the night.'

In his small, beautifully decorated oratory at the Savoy Palace, John of Gaunt knelt, head bowed in prayer, at his prie-dieu. Beside him, on a red and gold embroidered cushion, knelt his 'beloved nephew', Richard of England. Now and again the young king, his face like that of an angel, ivory-pale framed by gold hair, would blink his light-blue eyes and glance quickly at his uncle. He'd confided so often to his tutor, Sir Simon Burley, how much he hated 'dear Uncle' with a passion beyond all understanding. Did Gaunt really pray? the young king wondered. Or was the oratory a place of silence and seclusion, where he could plot? Richard lifted his eyes to the silver crucifix.

'Dear God,' he prayed silently. 'I am thirteen years of age. Three more years, only three, and I will be king in my own right!'

Richard smiled. And what would happen then to 'dear Uncle'? Yet three years was a long time: anything could happen! Richard, through his tutor, knew all about the peasants seething with discontent at being tied to the soil, at not being allowed to sell their labour in the markets, or bargain for what they were paid. Now a Parliament had convened at Westminster: the lords temporal and spiritual met by themselves; the Commons, assembled in the chapter-house, resolutely argued against levying taxes so 'beloved Uncle' could build more ships or raise more troops. Yet, what would happen if a storm broke which swept away not only Uncle but himself? Would the peasant rebels really lift their hands against the son of the Black Prince, their own anointed king? Beside him Gaunt sighed, lifted his head and blessed himself with a flourish. He turned to Richard.

'Beloved Nephew,' he purred, 'it was good of you to join me in prayer.'

'Dearest Uncle,' Richard replied just as sweetly, 'you need all the assistance God can send you.'

Gaunt's smile remained fixed. 'In three days' time, Sire, you are to go down to Westminster. You must walk amongst your Commons, tell them how much you love them. How you need their help.'

'And will you come, dearest Uncle?'

'As always, beloved Nephew, I will be at your right hand.'

'"And, if thine right hand be a cause for scandal,"' Richard quoted from the Gospels, '"cut it off."'

'Dearest Nephew, whatever do you mean?' Gaunt eased himself up from the prie-dieu but Richard remained kneeling.

'In three years' time, dearest Uncle, I come into my own: King in my own right.' Richard's voice hardened. 'I would like a kingdom to govern, not a realm rent by division and war.'

'The peasants will, in time, get what they want.'

Gaunt sat down on the altar steps, facing his nephew. 'I am not liked, Sire, but no man who exercises power is. The French and Spanish fleets ravage our southern coastline. The lords of the soil keep their boot on the peasants' neck. They, in turn, plot treason and revolt.'

Richard studied his uncle's leonine, arrogant face. He noticed the lines round the eyes and the furrows running into the silver beard. Am I wrong? the young king wondered. Was Gaunt plotting to seize the crown for himself, as his tutor Simon

Burley constantly warned him? Or was he just trying to steer the realm into calmer waters? Gaunt leaned forward and grasped his nephew's hand.

'Beloved Nephew, this kingdom is yours but, unless we raise these taxes, we will have neither the ships nor the troops to defend ourselves. Once I have this, I can settle the lords and provide relief for the peasants. When you go to the Parliament, do as I say. Speak kindly to the knights and burgesses. Tell them that my demands are yours.' Gaunt's face broke into a lopsided smile. 'After all, you are the son of the famous Black Prince, grandson of the great Edward III, conqueror of France.'

Richard removed his hand. 'I am also King of England in my own right.'

Gaunt was about to reply when there was a knock on the door. Sir Miles Coverdale came in and bowed. 'Your Graces, Sir Simon Burley is here. He insists the young king must return to his lessons.'

Gaunt rose to his feet and helped his nephew to his. 'Ah yes, your lessons.' Gaunt smiled. 'Give Sir Simon my regards, your Grace, but remind him of the famous saying: "It is easier to preach than to act".'

Richard shifted the gold cord round his slim waist, smoothing down the creases in his blue and gold silk gown. He bowed. 'Dearest Uncle.' He smiled back. 'You should have been a preacher.'

Coverdale stepped aside and Richard of England swept out of the oratory. Gaunt stood and listened to his footfalls fade into the distance.

'You have come from Westminster, Coverdale? I understand there have been more murders?'

'Yes, your Grace, but Sir John and Brother Athelstan have

matters in hand.' Coverdale smirked. 'The coroner has stirred up the knights: they are buzzing like bees.'

Gaunt knelt down on his prie-dieu. 'But they have made no progress in unmasking the assassin?' he asked.

'None, your Grace.'

Gaunt stared at the angel painted in the window high above the altar. 'I will stay here for a while,' he murmured. 'There will be two visitors. Keep them separate. Neither must know about the other's presence.'

Coverdale nodded and left. Gaunt returned to his meditations, calculating how the taxes, raised in the present Parliament, could be spent. He heard a tap on the door and glanced sideways as his hooded, masked visitor stepped into the oratory. By the sour smell, the mud on the hem of the man's ragged cloak, and his scuffed boots, Gaunt knew who it was.

'Every good dog finds its home,' he murmured.

'Your Grace,' Dogman declared, falling to his knees, 'am I not your most obedient servant?'

Gaunt's hand slipped to the dagger pushed into his belt, though he had no real fear. Dogman was a pathetic little traitor, terrified of being hanged. In any case, in the choir-loft behind him, two master bowmen stood hidden in the shadows, arrows notched to their bows.

'Stay where you are, knave,' Gaunt whispered, 'and do not move.'

Dogman folded his arms and knelt, trying to control the trembling which ran through his body. If the Great Community of the Realm knew he was here they would flay him alive as a warning to other traitors. Yet the Dogman was truly terrified of Gaunt: some time ago the Dogman had realised that, for all their secret names, hidden covens and close conspiracies, John of Gaunt knew exactly what the Great Community of the Realm was plotting. Dogman wondered how many others of the rebel leaders were in the regent's pay, yet he had no choice. He had been caught and given a choice: either be a Judas or be hanged, drawn and disembowelled at Tyburn as a traitor. Dogman had made his choice very quickly. He had agreed to what the regent's agents had offered. He now had no choice but to dance to their tune.

Gaunt turned. 'Well, well, Dogman, in three days' time, on Saturday morning, between the hours of eleven and twelve, my nephew and I will ride down to Westminster with a cavalcade of knights, squires and pages. The king will distribute alms and confer the King's Touch on the sick and infirm. You will be there . . .' Gaunt smirked. 'The Hare is as scabby and scrofulous as ever?'

Dogman nodded eagerly.

'And still hates those who ride on palfreys and clothed in silk?'

Again the fevered nodding.

'Make sure he's armed.'

Gaunt heard Dogman gasp, so he rose and walked over to him. 'What are you frightened of, Dogman?'

'The Hare will attack,' Judas whispered. 'Strike at the Lord's anointed.'

'Well, isn't that what you plotted in your covens and secret meetings in Southwark and elsewhere?' Gaunt dug a fingernail into the man's dirty cheek and laughed. 'Mad as a March hare. Just ensure he is there.' Gaunt patted the man's greasy hair. 'Oh, your comrade the Fox has been caught.' He spun a coin on to the floor. 'Your information was correct.'

'What will happen to him, my Lord?'

102

'I told my judges to give him a fair trial then hang him.'
Gaunt turned back. 'I must pray for his soul.'

Dogman grabbed the coin and scuttled out. Gaunt moved
over and picking up a jug of water, held his fingers over a bowl,
and let the rose-scented water pour over them. He wiped his
hands on a napkin and returned to his prie-dieu. He turned
abruptly, glared up into the shadowy choir-loft and, narrowing
his eyes, caught a glint of mail and knew the archers still waited
there.

Gaunt returned to his meditations. Cupping his chin in his
hand, he thought about the murders at the Gargoyle tavern.
Would Cranston, he wondered, be able to unearth the mystery?
Gaunt stared at a fly walking along the crisp white altar cloth.
Some men dismissed the coroner as a fat, drunken buffoon, but
Cranston's looks belied his wit. And that friar, Athelstan, with
his smooth, olive face and wary dark eyes! Gaunt closed his
eyes and smiled. In any other circumstances he would place a
wager that they would succeed, but whom could he tell?

There was another knock on the door. 'Come in! Come in!'

This time the visitor was cloaked and cowled, but the cloth
was pure wool and the boots peeping out beneath were costly
Burgundian leather.

'You may be a knight of the shire . . .' Gaunt murmured. He
pointed to the pyx; the gold, jewel-encrusted casket which hung
from a silver chain just above the altar. '. . . but, in the presence
of Christ our King, not to mention his lawful representative on
earth, you should kneel.'

The knight obeyed. Gaunt did not bother to turn.

'You speak loudly in the chapter-house,' he whispered.

'Your Grace, that is what you wanted.'

Gaunt pulled a face. 'Not too hotly,' he advised. 'Otherwise,

103

when you change tack, some might whisper.'

'And when do I do that, your Grace?'

'Oh, you'll know the time,' Gaunt replied. 'A sign will be given to you.'

'Your Grace.' The knight shuffled his feet as if he wanted to draw closer, but Gaunt stretched out his hands and snapped his fingers.

'No further,' he warned.

'Your Grace, the murders?'

'Ah yes, those two honourable Knights of the Swan, Sir Oliver Bouchon and Sir Henry Swynford. I have been kneeling here, praying for the repose of their souls.'

'Your Grace, there's an assassin on the loose. He intends to kill us all.'

'Not all of you,' Gaunt purred. 'Not all of you are guilty men.'

'We believed we were doing right.'

'What you believed and what the law decrees are two different things.'

'Your Grace,' the knight retorted hoarsely, 'we must leave London!'

'Leave?' Gaunt turned, one eyebrow raised. 'You and your companions, sir, are elected representatives.' He turned back. 'If you leave, I'll have the king's justices in Eyre dispatched to Shrewsbury. They will investigate, listen to the whispers, and dig down into all the dirt and refuse of your past. And what will the people say, eh, Sir Edmund Malmesbury? What will the people say? How you swept grandly up to London but fled because two of your companions had been murdered? And why had they been murdered? And who was responsible? They will whisper and gossip outside the church gate.'

104

Malmesbury pushed back his hood and stretched out his hands. 'Your Grace, we were young. We made a terrible mistake. We have vowed to go on pilgrimage, pay compensation . . .'

'Pilgrimage?' Gaunt snarled, half turning his head. 'Pilgrimage? This is your pilgrimage, Sir Edmund. This is your penance. You will stay. Cranston and Athelstan will unmask the murderer.'

'Cranston is a drunken buffoon.'

'I don't think so,' Gaunt replied softly. 'What you and the rest must do, Sir Edmund –' Gaunt lifted his hands together as if in prayer – 'is you must pray. You must really pray that Cranston and Athelstan unmask this assassin amongst you before he strikes again.' Gaunt snapped his fingers. 'A sign will be given to you on Saturday morning. On Monday you will know what is to be done. Make sure you do it!' Gaunt sighed. 'Of course, that is, if you are still alive. Yet, there again, if you are not, someone else will do it instead. Now go!'

Gaunt heard the man scuffle away, the oratory door closing behind him. The regent looked up at the crucifix and idly wondered who was responsible for the deaths of those two knights.

CHAPTER 6

Dame Mathilda Kirtles' house in Cottemore Lane was both stately and smart. Built on a foundation of brick, the broad beams which stretched up to the red-tiled roof were painted a glossy black, whilst the plaster in between was a dainty pink. Windows on all three floors were of the lattice type, filled with mullioned or leaded glass. The garden on either side of the pebble path had been tastefully laid out, with small rose-bushes interspersed with raised banks of fragrant-smelling herbs.

'And this is a brothel!' Athelstan exclaimed.

Banyard, grinning from ear to ear, pointed at the door-handle of yellow brass carved in the shape of a young, sensuous girl holding a pitcher of water. Athelstan gazed speechlessly at this, then at the end of the bell rope where the weights were carved in the shape of a man's penis. Cranston, huffing and puffing, not knowing whether to be embarrassed or laugh, pulled at the rope then moved his hand quickly away.

Thank God the Lady Maude can't see me here, he thought. Oh Lord and all his saints forfend she ever does!

The sweet sound of the bell inside the house was answered by a patter of footsteps and the door swung open. In any other circumstances Athelstan would have thought the young girl was a novice: a white, gold-edged veil covered her lustrous hair, and she was dressed in a high-necked grey gown, but this was flounced at the hem and her nails were painted a deep red. What Athelstan had first thought was a white cloth over her bosom, was instead a rather thin gauze veil over ripe, luscious breasts.

'Good morrow, sirs.' The girl smiled at them. She clutched at her gown and raised this slightly, showing the thick white petticoats beneath. She gestured airily to Athelstan. 'Come in, Father. You will not be the first friar we have had here.' She fought back the laughter in her voice. 'And you will certainly not be the last. Any friend of Master Banyard's is a friend of ours.'

'Master Banyard is leaving,' Cranston growled, regaining his wits and pushing by Athelstan. 'And you, my little hussy, should know that I am Sir John Cranston, Coroner of the city.'

'Coroners are also welcome,' the girl answered pertly. 'Though the lady of the house –' she pouted at Cranston's warbelt – 'does not permit swords.'

Banyard sniggered, but when Sir John whirled round, pulled his face straight. 'Sir John, I have to go back.'

'Dame Mathilda Kirtles,' Cranston pushed his face towards the young woman. 'I want to see her now or it will be the bailiffs. And don't tell me they'd be most welcome as well!'

The young girl, covering her mouth with her hand, stepped back and led them along an airy passageway and into a sweet-smelling parlour. She told them to wait, closed the door behind her. Athelstan sat in a cushioned windowseat, mouth half open as he stared around.

'Oh, come, come, Brother,' Cranston called out. 'Don't tell me you haven't been in a molly-house before!'

Athelstan quietly raised his hands. 'Sir John, I swear, I have never seen a place like this.'

The friar stared down at the floor where the boards were so highly polished that they caught the sunlight. Here and there lay thick woollen rugs. The walls were half covered with wooden panelling, above this the plaster had been painted a rich cream shade. Tapestries, full of colour, hung there. Athelstan, craning his neck, studied one. At first he thought it was a young maiden listening to the song of a troubadour, but he blushed as he realised the troubadour was naked, whilst the young lady had her dress split down the middle.

'Yes, yes, quite,' he murmured.

'Have you ever been with a maid?' Cranston asked.

'Sir John, that's for me to think about and you to wonder . . .' Athelstan shook his head. 'At first glance, this could have been an abbess's parlour.'

'Knowing some of the abbesses I do,' Cranston growled, 'you're probably right!'

'Doesn't the city try to close them down?' As he spoke Athelstan heard a sound from the wall just next to the canopied hearth. He glanced quickly over; he was sure he glimpsed a wooden shutter being drawn closed.

'Who would shut a place like this down?' Cranston answered. 'Dame Mathilda and her "*Jolies filles*" could sing a song which would embarrass many an alderman.'

'Aye, and a few others!'

Cranston whirled round. A tall, severe lady, dressed in a white veil and grey dress, stood just within the doorway. Her hair was grey, her face thin and haughty, her eyes sharp and watchful. She walked across, fingering the golden girdle tied round her waist. Athelstan felt like pinching himself: she

109

walked and talked like some venerable mother superior.

'I am Dame Mathilda Kirtles.' She stared down at Athelstan. 'You are the Dominican from St Erconwald's, aren't you? One of your parishioners, Cecily, often talks about you.'

Athelstan was too tongue-tied to reply.

'And you, of course, must be Sir John Cranston: the fattest, loudest and most bibulous of coroners!' She held a hand out. Cranston grasped and kissed it.

'Madame, I am your servant.'

'No you are not,' Dame Mathilda snapped, 'you have nothing to do with whores, Sir John, more's the pity.' Her eyes softened a little. 'But they say you can't be bribed, and that makes you unique.' Dame Mathilda swept away and sat down on a small cushioned chair before the fireplace.

'Sir John, you are not here for pleasure, so what is your business?'

Cranston sat down in the windowseat next to Athelstan. For some strange reason he felt like a little boy again, quietly throwing stones into the stewponds and being reproved by one of his elderly aunts.

'I'd offer you some refreshment,' Dame Mathilda declared, 'but I'll be honest, Sir John, the sooner you're gone the better!' She smiled thinly. 'Banyard cackles like a goose. No one will dare come near the house whilst you are here.'

'Including the honourable representatives from Shrewsbury?' Cranston asked. 'They were here last Monday night, Dame Mathilda. Bellies full, deep in their cups.'

'Aye, and their purses full of silver. They came here about two hours before midnight.' She continued. 'My girls entertained them . . .' She indicated with her head at the ceiling. 'Each went their separate ways with the girl of his choice.'

110

'All of them?'

'One left.'

'Who?' Athelstan asked.

'The small, funny one. He sat for a while with one of my girls, boring her to sleep with chatter about animals, beasteries and what he had seen in the Tower. He looked at the hour-candle, gabbled an excuse and left.'

'And he did not return?'

'I did not say that. He came back just before the rest left. And, before you ask, Cranston, I don't know where he'd gone or what he'd been doing: his cloak was damp so I think he had been on the river. Mind you, if he stayed,' she continued tersely, 'he'd have been as useful as the rest.'

'What do you mean?' Cranston asked.

'Sir John, these are men of middle years, mature in wisdom, their bellies full. They may still hold their lances straight, but not in the bedchamber.'

'Yes.' Cranston glanced quickly at Athelstan, but the friar seemed totally bemused at what Dame Mathilda was saying. 'And I suppose, good lady, when your guests stay here, you keep an eye on them?' The coroner gazed round. 'Even in this room there must be eyelets and hidden peep-holes?'

'Sir John, you are wiser than you look.'

'And they talked to the girls?'

'Sir John, come, come!' Dame Mathilda clasped her hands demurely in front of her. 'Do you really expect me to tell you that?'

'Well . . .' Sir John stretched out his legs and folded his arms. 'You can either tell me here or I could ask the bailiffs to accompany you to the Guildhall tomorrow.'

'They boasted, Sir John, like all men do: what barns they

had, what granges, how fat their sheep, how high their own standing . . .'

'And what?'

'How they were members of the Commons and would not lift a finger to help the regent unless he met their demands.' Dame Mathilda got to her feet. 'And that, Sir John, is all I can tell you, either here or in your Guildhall.' She walked towards the door then turned. 'Brother Athelstan, have you found out where Perline Brasenose is?'

'Why no.' The friar got to his feet. 'You know him?'

'Yes, I do.' Dame Mathilda came back. 'Years ago his mother worked here. Perline was, how can I put it, an unexpected result of a night's work here.'

'He's a member of my parish, he's married to Simplicatas.'

'Oh, is that what she's calling herself now?'

'I hadn't thought of that.' Athelstan smiled and stared down at his hands.

Perline and his mother had come to Southwark a few years ago, then Simplicatas had suddenly appeared in their household. Perline had always claimed she was a very distant kinswoman. When he had married her at the church door of St Erconwald's, all Athelstan had been concerned about was that there was no kinship of blood between them, as laid down by canon law. He closed his eyes and recalled Simplicatas's pale, elfin face, her blonde hair and green smiling eyes.

'Well I never,' he murmured. He glanced up. 'You know Perline is still missing?'

'Yes, yes, I do.' Dame Mathilda opened the door. 'It's a small world, Brother Athelstan, especially if you are a whore. Simplicatas has asked for our help.' The woman glanced impishly at Sir John. 'There is little that happens in London

112

that we whores do not know about. Now, Sir John, I really must insist . . .'

Once outside the house, Cranston put his arm round Athelstan's shoulders and roared with laughter. He held the small friar away. 'Brother, Brother.' He swallowed hard and blinked his popping blue eyes, watering after laughing so much. 'Don't you know anything about your parishioners?'

'Apparently not, Sir John.' Athelstan's shoulders sagged. 'Simplicatas seemed so demure.'

'And so she is,' Cranston linked one arm through Athelstan's and walked back into Cottemore Lane. 'If you are a woman, poor and lonely in London, being a whore is better than starving. Simplicatas is not a prostitute. She probably earned her dowry and left as soon as she could. But,' he asked, 'now her husband has fled?'

'Yes, and it's not like him,' Athelstan replied. 'Perline is a madcap but he loves Simplicatas. No one seems to know where he is. He liked his job as a soldier in the Tower. He was paid and well fed.'

'And if he's not back soon,' Cranston muttered, 'they'll hang him for desertion.'

At the end of Cottemore Lane, Athelstan withdrew his arm and stared back towards the riverside.

'You look tired, Brother,' Cranston remarked, staring at the dark circles under the friar's eyes.

'I am worried, Sir John – about Perline, Simplicatas, the devil loose in Southwark, not to mention Pike the ditcher whispering about the great revolt in the corners of taverns. He thinks he's so clever, yet the tapboy who serves his ale could be the regent's spy.' Athelstan pointed to the soaring towers of Westminster. 'And now there are these murders.'

113

He allowed Cranston to steer him up a narrow alleyway leading towards Fleet Street. 'And what do you make of this business?' Cranston asked.

'Well . . .' Athelstan paused to collect his thoughts. 'We know our noble representatives are lying, Sir John. The knights have got a great deal to hide, but I suspect they are frightened men and cluster together, except for Sir Francis Harnett. The night Bouchon died, he left Dame Mathilda's and went upriver. Now, whether it was to meet Bouchon or on some other business, I don't know. What I also keep wondering about,' he continued, 'is why should the killer chant the "*Dies Irae*" as he throttled Swynford's life out?'

'Do you think he could be a priest? Or even a monk?'

'Such as Father Benedict?' Athelstan recalled the tall, severe Benedictine monk. 'But why should he hate Swynford or Bouchon? The only connection between him and those knights is that a former friend, Father Antony, once served in the same Shropshire abbey where these knights once held their Round Tables.'

Athelstan blew his cheeks out. 'So far, Sir John, we haven't learnt enough. If we returned to the Gargoyle, Sir Francis would spin us a story which would neither prove nor disprove why he left the brothel. I am sure that one of his companions would solemnly swear that Sir Francis was telling the truth.' He nudged the coroner. 'What we have to do, Sir John, is wait. There will be another murder.' He sighed. 'And there's little we can do to stop it.'

'What about Coverdale?' Cranston asked. 'He's young, strong and hails from Shropshire. He could have met Bouchon, knocked him on the head and thrown him in the river. He could also have entered the Gargoyle dressed as a priest and garrotted

114

Swynford. We could go back and question him.'

'And he would ask us why,' Athelstan replied. 'What motive does he have for killing two knights?'

'Revenge?' Cranston answered. 'His father was a petty landowner in Shropshire. Coverdale, nursing wrongs and grievances, may have seized this opportunity to settle scores. And, of course, he is one of Gaunt's henchmen.'

'And that is the weakness of your case,' Athelstan replied. 'Why should Bouchon agree to meet one of Gaunt's men at night? And Coverdale entering a busy taproom, even disguised as a priest, would be highly dangerous. Moreover,' Athelstan stopped and stared up at the red-streaked sky, 'Coverdale is shrewd. We are here investigating these murders precisely because Gaunt does not wish to be blamed for them. Unless, of course, Coverdale is not really Gaunt's friend,' he added. 'In which case, Sir John, we are like dogs chasing our tails.'

'Which is why I am returning to Cheapside.' Cranston called over his shoulder as he strode on. 'I may not be able to help my lord Regent . . .' he stopped and tapped his fleshy nose. 'But perhaps I can assist your search for Perline Brasenose.'

They went up on to Holborn Street. The sun was beginning to set, and that broad thoroughfare which swept out of Newgate was full of traders, carters, hucksters and peasants making their weary way home after a day's business. A hedge-priest, his battered wheelbarrow full of tattered belongings, stopped and begged a penny off Athelstan.

'Blessings on you, Brother!' He sketched a benediction. 'And if I were you I would hurry. The crowds around Newgate are thicker than flies on a cowpat. They're getting ready to hang a man.' He then seized his wheelbarrow and hurried on.

Cranston and Athelstan crossed the street where the coroner,

115

using his ponderous bulk and booming voice, stopped a wine cart loaded with tuns and casks. The lord Coroner of the city, together with his secretarius, sat like two boys at the end of the cart, legs dangling, as the wine trader, eager to be in London before curfew, cracked his whip and urged the great dray horses forward. They rattled by Pontypool Street, Leveroune Lane, the Bishop of Ely's inn, then turned right at Smithfield, past Cock Lane where the whores thronged. One of them recognised Cranston. She steadied the orange wig on her bald head and turned to her sisters. 'There goes Lord Fat Arse!'

The rest of the group took up the shouts. Cranston smiled beatifically back, sketching a sign of the cross in the air towards them. Athelstan hid his face and just prayed they would reach Newgate without further mishap. They were forced to stop just alongside the great city ditch where the stinking refuse was piled in mounds as high as their heads. The stench was indescribable. Convicted felons, under the supervision of bailiffs, their mouths and eyes covered by scraps of dirty rags, were sprinkling saltpetre over the mounds of slime. Others, armed with bellows, stood round great roaring braziers, fanning the burning charcoal. Athelstan pinched his nostrils and tried not to look at the corpses of rats and other animals which protruded out of the heaps. Cranston, however, shouted encouragement to the bailiffs.

'Good lads! Lovely boys! It will be ready before nightfall?'

'Oh yes, Sir John,' one of them shouted back, leaning on his shovel, 'Once the curfew bell tolls, we will light the fire.'

'Thank God,' Cranston breathed. 'The ditch is full enough: when the winds come from the north-west, they make Lady Maude sick.'

One of the felons shouted, pulling down the muffler from his

116

face. 'It's good to see, how the lord Coroner has now got his own carriage, suitably furnished.'

Cranston peered through the shifting columns of smoke. 'Is that Tolpuddle? So, you've been caught again, you little bastard!'

'Not really, Sir John,' the felon shouted cheerily back. 'Just a little misunderstanding over a baby pig I found.' Tolpuddle came closer. Athelstan noticed how one eye was sewn up, the other was bright with mischief.

'Misunderstanding?' Cranston asked.

'Aye, the bailiffs caught me with it two nights ago.'

'So you had stolen it?'

'No, Sir John.' The felon leaned on his rake. 'The saints be my witness, Sir John. I found the little pig wandering alone in the streets. It looked so lonesome. I simply picked it up, put it under my cloak. I was going to take it back to its mother.'

Cranston laughed, dug into his purse, and flicked the man a penny. At last the wine trader saw an opening in the crowds. He cracked his whip and the cart trundled on. Tolpuddle stood, cheerily waving goodbye, until a bailiff clapped him on the ear and sent him back to his work.

The cart rattled on through the old city walls, and Cranston and Athelstan got down in front of Newgate. The great bell of the prison was tolling. On a high-branched scaffold just outside the double gates, a man was about to be turned off. Around the foot of the scaffold thronged men-at-arms and archers wearing the regent's livery; these held back the crowds, even as a herald in a royal tabard proclaimed how Robert atte Thurlstain, known as the 'Fox' and self-proclaimed leader of the so-called 'Great Community of the Realm' had been found guilty of the horrible crimes of conspiracy, treason, etc. On a platform next

117

to the scaffold a red-garbed executioner was already sharpening his fleshing knives, laying them out on the great table. The hapless felon would be thrown there after he had been half hung: his body would be cut open, disembowelled, quartered, salted, and then placed in barrels of pickle before being displayed over the principal gateways of London and other cities.

Athelstan watched as the priest at the foot of the ladder quickly gabbled the prayers for the dying, whilst the executioner's assistant, who bestraddled the jutting arc of the gibbet, placed the noose over the prisoner. The executioner bawled at the priest to hurry up; the crowd didn't like this and grew restless. Bits of refuse and rotten fruit were thrown at the hangman even as the herald stopped his declamation and a drumbeat began to roll. Athelstan went cold as he recalled the warnings given by Joscelyn, the one-armed taverner of the Piebald. Hadn't he said that a man calling himself the 'Fox' had been one of those Pike had secretly met? He tugged at the coroner's sleeve.

'Come on, Sir John,' he whispered. 'Let's be away.'

Cranston agreed, though he paused to grasp the hand of a foist who was busy threading his way through the streets. The coroner seized the man's wrist, drew out the very thin dagger the felon had concealed up his sleeve, and sent it spinning into a pile of refuse. Sir John tapped the man on the head with his knuckles.

'Now be a good boy and trot off!' the coroner growled, and shoved the pickpocket after his knife into the pile of refuse.

'Did you know anything about that execution?' Athelstan asked as they hastened down the Shambles into Cheapside.

'Not a whit,' Cranston replied. 'The poor bastard was

probably tried before King's Bench: the regent always demands immediate execution.'

They turned a corner into the broad thoroughfare, which was now emptying as traders dismounted stalls and weary-eyed apprentices stowed away their masters' belongings into baskets and hampers. Even the stocks had been emptied, and the city bellman strode up and down ringing his bell and proclaiming:

'All you loyal subjects of the king. Your business is done. Thank the Lord for a good day's trade and hasten to your homes!'

Rakers were busy cleaning up the refuse and rubbish. Cranston stopped and, shading his eyes against the sunlight, looked down Cheapside.

'Aren't you going home?' Athelstan asked hopefully.

'I'd discover nothing about Perline Brasenose there.' Cranston smiled. 'But it would be good to kiss the poppets.'

They walked towards Cranston's house.

'I want Leif the beggar, the idle bugger,' Cranston growled. 'I want him to deliver a message.'

The words were hardly out of his mouth when the tall, emaciated, red-haired beggar hopped like a frog out of an alleyway.

'Sir John, Sir John, God bless you! Brother Athelstan, may you send all demons back to hell!'

'So, you have heard?'

'Aye I have,' Leif replied, resting on his crutch, head cocked to one side. 'They say a butcher in Southwark caught the demon in a cellar. It was in the shape of a goat: the butcher cut his throat, sliced the goat into collops and invited everyone—'

119

'That's enough,' Cranston interrupted. 'How is the Lady Maude?'

Leif smiled slyly. 'In a fair rage, Sir John. The two dogs have eaten your pie: left out on the table, it was, cooling for supper, broad and golden with a tasty crust. She thinks the poppets took it down and gave it to the dogs. The Lady Maude is also complaining about the stench from the ditch. She says if they fire the refuse tonight, it will be impossible to dry sheets in the morning.'

'Yes, yes, quite,' Cranston growled, and glanced hurriedly down the street to the Holy Lamb of God inn. He cleared his throat. 'Perhaps, Brother, it's best if we let the Lady Maude's anger cool for a while.'

'I am all a-hungered, Sir John,' Leif wailed. He peered at Athelstan. 'And so are you, aren't you, Father?'

Athelstan nodded. He felt hungry, his legs were aching, and he couldn't refuse Sir John's generous offer to help.

'Perhaps ale and something to eat at the Holy Lamb, Sir John?'

'Shouldn't you go home?' Leif asked innocently.

'Affairs of state. Affairs of state,' Cranston breathed.

'I am hungry as well, Sir John,' Leif slyly added. 'The Lady Maude is waiting for me.'

'Well, you can join us,' Cranston replied. 'But first go round the streets. Seek out the Harrower of the Dead. Tell him Sir John requires his presence at the Holy Lamb of God! Yes, yes.' He thrust a penny into Leif's outstretched hand. 'I understand, you'll need some sustenance on the way.'

The beggar was about to scamper off, but Cranston seized his arm. 'And what news in Cheapside, Leif?'

The beggar scratched his nose. 'More cats have gone, Sir John.' Leif pointed down to a great, high-sided dung cart.

'People have lost confidence, Sir John. They are even paying Hengist and Horsa to look for their cats.'

'Are they now?' Cranston murmured. 'Well, you trot off, Leif, and deliver my message.'

The beggar left as fast as a whippet, eager to be back at the Holy Lamb for the supper Sir John had promised. Cranston marched down towards the two dung-collectors. They were cleaning the sewer in the centre of Cheapside, digging out the mess and slops, cheerily throwing the muck into their huge, stinking cart.

'God bless you, sirs,' Cranston greeted them.

Both men paused, pushing back their hoods.

'Lovely lads!' Cranston breathed. 'Brother Athelstan, this is Hengist and Horsa. Dung-collectors of Cheapside.'

Both men grinned in embarrassment. Twin brothers, their dirty, wart-covered faces were identical, except that Hengist had one tooth whilst Horsa had none.

'Good morrow, Sir John,' they chorused.

'So, you are searching for the stolen cats?' Cranston asked.

'Aye, Sir John, and a great pity it is how the poor animals are disappearing.'

Hengist leaned his shovel against the cart and wiped his fingers on his red leather apron. Athelstan noticed that Horsa's leather apron was cut much shorter. The fellow noticed Athelstan's gaze.

'It's cut like that, Father, so people can tell us one from the other.'

'Have you found the cats?' Cranston growled.

'No, Sir John.' Hengist clasped his hands together as if in prayer. 'The poor creatures seem to have disappeared into thin air.'

121

'And you have found no signs to indicate who has taken them?'

'None whatsoever, Sir John.' The fellow's eyes grew large. 'But we have all heard about the demon in Southwark.'

'You're taking payment for your searches?' Cranston insisted.

'Oh yes, Sir John, but not hide nor hair can be seen.'

Cranston took a step closer and stared into the dung-collector's watery eyes.

'Now, my bucko,' he said quietly, 'if you can discover neither hide or hair, why are you taking pennies from petty traders and poor old ladies?'

'Sir John, we haven't taken much. People have only asked for our help.'

'Aye, in which case,' Cranston grated, 'they must be truly desperate.' And, shouldering past the man, he made his way further down Cheapside.

'Sir John, you were unduly harsh,' Athelstan declared, hurrying up beside him.

Cranston just shook his head and lengthened his stride, heading like an arrow for the Holy Lamb of God. Once inside, he took off his cloak and tossed the empty wineskin at the landlord's wife; she came bustling out from the kitchen to greet Sir John as if he was a long-lost brother.

'Some ale!' Cranston tweaked her plump cheek. And one of your pies – freshly baked, mind you, not yesterday's.'

'Sir John, as if we'd ever . . .' the woman simpered back.

Cranston moved his bulk towards the windowseat quickly vacated by two traders who knew Sir John and his habits. The coroner sat down and stared out through the open window at the garden beyond.

'So, you think I'm harsh, Brother. I wouldn't trust either of that precious pair as far as I could spit.' He paused as the ale-wife brought over two brimming tankards of ale. Cranston sipped at his and leaned back against the wall. 'But there again, my dear friar, perhaps I am harsh. Except as far as those two are concerned, it's a case of much suspected but little proved. Anyway, "sufficient unto the day is the evil thereof". Come on, Brother, relax.' He cradled his tankard in his hands and watched Athelstan under half-closed eyelids. 'I just wonder what our beloved regent is plotting.' He murmured. 'All this hubbub, deaths at Westminster, and a public execution. I suspect there's a purpose behind it all but I'm damned if I can see it!'

'And young Perline?' Athelstan asked hopefully.

'I've sent for the Harrower of the Dead,' Cranston replied. 'Perline lived and worked at the Tower, and there's nothing that happens along the alleyways of the city which the Harrower doesn't know about.' He sat up as the ale-wife brought back two bowls, each containing a pie hot and spicy, neatly cut in four and covered with an onion sauce. Cranston took his horn spoon out, cleaned it carefully on a napkin, and began to eat.

'And there's also the cats?' Athelstan asked.

'Aye, Brother, the Harrower might know something about that.'

They continued their meal in silence and were almost finished when Leif hopped into the tavern. 'Sir John, he's coming! He's coming!'

The coroner pointed to a far corner of the tavern. 'Well, Leif, bugger off and sit over there! Eat and drink what you want but don't go back to the Lady Maude and tell her where I am! Do you understand?'

Leif raised his right hand and solemnly swore. The beggar was hardly settled in his favourite nook when a cowled, hooded figure slipped like a shadow into the room.

CHAPTER 7

The Harrower of the Dead sat on a stool before Athelstan and Cranston. He did not pull back the cowl of his cloak or unwrap the black silk mask which covered the lower half of his face. Athelstan noticed the very fine brows over heavy-lidded eyes: strange eyes, close-set and chillingly blue, they never flickered in their gaze.

'My lord Coroner.' The voice was well modulated, just above a whisper through the slit in the silken mask. 'What do you want from the Harrower of the Dead?'

'We, er . . .' Athelstan stammered. 'I need your help.'

The Harrower's eyes never left Cranston's. 'I only come when the coroner calls.' He shifted his gaze; Athelstan was sure the man was smiling. 'Nevertheless, Brother Athelstan, priest of St Erconwald's, you need all the help there is, don't you?'

Athelstan felt the hair on the back of his neck prickle. He silently cursed his fears: it was those eyes and the sweet, perfumed smell which came from the man's black woollen robes which unnerved him.

'Don't you ever take your mask off?' Athelstan snapped, fighting hard to steady his voice.

'Do you ever take off your Dominican robes?' the Harrower

replied. The eyes flickered back to Sir John. 'Tell him, my lord Coroner.'

Cranston sipped from his tankard but, beneath the table, one hand gripped the pommel of his dagger.

'The Harrower of the Dead,' Cranston began, holding the visitor's gaze, 'is a mysterious figure. Some people claim he is a defrocked priest who committed a terrible blasphemy and suffered God's vengeance with a malingering disease which has eaten away the lower half of his face. Others say he is a knight who fought in the king's wars and received an arrow bolt through his mouth. Whatever,' Cranston placed his tankard down, 'when the great pestilence visited the city, no one came forward to move the infected corpses except the man now sitting before us. He appeared in the Guildhall and the mayor and the aldermen hired his services. As the great death raged, the Harrower, as he came to be called, took the corpses out to the huge pits near Charterhouse and burnt them. In return, the city council signed an indenture with him; for a monthly payment, the Harrower of the Dead walks the streets of London at night removing any corpses he finds there. The victims of violence, the aged beggar, the unknown foreigner or those who simply die of some terrible sickness, all alone, bereft of any help. The Harrower of the Dead collects them in his red painted cart; with his black handbell he prowls the streets like Death itself. For every corpse he receives twopence. For those who've suffered violence, the city fathers pay him sixpence.'

Cranston sipped at his tankard, staring into the Harrower's light-blue eyes. 'No one really knows where he comes from, and I don't care. Sometimes . . .' Cranston's voice fell to a whisper. 'Sometimes they say that, if the Harrower finds you lingering between life and death, death will always have you.'

126

'Such men are liars, my lord Coroner.'

'Perhaps they are,' Cranston replied wearily. 'But the Harrower of the Dead picks up the corpses in the streets and alleyways of the city whilst his comrade, the Fisher of Men, nets those from the river.'

'What do you want, Cranston?'

'Brother Athelstan has a parishioner, a young soldier called Perline Brasenose, a member of the Tower garrison. He has disappeared.' Cranston turned to Athelstan. 'Give him a description.'

Athelstan obliged and the Harrower of the Dead, chin resting in the palm of his gloved hand, listened attentively.

'I have discovered no corpse fitting your description, Brother, but . . .'

'But what?' Cranston asked.

'Sir John, I am your guest. You have offered me neither food nor drink.'

Cranston apologised and called across the taproom but the ale-wife, standing near the casks and tuns, just shook her head: her eyes were rounded in fright as she stared at the Harrower of the Dead.

'Now you know why I didn't offer you anything to eat or drink,' Cranston grated. Heaving his bulk out of the windowseat, the coroner walked across to the ale-wife, then returned with a pewter goblet brimming with claret. 'She'll boil the cup after you have left,' Cranston added.

The Harrower of the Dead sipped delicately at the wine. Athelstan realised there must be something wrong with his lower lip, for the man made a strange sipping noise; eyes closed momentarily in pleasure, the Harrower breathed a sigh of satisfaction.

'When did the young soldier disappear?' he asked.

'About three nights ago.'

The Harrower rocked himself gently to and fro, his eyes never leaving those of Cranston. 'I'm a busy man, Sir John. I spend my time with you whilst the dead wait for me.'

Cranston slid a coin across the table. The Harrower deftly plucked it up.

'On Monday night last,' he replied. 'I was down near the steel yard where the Hanse berth their ships. There had been a tavern brawl. A sailor from a Lübeck ship had been killed and his corpse stripped. Now usually I don't go so near the river.' He smiled beneath his mask. 'The Fisher of Men is most sensitive about his territory, but the corpse was mine. Now I was tired and drew my cart into the shadows.' He tapped the bottle beneath his cloak. 'Like you, Sir John, I need my refreshment. A skiff came to the river steps. A soldier – I recognised him as such because of his livery – came up, accompanied by a small, well-dressed man.' The Harrower paused to sip from his cup. 'For a while the two stood there, unaware of me in the shadows. The short, well-dressed man called the soldier "Brasenose"; he in turn called his companion "Sir Francis".'

'Sir Francis Harnett!' Athelstan exclaimed.

The Harrower shrugged. 'God knows, Brother, but the two were locked in argument. Sir Francis, drumming his fingers on his sword-hilt, accused Brasenose of robbing him.'

'And Perline?' Athelstan asked.

'He seemed subdued, wary, retreating before the other's accusations. The discussion ended. The one you call Perline turned on his heels and strode away down towards London Bridge. Harnett shouted after him to come back, that he was a

128

thief, but the young man walked on. After a while Harnett went down the river steps and into a waiting skiff.' The Harrower sipped from the goblet in his eerie manner. 'That's all I know, Sir John, but, if you wish, I shall ask my comrade the Fisher of Men. The river may have the soldier's corpse.'

'I'd be grateful,' Cranston replied. 'And you know nothing else?'

The Harrower shook his head and drained his cup. He was about to rise when Cranston leaned across and seized him by the wrist.

'You walk the street,' the coroner said. 'I have a little mystery of my own. You have heard, no doubt, of the cats which are disappearing?'

The Harrower chuckled. 'Sir John, what are you saying? Are you asking for my help or making an allegation?'

'I am asking a question,' Cranston declared.

'I know nothing about your cats, Sir John, except that their disappearance is making my work all the more difficult. The rats and mice have increased four-fold. Yet I have something to tell you.'

Cranston passed a coin across the table. This time the Harrower dug into a small leather bag slung beneath his cloak. He laid two black leather muzzles on the table.

'Down near Thames Street,' he declared, 'I found the corpse of a cat, scarred and wounded, beneath a midden-heap. This muzzle was tight about its jaw. What I suspect is that someone placed the muzzle over its mouth to keep it silent: the animal must have escaped but, unable to take the muzzle off, either starved to death or became so weak that it could not defend itself against the dogs which prowl there.'

Cranston stared at the muzzles distastefully. 'And the second?'

'I found it near the stocks in Poultry, just lying there.' The Harrower rose to his feet. 'That's all I know, Sir John. You've got what you paid for.' And, spinning on his heel, the Harrower of the Dead left the tavern as quickly as he came.

Athelstan let out a sigh of relief. 'Sir John, I do not like some of your acquaintances.'

'In keeping the king's peace, dear monk, you end up having some very strange bedfellows. The Harrower is not as fearful as he looks.' Cranston called over to the ale-wife to refill their blackjacks. 'What really concerns me is what Sir Francis Harnett, knight of the shire from Shropshire and a member of the Commons, would have to do with young Perline Brasenose.'

Athelstan stared through the doorway: the light was dying, dusk was beginning to fall.

'Sir John, are you refreshed?'

'For what?' Cranston asked.

'A walk to the Tower.'

Cranston stretched his great legs until the muscles cracked. 'Why there? Yes, I know Perline was a member of the garrison, but what could we learn?'

'About Perline, Sir John, very little.' Athelstan sat up in his seat and rubbed his eyes. 'Remember, Sir John, on the Sunday before Sir Oliver Bouchon was killed, all the representatives from Shropshire were taken by Coverdale to see the king's beasts at the Tower. Harnett was amongst them. Since that visit, Perline Brasenose has disappeared and these murders have taken place.' He plucked at the coroner's sleeve. 'Please, Sir John, I have drunk enough, we should be there before dark.'

Cranston hid his annoyance and agreed, calling for the ale-wife to leave his order for another time. They left the Holy Lamb of God, walking briskly along Cheapside, down Lombard

Street, into Eastcheap and towards Petty Wales. The evening proved to be warm. The ale-houses were full, doors and windows open, the babble of voices and laughter pouring out. Bailiffs and wardsmen patrolled the narrow alleyways. Athelstan felt safe as they threaded through these, under the overhanging houses disturbed by little more than a barking dog or children chasing each other in wild, antic games of Hodsman Bluff. They walked into Tower Street, past a church where two beadsmen knelt on the hard stone steps, hands clutching their rosary beads as they prayed in atonement for some sin. Further along, a group of men sat in the doorway of a tavern idly watching two puppies play. They called out as Athelstan passed and the friar blessed them. They went down an alleyway and into Petty Wales: a young boy's voice, clear and lilting, broke into song from a window high above them. They paused for a while to listen. Athelstan closed his eyes; the song was one of his favourites. He remembered how his dead brother Stephen had sung it as they helped their father bring the harvest in during those long, sun-drenched autumn days before he and Athelstan had gone to the wars. Stephen had been killed, only Athelstan had returned.

The friar's heart lurched with sadness: the boy's voice was pure and clear, just as Stephen's had been. Everyone had praised his brother's singing, especially at Christmas, when he would stand before the crib in the village church and make the rafters ring with some merry carol.

'Brother?'

Athelstan opened his eyes. Cranston was staring down at him curiously. The song had finished.

'Are you well?' Cranston asked solicitously.

Athelstan shivered and crossed his arms. 'Nothing, Sir

John, just a ghost from the past.'

They crossed a deserted square. Above them soared the sheer crenellated walls, turrets, bastions and bulwarks of the Tower. A mass of carved stone, a huge fortress built not to defend London but to overawe it. They followed the line of the wall round and crossed the drawbridge: beneath them the moat was full of dirty, slimy water. They went through the black arch of Middle Tower, whose huge gateway stood like an open mouth, its teeth the half-lowered iron portcullis. The entrance was guarded by sentries, who stood in the shadows wrapped in brown serge cloaks.

'Sir John Cranston, Coroner,' Athelstan explained to one of the guards. 'We need to see the constable.'

The man groaned, but one glance at Cranston's angry eyes and he scampered off up the cobbled trackway as his companion took them into the gatehouse. Cranston and Athelstan sat on a bench and cooled their heels until the guard returned, accompanied by a fussy little man dabbing at his face with the hem of his cloak.

'What's this?' What's this?' the constable asked, bustling in. 'Sir John, you have no jurisdiction here.'

'Oh, don't be so bloody pompous,' the coroner snapped. 'You have a guardsman Perline Brasenose?'

The constable must have been eating; he stood, cleaning his teeth with his tongue in a most disgusting fashion. Cranston pushed his face closer. 'I have no jurisdiction here,' he whispered sweetly, 'but I am on business from His Grace the Regent.'

The constable's head came up. He forced a smile. 'Sir John, Sir John. I am sorry,' he blustered. 'But Perline Brasenose is a member of the garrison, or I should say was. He's been absent from his post for days.'·

'And so he is a deserter?' Athelstan asked anxiously.

The constable patted him kindly on the shoulder. 'Don't fret, Brother. The French haven't landed and the Tower is safe. It's common for a young man to disappear.' The constable's face became grave. 'Well, within reason. If he isn't back within the week, I'll have him proclaimed as a deserter, yes.'

'Was he on duty?' Athelstan asked. 'Last Sunday when members of the Commons visited the Tower?'

The constable pursed his lips together and stared up at the wall behind him. 'Yes, yes he was. He was one of those who escorted them as they went round the Tower, inspecting the royal muniments, the siege machines and, of course, the royal beastery.'

'Did anything untoward happen?'

The constable shook his head. 'The Tower's a lonely place, Brother. All we do is wait here for an enemy who never attacks. We guard some prisoners lodged in the dungeons and, now and again, make a foray into the city or countryside.'

'You should be more vigilant,' Cranston urged. 'If you go into the countryside, you must have heard about the plots and conspiracies amongst the peasants?'

The constable made a rude sound with his lips. 'Sir John, the Tower has stood for three hundred years. No one has ever taken it, let alone a bunch of ragged-arsed peasants. If they come, our drawbridge will go up, and they can sit outside until the Second Coming. That's as far as they'll get.'

'And the menagerie?' Athelstan asked.

'The royal beastery . . .' the constable scoffed. He stuck his thumbs in his belt and leaned closer. 'It's nothing more than a collection of pits and cages at the other end of the Tower. An elephant, bears, some mangy cats, monkeys and baboons.

Since the old king died there's very little been done to care for them.' He smirked. 'But, there again, they impress our visitors. One knight in particular, Sir Francis Harnett, was much taken by what he saw.'

'And nothing untoward happened?' Athelstan repeated.

'Brother, they came and they went. I have nothing more to add. Now, I must go!' And he bustled off back to his meal.

Athelstan and Cranston walked back through an alleyway into Petty Wales.

'Not very helpful,' Athelstan observed.

Cranston stared back at the Tower through narrowing eyes. He had not liked what he had seen: sleeping guards, a constable more interested in his belly, the way they had been kept in the gatehouse and allowed no further in.

'Next time I see Gaunt,' he growled, 'I'll have a chat about the Tower. He needs to send the royal commissioners in to check the stores and the muster roll. Our little fat constable is, I believe, not above taking bribes; not only for people to see the royal beastery, but also from members of his own garrison in order that they can slip away.'

'Do you think that?' Athelstan asked.

'I know that,' Cranston replied. 'According to the law of arms, and all its usages, Perline Brasenose is a deserter and his name should be posted throughout the city.' He clapped Athelstan on the shoulder. 'Which means, my little friar, that Perline is not dead. What he has done is slipped away and paid the constable a few coins not to look for him.'

They continued along Thames Street and into Billingsgate. The air smelt tangy with fish and salt. Here the streets were busy as men prepared for the late-night fishing. The merchants and fishmongers were already preparing their stalls and barrels

134

of brine and salt for the morning's catch.

On the corner of Bridge Street, Cranston and Athelstan parted, the coroner still fulminating against the constable and promising Athelstan that tomorrow he would make inquiries to learn if the Fisher of Men could contribute anything to the mysteries which confronted them. Athelstan thanked him and walked down to the entrance to the bridge. He stopped at the barrier before the entrance, where soldiers lounged or played dice, impervious to the great poles jutting out over either side of the bridge: each bore the severed head of a pirate caught plundering boats in the Thames estuary. Athelstan showed the pass which Cranston had given him. The barrier was opened and he passed on to the bridge, past the silent shops and houses built on either side.

Half-way across, just near the Chapel of St Thomas à Becket, Athelstan went and stood by the rails; he looked out over the Thames, back towards the Tower. The sky was still lit with the fading rays of the setting sun. He always liked to stop here, with the water rushing past the starlings below and, above him, the sky already peppered with the first stars. It was like being caught between heaven and earth. Athelstan breathed in deeply, his gaze fixed on the evening star. The breeze which curled his hair cooled the sweat on his brow and, for a short while, seemed to blow away the weariness and problems of the day.

'I wish I could go to the halls of Oxford,' Athelstan murmured. 'Study the manuscripts of Roger Bacon.'

Athelstan stared at the star. Bacon had built an observatory on Folly Bridge and written a fascinating work on the stars and the planets. Where had they come from? Why did they move? And, if they did, what kept them fixed in the heavens? Why

135

were some stars brighter than others? And did the moon move? Athelstan leaned against the rail and closed his eyes. He wondered if Father Prior would allow him just a short break from his duties in London. Athelstan had heard the whispers: how newly discovered manuscripts of the Ancients, discovered, copied and translated in Italy, were already causing excited debate amongst the scholars. Some even whispered that these proved that the stars did affect man's behaviour. Others, citing the great Ptolemy, argued that the earth was not flat but a veritable sphere, one amongst many in the heavens.

Athelstan opened his eyes and smiled. 'There again,' he whispered, 'each way of life has its own problems.'

His own Order played a prominent part in the Inquisition, both in Italy and elsewhere. Yet the Inquisition took a very dim view of whatever was new. And, of course, there was Cranston, St Erconwald's, and all its parishioners. Athelstan walked on briskly. He stopped at the wicker gate just near the gatehouse on the other side of the bridge. The guards, as usual, began to indulge in some good-natured banter about wandering friars and what they could possibly be up to at the dead of night. Suddenly, a window high in the gatehouse was flung open. Burdon, the diminutive keeper, thrust his head out, hair all spiked.

'For the love of God,' he roared, 'will you shut up! Can't a man and his wife, not to mention his children, sleep in peace?'

The guards pulled faces and sniggered behind their hands.

'Master Burdon!' Athelstan called. 'I am sorry. It's my fault!'

The little head turned. 'Oh, it's you, Brother. Sorry!' he sang out, and the window was drawn sharply shut.

Athelstan left the guards and walked up past the priory of

St Mary Overy and along an alleyway leading to St Erconwald's. At night Southwark never slept. The streets were full of whores, pedlars and hucksters still trying to sell their tawdry goods, most of which, Athelstan knew for a certainty, had been stolen from across the river. Tavern doors stood open, the noise, light and laughter pouring out into the streets. Whores flounced by in their tawdry finery, simpering and winking at him. Two men were involved in a fight over a game of dice. Athelstan looked round. Something was wrong. Usually he'd see at least one of his parishioners: Ursula the pig-woman and her demon sow who followed her everywhere and feasted like a king amongst the cabbages in Athelstan's garden. But there was none. The bench outside the Piebald tavern was not occupied by Tab the tinker, Manyer the hangman, Mugwort the bell clerk, or even Pernell the old Flemish lady, who dyed her hair orange and spent the night crooning over a tankard of ale.

Athelstan, his heart heavy, turned a corner. He could see the flicker of torchlight and hear the shouts and his anxiety grew. Something was wrong. He hurried on, trying hard to control the beating in his heart, but the scene in front of St Erconwald's stopped him full in his tracks. The church doors were closed, but a large crowd of his parishioners was assembled on the steps, torches in hand, listening to a speech from Watkin the dung-collector.

'Oh, no!' Athelstan groaned. 'He's gone and armed himself!'

Watkin was striding backwards and forwards, a small metal cooking-pot on his head, a battered leather sallet round his shoulders, a rusty sword poked into the belt which held in his bulging belly. On either side stood his two lieutenants: Pike the ditcher holding a spear. He also had a cooking-pot on his head whilst, on the other side, Ranulf the rat-catcher had armed himself with a longbow and a quiver full of arrows.

'We must arm ourselves,' Watkin repeated, jabbing the air with his stubby fingers and beaming at the chorus of approval. 'If Father Athelstan does not come back.' His voice dropped. 'And who knows if he will, eh? For all we know the demon could have taken him.'

A roar of disapproval greeted his words.

'We must hunt for the demon.'

Again there was a roar of agreement. Athelstan noticed with a sinking heart how Tab the tinker had taken the statue of St Erconwald from its plinth inside the church, whilst Huddle the painter grasped the processional cross as if it was a spear.

'Benedicta! Benedicta!' Athelstan groaned. 'Where are you?'

He searched the crowd and glimpsed the widow at the far back. She seemed to sense his presence, turned and looked straight at him. Athelstan moved out of the shadows. 'Watkin!' he shouted.

The dung-collector jumped in surprise. 'It's Father!' he yelled. 'The demon has released him!'

Athelstan strode across, shouldering his way through the crowd, ignoring the pats and cries of good wishes. He stared up into the dung-collector's fat, bulbous face.

'Watkin, Watkin,' he whispered. 'In God's name what are you doing?'

'We have seen the demon,' Pike came forward. 'Just before dusk, Father, a black shape in the cemetery.'

'Have you been drinking?' Athelstan accused.

Pike looked stricken. 'Father, I swear, by the cross!'

'Don't blaspheme,' Athelstan whispered hoarsely. 'I have come from Newgate where they have just hanged your friend the Fox.'

Pike's jaw sank.

'It's really my fault, Father.' Ranulf edged nervously forward. 'Early in the day I was in that house in Stinking Alley. You know, the one the merchant wants to buy. I saw the demon there, it was at the top of the stairs.'

'And did you go back and search?'

'Oh yes, Father, we did: it was gone but the stench was terrible.'

'And who saw it tonight?'

'I did.' Cecily the courtesan came up to the steps, hips swaying, her face as innocent as an angel's. 'Father, you told me to come back and help, so I did.'

'And what were you doing in the cemetery?' Athelstan asked, glancing quickly at Pike the ditcher.

'Now, Father, don't be like that. I was all by myself: there was some mouldering fruit left upon a grave so I collected that. It was very quiet.' She babbled on. 'Then I heard a sound. Cross my heart, Father.' She blessed herself. 'I saw the shape, down near the wall, prowling amongst the trees.'

'And what do you all intend to do now?'

Watkin pointed to the statue of St Erconwald and the cross that Huddle still grasped. 'We are going into the cemetery, Father, to hunt the demon!'

Athelstan turned and stretched his hands out above his parishioners. 'Brothers, sisters,' he called. 'What stupidity is this?'

'We want to hunt the demon!' Hig the pigman shouted. 'It's only a matter of time, Father, before he attacks someone else. Who knows, this time he might take them off to hell?' Hig lowered his voice and stared around. 'Perhaps he's hunting Pike?'

'Don't you say anything about my husband!' the ditcher's wife shouted back. 'You can talk, Hig! I saw you this morning outside the Piebald!'

'What do you mean?' the pigman called back.

'Well, that wasn't your daughter!'

A vicious row would have ensued, but Athelstan clapped his hands for silence. 'Tomorrow morning,' he shouted, 'I will celebrate Mass and ask for God's help in this matter.'

A groan of disapproval greeted his words.

'However, to make sure we all sleep peacefully in our beds, I will inspect the cemetery.'

Athelstan meant to go by himself, but Watkin's control over the crowd was too strong. Huddle went first, rather nervously, holding the cross, followed by Tab the tinker carrying the statue of St Erconwald. He was flanked on one side by Crim the altar-boy carrying a flaring torch and Amisias the fuller carrying another. Athelstan closed his eyes and sighed as Watkin took up position beside him, marching like an earl ready to do battle. Ursula's sow suddenly lurched forward, brushed past Tab and headed straight for Athelstan's garden, pursued by Ursula screeching at the top of her voice.

At last they entered the cemetery. Watkin's courage seemed to fail, he hung back, indicating that Pike should take his position. Huddle and Tab drew to one side and Athelstan walked along the beaten trackway which snaked amongst the graves.

Crim the altar-boy came pattering after him, holding a torch. 'There's nothing here, Father,' he whispered. 'Any demon with half a brain would have fled ages ago.'

Athelstan smiled and stared into the darkness. 'Is there anyone there?' he called.

But only the evening wind rustled the branches of the yew trees and bent the long grass between the headstones. An owl hooted. Athelstan was glad he didn't jump or start, though, behind him, his parishioners hastily stepped back.

'Is there anyone there?' Athelstan repeated. 'In the name of God, show yourself!'

He felt slightly ridiculous shouting into the darkness. He silently thanked God that none of his brothers from Blackfriars or, even worse, Sir John Cranston were present.

'The lord Coroner would love this,' a voice whispered.

Athelstan turned and stared down at Benedicta's smiling face.

'He'd draw his sword,' the widow woman continued. 'And charge like a paladin round the graveyard.'

'Aye,' Athelstan replied. 'And then we'd never get them to bed.' He frowned at her. 'Benedicta, couldn't you have stopped them?'

'Father, you know what they are like. Once Watkin gets an idea into his head.' She grinned. 'You were gone so long, they really did think the demon had taken you.'

'He had,' Athelstan replied. 'He's big, fat, drinks, and calls himself John Cranston.' He touched Benedicta's face with the tip of his finger. 'I'll tell you tomorrow what happened.'

'Give one of your blessings!' Watkin shouted. 'You know, Father, three crosses in the air!'

'Aye,' Pike shouted, unwilling to let Watkin have the last say. 'And a big bucket of holy water, Father!'

'I shall give my most solemn blessing,' Athelstan shouted back. 'God forgive my lie,' he whispered, winking at Benedicta. 'It's the most solemn blessing a Dominican can give,' he shouted. 'He is only allowed to give it five times throughout his priestly life, and this is my first!'

His words were greeted by a murmur of approval from his parishioners, sheltering by the side of the church. Athelstan turned and stared into the darkness. To impress his parishioners, he chanted the first five verses of Psalm Fifty-one and then, raising his hand, delivered four blessings: one to the north, another to the south, then to the east and west. Watkin was satisfied. The parishioners drifted away. Benedicta would have stayed to question him, but Athelstan shook his head.

'I have talked and walked enough,' he apologised. 'Oh, where's Bonaventure?'

'He's got more sense,' Benedicta smiled. 'As soon as Watkin appeared, he went hunting.'

'Sensible cat,' Athelstan growled, imitating Cranston.

He and Benedicta walked over to the stable to check on Philomel, his old war-horse. Behind them, in the graveyard, the 'demon' of St Erconwald's lurked beneath the trees and glared through the darkness at them.

CHAPTER 8

As Athelstan built up the fire in the heart of his small priest's house, Sir Francis Harnett was hurrying along the deserted vestibule leading to the chapter-house of Westminster Abbey. The knight was vexed at being stopped so many times by the guards and archers. However, once through, and into the abbey precincts, this irritation gave way to a small glow of pleasure at the prospect of meeting the elusive Perline Brasenose. Harnett stopped just before the steps leading into the chapter-house and, turning right, went down the long flight of stairs into the Pyx chamber. At the bottom he cautiously pushed open the metal-studded door. The chamber inside was bare stone and vaulted, really nothing more than a huge cellar, dry and clean with two sconce torches glowing from their brackets on the wall.

'Perline?' Harnett whispered. The knight's brow knit together in displeasure. 'Where in God's name are you?' he hissed, but his words echoed emptily around the chamber.

Harnett sighed in exasperation and, mopping his face with the hem of his cloak, went and sat on a stone plinth at the far end of the chamber. Perhaps the soldier had gone elsewhere? When he returned, Harnett intended to give Brasenose the rough edge of his tongue. Above him the abbey bells began to toll for Vespers. Despite the thickness of the walls, Harnett heard the patter of feet as the monks moved down. There was silence and then, faintly, the sound of the choir beginning its chant:

'*Exsurge Domine, exsurge, et vindica causam meam.*'

'Arise, O Lord, arise and judge my cause.'

Harnett heard the words and smiled weakly. Had God risen to judge him and the others? Suddenly he felt weary and, leaning back against the wall, stared into the darkness. So many things had gone wrong. Twenty, thirty years ago, he and the others had been young paladins, the spiritual successors of Arthur and his knights. They had even paid a monastic chronicler to prove that Arthur had built his palace in Shropshire. And wasn't Guinevere reputed to be buried at the nunnery at White Ladies, amongst the oaks around Boscobel? The Knights of the Swan had held their Round Table at Lilleshall Abbey. They had their tourneys and tournaments in a blaze of colour and the shrill blast of silver trumpets. Then they had found the cup. At first Sir Edmund Malmesbury had been mistrustful. He had scoffed at the relic-seller who had brought the cup for sale. Sir Henry Swynford, however, had taken it to a learned monk, who had pronounced that the cedar chalice was indeed of great age and may well have been the Grail for which Arthur and his knights had searched. Oh, how they had been pleased!

Harnett stretched out his legs, easing the cramp in his muscles. They had met in the great refectory of Lilleshall, seated around the table with the chalice on a plinth, covered by a purple, damask cloth. Each knight, in turn, had been given the privilege of owning the chalice for a month, but then it had gone. One night, as they rested at the abbey, Malmesbury had burst in where they were supping and feasting, screaming:

'The chalice has gone! The chalice has gone!'

They had searched high and low but never found it, and the seeds of discord had been sown. Nobody levelled open accusation, but the Knights of the Swan had begun to whisper amongst themselves. The finger of accusation had been pointed to this person and then another: the rottenness had spread, like a canker in a flower, seeping through their lives, creating further discord.

One thing had led to another. The war in France turned sour and, with news of defeats, came the effects of the ravages of the great pestilence: a shortage of labour and demands by the peasants for higher wages and better privileges. Harnett and the rest had let their souls slip into darkness . . .

Harnett sighed and leaned forward: that, surely, had all been forgotten? He had cultivated his fields, bought books, and developed an interest in strange and exotic animals. He had not wanted to come to this Parliament. Indeed, quietly, he had striven not to be elected, but the sheriff had been Gaunt's man. When the returns had been counted in the guildhall at Shrewsbury, Harnett had been as surprised at the result as the rest. Oh, Malmesbury had told them to put a brave face on it, trumpeting about what they would do once they arrived at Westminster, yet something was wrong.

Harnett and Aylebore had quietly protested: the sheriff had just smiled from behind his great table on the guildhall dais and spread his hands. 'You are elected,' he had declared. 'Are you saying that I am corrupt?'

What could Harnett do? To protest would have been strange. So, instead, he and the rest had accepted the result and journeyed up to Westminster, staying as usual at the Gargoyle tavern.

Harnett stirred as he heard a sound from the vestibule outside, a faint footstep. He got to his feet but all he could hear was the faint chanting from the choir-stalls. He heard another sound and walked slowly to the door. Surprisingly, the sconce torch fixed in the wall above the steps had gone out.

'Is there anybody there?' he called. A shiver of fear ran down his spine. Harnett, grasping the hilt of his dagger, walked slowly up the steps. 'Perline?' he whispered.

At the top he looked round. Nothing but shadows dancing in the torchlight, turning the gargoyle faces at the top of the pillars even more grotesque: demons laughed down at him; satyrs bared their teeth. Harnett tried to control his breathing. Should he wait or go? He went back down the steps, vowing that if Perline did not arrive soon, he would leave to plot his revenge. Harnett clenched his hands in anger: he had given Perline a special letter allowing him entrance to the chapter-house. Why hadn't the soldier used that and just come, instead of sending Harnett a message saying they should meet here? Harnett went back and sat on the stone plinth. He no longer wondered about the secret agreement he had made with the young soldier from the Tower, his mind kept going back to Sir Henry Swynford, his face a mask of horror, the garrotte string tight round his neck. Or Bouchon's corpse, covered in river slime, his face a liverish-green. Those horrid red crosses carved on their skin! Those terrible mementoes from the past.

He and the rest had protested to Malmesbury, whispering that they should flee. Malmesbury, just as frightened, had shaken his head. 'You know what will happen,' he warned. 'We have no choice.'

'But the arrowhead, the candle?' Aylebore had retorted. 'Who could know about that?'

'The regent does,' Malmesbury replied.

'Has he brought us here to kill us?' Goldingham had asked. 'Why don't we change, Sir Edmund? Perhaps the regent is punishing us for our opposition?'

Malmesbury had shook his head and put his face in his hands. 'There's nothing he can do,' he'd murmured. 'The regent has promised a sign.'

'This is preposterous,' Goldingham had stuttered. 'We wait here like lambs waiting for our throats to be cut!'

Harnett stared down at his fingers. The regent had told Malmesbury to put his confidence in Cranston. The knights had agreed not to separate; except – Harnett beat his fist against his leg – he *had* to see Brasenose. He had paid good silver and he wanted a return! Harnett heard a sound in the doorway. He lifted his head, his heart skipped a beat and his blood ran cold. A cowled figure stood there.

'Brasenose?' Harnett's voice was a whisper.

'Oh day of wrath!' the figure intoned as it walked slowly forwards. 'Oh day of mourning! See fulfilled the prophet's warning! Heaven and earth in ashes burning! See what fear man's bosom rendeth, when from heaven the Judge descendeth, on whose sentence all dependeth!'

Harnett backed into the corner, his hand flailing out. The figure tossed something at him: the arrowhead fell at Harnett's feet, followed by the candle and scrap of parchment.

Harnett went down on his knees, hands clenched. '*Please!*' he begged.

The figure swept closer. Harnett couldn't make out his features: the light was poor, the door to the chamber closed whilst the torchlight flickered behind this awesome, horrid shape. A phantasm which stirred hidden terrors in Harnett's

147

soul and brought back images from his past. Mounted horsemen, mailed and coiffed, torches in their hands, gathered beneath the outstretched branches of a great oak tree from which figures dangled and danced.

'It's so long!' Harnett moaned.

'Nothing remains in the past, Sir Francis,' the figure replied. Harnett's head came up. He recognised that voice!

'Oh no, not you, for pity's sake!'

'Make your peace with God.'

The axe came from beneath the man's cloak. Sir Francis crouched. The axe fell and, with one clean swipe, Harnett's head bounced on to the chamber floor.

Athelstan sat at his table in the priest's house and stared into the fire.

'I should be in bed,' he whispered to Bonaventure.

The great tom-cat, quite fatigued after a night's hunting, lay stretched in front of the hearth, purring at the warmth. Athelstan stared down at the piece of parchment before him. He had tried to make sense of the day's happenings. So much had occurred! Images and pictures still remained. Those two dreadful corpses lying in their coffins; once powerful men now so pathetic in death. Banyard, taking them down to Dame Mathilda's: that young whore, her beautiful breasts exposed.

Athelstan smiled. 'She was very beautiful, Bonaventure,' he murmured. 'Hair black as night and a body which would tempt a saint.'

The cat lifted its head as if to acknowledge him, then flopped back. Athelstan stared into the flames. If only Bonaventure could speak and tell him what he saw in the dark alleyways and runnels of Southwark! That would solve the mystery of the demon. Athelstan pressed his lips together. Well, the demon would have to wait until he received advice from Father Anselm. He wondered if Sir John was asleep, and recalled their meeting with the Harrower of the Dead. Thank God the fellow had not discovered Perline's corpse! Cranston was probably correct: Perline had not deserted the Tower garrison, but paid the constable to look the other way whilst he absconded to do something else. But what? And why should Perline be meeting a knight of the shire on a dark, lonely quayside? Athelstan scratched his chin: apparently Harnett had gone to Southwark to meet Perline and they had both crossed the river to the steel yard, but why? Could Perline be involved in the macabre deaths of these knights?

Bonaventure stirred and stretched, Athelstan recalled Cranston's worries about the disappearing cats in Cheapside. He leaned down and stroked Bonaventure.

'A sea of troubles, Bonaventure! A sea of troubles!'

And, going back to the table, he sat down, picked up his quill, closing his eyes to concentrate. I have finished my Office, he thought; Philomel is snoring fit to burst. I can't do anything about our demon until Prior Anselm answers. Sir John and his cats? Well, they will just have to wait. So what about the murders at Westminster?

Athelstan sighed, opened his eyes and wrote down his thoughts.

Item: Bouchon and Swynford belonged to a powerful group of men who formed a company called the Knights of the Swan.

Item: What happened to this company?

Item: Does the arrowhead, the candle and that scrap of

149

parchment have anything to do with these knights' chivalric pursuits?

Item: Are the deaths of Bouchon and Swynford connected to the break-up of the company of the Knights of the Swan?

Item: What other antagonisms exist between the knights, besides the failure of a business venture at sea?

Item: What were the knights trying to hide from their past? What terrible secrets did they share?

Item: Was it just coincidence that Father Benedict, Chaplain to the Commons, knew, through his dead colleague Father Antony, these powerful men from Shropshire?

Item: What was Harnett doing visiting Perline Brasenose? Why didn't he just tell Cranston the truth?

Item: Whom had Bouchon met last Monday night? Where did that black dirt under his fingernails come from?

Athelstan threw down the pen and stretched. Bouchon's body, he thought, had been found down near Tothill Fields: that meant he must have been killed and thrown into the Thames when the river tide was running full towards the sea. Otherwise the body would have been swept back, up towards the city. Athelstan rubbed his lips. But did that say anything about where he had been killed? The corpse had been found trapped amongst reeds. Athelstan shook his head. He would remember that.

Athelstan picked up his quill and continued writing.

Item: That mysterious priest who appeared entering and leaving the Gargoyle tavern without anyone really noticing? Why was he so confident he would escape undetected? Unless, of course, it was one of the knights themselves?

Athelstan threw his pen down in exasperation.

'Oh, Bonaventure,' he spoke as the cat leapt up from the table and nuzzled his hand. 'That's the real mystery, most cunning of cats. Why don't these knights leave Westminster and return to Shrewsbury? After all, they are avowed opponents of the regent. Unless, of course . . .' Athelstan stroked Bonaventure and stared down at what he had written. 'Unless, most faithful of cats, the regent himself knows their terrible secrets and is forcing them to stay at Westminster.'

Athelstan placed the cat gently back on the floor. He went to the buttery, poured some milk into a metal dish and placed this before the hearth. Bonaventure leapt down from the table and crouched, sipping the milk with his little pink tongue.

Athelstan knelt beside it, listening to the cat's purrs of pleasure. He spoke into the darkness. 'But why does Gaunt want these knights, his avowed enemies, present at Westminster?'

Athelstan knelt back on his heels. Should he and Cranston demand an audience with the regent? Insist that John of Gaunt tell them everything he knew about these men? Or would Gaunt simply raise his delicate eyebrows, shrug and claim complete ignorance?

Athelstan returned to his writing. He paused, listening to the wind outside moaning through the trees in the cemetery. He remembered Watkin's little army: Simplicatas hadn't been there, yet she was for ever hanging round the church, asking Athelstan for news. The friar tucked his chin in his hands.

'Time,' he murmured. 'All these mysteries depend on time.'

They were like designs on a piece of tapestry which was being slowly unrolled. So far he couldn't even see a glimmer which might lead him through this maze of mysteries. He glanced at the hour-candle. If he stayed working any longer, he would only become more agitated. He went to the hearth and put up the crude wire mesh so no flames or cinders would escape. He patted Bonaventure on the head, picked up his writing-bag and went towards the stairs. He sighed and returned to the table. Once he had left the inkstand out and Bonaventure had knocked it flying. Athelstan placed the cap on it, opened his writing-bag and, in the light of the fire, glimpsed the two muzzles the Harrower of the Dead had left on the table in the Holy Lamb of God. Athelstan took these out and examined them carefully. The leather was black and scuffed.

'How could anyone inflict such cruelty on God's poor creatures?' he asked Bonaventure.

Athelstan tore one of the muzzles apart and studied the red leather inside. The friar grinned. He knelt down to stroke Bonaventure's head. 'There must be an angel who guards cats,' he said.

And, putting the torn muzzle back in the bag, the friar went up the stairs singing under his breath. Tomorrow he might resolve at least one of the mysteries confronting himself and Cranston.

'*Ite Missa est*, Our Mass is finished.'

Athelstan stared down at his parishioners who, surprisingly enough, had all turned up for the dawn Mass, eager and expectant to know what their parish priest had decided to do about their demon. Athelstan finished the benediction. He was about to go down the altar steps, genuflect to the host, when he caught the look of desperation in Watkin's eyes. Athelstan sighed, came down and sat on the altar steps, Crim the altar-

152

boy on his right, Bonaventure on his left. The cat sat erect, staring disapprovingly with his one good eye at these people who were delaying the arrival of his early morning dish of milk.

'Brother and Sisters,' Athelstan began, 'I really don't know what to say. I have sent for help from Prior Anselm.'

'And that help has arrived, Father!'

Athelstan's head snapped up. He peered round the rood-screen at the burly, thickset friar who came ambling up the nave. He pulled back his cowl and Athelstan recognised the pleasant, smiling face of one of his Dominican brothers, John Armitage. Athelstan got to his feet as Armitage swept under the rood-screen, the parishioners moving swiftly to one side. Armitage grasped Athelstan's hand.

'I have been here for some time, Brother, in the shadows at the back. Who's your artist?'

Athelstan pointed to a nervous-looking Huddle.

'You've got a good eye, man.' Armitage scratched his shaven cheek. 'Have you ever thought of becoming a Dominican? We need good artists.'

Huddle, rather frightened by this bustling friar who stared at him so intently, shook his head.

'We need good artists,' Armitage repeated. 'If all our churches looked like this, perhaps we could get more people attending Mass.' He eased the cord round his considerable bulk, though, for a heavy, thickset man, Athelstan knew Armitage could move very quickly. 'Father Prior sent me,' Armitage murmured. 'But I don't feel like having a discussion in the presence of all.'

'What concerns Father Athelstan,' Watkin trumpeted, having overheard this conversation, 'concerns us all, especially if it's about our demon!'

'He's a leader of the parish council,' Athelstan whispered

quickly, catching the warning look in Armitage's eyes.

Father John walked across and looked down at Watkin, who glared defiantly back. The friar leaned down and whispered in the dung-collector's ear. Watkin's face changed: he beamed from ear to ear and nodded solemnly. Armitage then genuflected before the pyx and Athelstan, Crim and Bonaventure followed him into the sacristy. Athelstan quickly divested and took his visitor across to the priest's house.

'I have some oatmeal,' he offered.

Armitage licked his lips. 'Any milk and honey?' he asked.

'In abundance,' Athelstan smiled back.

'Then truly my cup is pressed down and overflowing,' Armitage replied.

'What did you say to Watkin?' Athelstan asked as he served his visitor.

Armitage's eyes twinkled. 'I told him to guard the sanctuary: if the demon attacked, he would strike at the high altar. Only a man such as Watkin would be strong enough to resist it.'

Athelstan grinned and, for a while, they sat and broke their fast. It wasn't much, but Armitage declared it was a thousand times better than what Blackfriars refectory served. Once he'd finished, he leaned his elbows on the table and stared across at Athelstan. His dark eyes were not so merry now.

'Prior Anselm told me about your problem.'

Athelstan nodded warily. 'I thought you were lecturing in the halls of Oxford?' he asked evasively.

'The food was terrible so I asked to be transferred back,' Armitage joked. He patted his stomach. 'Now I am at Blackfriars, ostensibly as librarian and archivist. I am also exorcist for the eastern part of London. Well, most of it, except for those parishes north of St Mary of Bethlehem.'

Athelstan stared disbelievingly back. He remembered Armitage from his novitiate days as a merry, practical priest, not the sort to be involved with demons, incantations and exorcism.

'I know what you are thinking, Athelstan.' Armitage picked a crumb up from his platter and popped it into his mouth. 'But my task is not as frightening as it appears.' He smiled thinly. 'You can't imagine how many people, with two quarts of ale down them, manage to see demons and sprites in every corner.'

'This is different,' Athelstan replied.

'I know, I know, Father Prior told me. One of your parishioners was actually attacked and others have seen a dark, hideous shape; you yourself detected a terrible stench in the death-house. Before I went into your church I visited it, but I could neither smell nor see anything untoward.'

'That's because it has been scrubbed and cleaned,' Athelstan replied sharply.

Armitage grasped his hand. 'Brother, I am not mocking you. I have been an exorcist now for eighteen months. There have been over fifty incidents I have attended. All of them could be explained by natural phenomena. But,' he added slowly, 'there are others.' He supped at his jug of ale. 'Ten days ago I went to a house near St Giles Cripplegate. The mother had talked of strange sounds and cries in the night. A sense of evil, of deep foreboding. Athelstan, I experienced the same. I searched that house. I blessed it. I exorcised it but I could discover nothing wrong. The woman was a widow; gentle, prayerful, rather anxious, but basically a good woman.

'I was about to leave when her twenty-year-old son came in. He was dressed in the latest fashion, his hair crimped and curled. He was ever so polite.' Armitage blinked and Athelstan

155

saw the fear in his eyes. 'This young man,' the exorcist continued, 'grasped my hand and asked how I was? Wouldn't I stay for another stoup of ale? Take some silver for the poor?' Armitage closed his eyes as he chewed the corner of his lip. 'That young man,' he continued hoarsely, 'really frightened me. His eyes were dead, Brother. You had the impression that his entire face was a mask and something else lay behind it: a presence, dark and sinister, sneering at both me and his mother.'

The exorcist put his ale down. 'I have yet to pluck up courage to go back and tell that woman how, in my opinion as an exorcist, her son's soul is shrouded in darkness. He has been dabbling in some vice which has opened the door to let other powers in.' He pushed his tankard away. 'Now, I tell you this, Athelstan, because that's my view of a demon, of possession. Someone cool, logical, rational, even pleasant in appearance and attitude.'

Athelstan was now stroking Bonaventure who had leapt into his lap. 'And so you are saying we have no demon in Southwark?'

Armitage smiled. 'Do you really believe that, Brother?'

Athelstan shook his head.

'Then follow your heart, Athelstan. When you meet a devil, it won't be some dark shape leaping amongst the graves. Surely you know what I mean?'

Athelstan recalled those powerful knights at Westminster; their easy smirks, their lying ways, the duplicity of their lives. 'I understand.'

Armitage sighed. 'I thought you would. You are the lord coroner's clerk, aren't you? Your reputation goes before you, Brother Athelstan. Think of the murderers you have hunted: those men and women who can wipe out another life without a flicker of an eyelid, then wipe their lips and proudly proclaim their innocence to the world. There are your demons. However,' he pulled up his cowl, 'at the same time your parishioners could be correct: there may be a presence loose in Southwark, though I really doubt it.'

'Then what shall I do?' Athelstan asked.

'Apply that logic for which you are famous.' Armitage got to his feet. 'Keep your parishioners calm. Study all the evidence given to you. Look for the weakness and, when you find it, the mystery will unravel.' Armitage picked up his cloak. 'I am sorry I have been of little comfort, Brother. Father Prior was sending me to Eltham, he asked me to stop off here and see you.' Armitage grinned. 'Accept my wager, Brother; if you haven't found your demon in a week, I'll come back and stay until you do.'

'And if I do find it . . .?'

Armitage extended his hand. 'Send your painter to Blackfriars: there's a stretch of bare wall just near the vestry, and every time I pass it, I imagine this beautiful picture of Christ talking to the Samaritan woman. Don't worry, he'll be well paid!'

Athelstan clasped his outstretched hand. 'Wager accepted!'

Armitage thanked Athelstan and Bonaventure for their company, gave them his blessing and left the priest's house.

For a while Athelstan sat and reflected on what the exorcist had said.

'Brother John spoke the truth,' he declared finally. 'But where's the weakness in all of this?'

He cradled the cat and stared at the stark crucifix above the hearth. Watkin and the rest had first seen the demon on Monday evening. Later that same night Sir Oliver Bouchon had been killed; Perline Brasenose, who'd not been home since Saturday, apparently met Sir Francis Harnett on the quayside across the river. Since Monday evening, the demon had been seen near Benedicta's house – another lonely, deserted place; in the empty house by Ranulf the rat-catcher, and again, yesterday evening, in the parish cemetery. So where was the weakness in all this? He heard a knock on the door.

'Come in,' Athelstan shouted.

He half expected Cranston, but Benedicta slipped in, a shopping basket over her arm. For a while all was confusion as Bonaventure hastily leapt into this, looking for something to eat.

'I have brought food,' Benedicta smiled, putting the basket on the table. She took out small, linen-covered bundles and laid them out: bread, cheese, a small jar of home-made jam, a piece of cured ham, slices of salted bacon, onions and a small bag of oatmeal. Athelstan couldn't refuse. Indeed, as Cranston constantly teased him, he was only too pleased to see Benedicta's lovely face. She took the food into the buttery and helped Athelstan clear the table. He brought fresh jugs of ale, then sat and told her about what was happening at Westminster. Benedicta heard him out: her smooth, olive face lost some of its laughter lines as Athelstan described the deaths of the two knights and the possible sinister intrigues of the regent, John of Gaunt.

'You should be more careful, Athelstan,' she warned. 'When you go into the marketplace people smile and greet you, and so they should. But when you are gone, the whispering continues, fed and fanned by the peasants who bring their produce in to be sold. There's been unrest in Essex; at Coggeshall a tax-collector was assaulted, whilst at Colchester they barred the gates against royal messengers. There's talk of people collecting arms, hiding swords and daggers. Yew trees are being stripped to fashion new bows and arrows. Scythes and bill-hooks have been sharpened, and it's not for the harvest.' She leaned across the table and laid one soft hand on Athelstan's. 'There's a storm coming, Father. This city is going to see terrible violence.'

'And, before you ask, Benedicta.' Athelstan self-consciously moved his hand; he got to his feet and went to stand before the fire. 'I will stay where I am, unless Father Prior orders otherwise.'

Benedicta saw the stubborn line to his mouth, and knew any further discussion was closed.

'And the demon?' she asked quickly.

'I am still hunting it.'

'And Perline?'

Athelstan shook his head.

'I met Simplicatas in the marketplace,' Benedicta continued. 'She still looks worried. I asked her if there was any news but she shook her head and continued shopping.' Benedicta laughed self-consciously and played with the silver chain round her neck. 'I would have been here earlier, but I helped to carry her basket.'

Benedicta jumped as the door was flung open and Cranston came crashing in like the north wind. He crowed with delight when he saw Benedicta and, gripping her by the shoulders, bent down and planted a juicy kiss on each cheek.

'Thank God for pretty women!' he bellowed, and turned, legs apart, thumbs tucked in his belt. 'Well, Athelstan, pack your bags. Lock your church, we are off to Westminster!'

Athelstan groaned.

'The regent's orders,' Cranston continued. 'Last night Sir

Francis Harnett, knight, was found in the Pyx chamber. His body lay on the floor. His head was tied by the hair to a torch-holder in the wall.' He grimaced at Athelstan. 'Apparently yesterevening our good knight went down there to meet someone. God knows who. The guards let him through. This morning one of the archers saw a door open and went down to investigate. He came rushing out, screaming himself witless.'

'But why was Harnett so stupid as to go to such a lonely place?'

Cranston shrugged. 'God knows. Malmesbury had told the knights to stay together. Anyway, that is what we have to search out.' He patted Athelstan on the shoulder. 'I am sorry, Brother, both you and I have no choice but to take chambers at the Gargoyle. It's the regent's orders.'

Athelstan opened his mouth to protest but Cranston shook his head. 'There's no debate, Brother. Everything here will have to wait.' He grinned over at Benedicta. 'You'll have to look after the parish and, if you sit there long enough, looking as pretty as you do, you might even trap this demon.' He turned back to Athelstan. 'There's a further order. On Saturday morning, Gaunt and the young king intend to ride in procession to meet the Commons at Westminster.' He puffed his chest out. 'I, as the king's law officer, will be part of that procession, and of course, dear Athelstan, you will have to go with me.'

Athelstan stared into the fire. He felt like screaming his refusal, yet that would only upset Cranston and achieve nothing.

'Benedicta, I'll leave you the keys.' He got to his feet. 'Look after Bonaventure. Remember to feed Philomel and ask the priest at St Swithin's if he would be so kind as to come and say a morning Mass.'

Benedicta said she would. Athelstan went over to the hearth

and, grasping a poker, began to sift amongst the cinders. 'It will go out soon,' he said absentmindedly.

'Don't worry, Brother,' Benedicta offered, 'I will make sure that all's well.'

Athelstan climbed the makeshift ladder into his bedroom. As he filled the saddlebags at the foot of his bed, he wondered, not about Westminster, but Simplicatas. Why should a lonely young woman, supposedly riven with anxiety about her missing husband, buy so much in the marketplace that Benedicta had to help her carry it!

CHAPTER 9

'There's little the corpse-dresser can do with that.' Banyard pointed to the severed torso of Sir Francis Harnett. His remains lay sprawled on a shoddy tarpaulin in an outhouse behind the tavern: the head lolled to one side like a ball, the eyes were half open, and bruises marked the cheek where the head had rolled along the floor of the crypt.

'For heaven's sake, show some respect,' Cranston murmured.

'I merely describe things as they are, my lord Coroner, not as they should be.'

Athelstan knelt down. He crossed himself, closed his eyes and whispered the requiem: '"Eternal rest grant unto him, O Lord, and let perpetual light shine upon him. May he rest in peace."'

'Amen,' Cranston intoned.

'What on earth was he doing in the Pyx chamber?' Athelstan asked, getting to his feet.

'God knows,' Sir Miles Coverdale replied. 'The Commons sat late yesterday. The abbey then became deserted, though, of course, members stayed around the precincts gossiping and talking.'

'And your guards were still on duty?' Cranston asked.

'Oh yes. Even at night. No one can enter or leave the

163

cloisters without showing the special seal each of the representatives carries.'

'And who went into the cloisters last night?' Cranston persisted. 'Come on, man, you know what we are after.'

Coverdale, his face pale, shook his head. 'I can't honestly answer that, Sir John. Representatives are constantly going in and out. As you know, the evening can be cold and many are cowled or hooded. But I can state two things. First, no one entered or left those cloisters, or the area around the chapter-house, without showing the special pass.'

'And the vestibule?' Athelstan asked. 'Are those double doors still guarded?'

'At night, not as strictly as during the day when the Commons sit, but there are guards in the gallery leading to it.'

'And did anyone remember Sir Francis going there?'

'One of my men, vaguely; others followed but it was dark. As I said, members are cowled and hooded, arrogant and peremptory. They show their seal, pull back cloaks to show they carry no swords, and doors are opened.'

'You were going to tell us two things?' Cranston asked.

'Ah well.' Coverdale waved at Harnett's decapitated corpse. 'Sir John, you have seen executions or beheadings after battle. To take a man's head off, you need either a broadsword or a two-headed axe, yet anyone who enters the abbey precincts must show he carries no such weapon. Only dress-daggers are permitted.'

Athelstan covered the decapitated body with the edges of the dark tarpaulin. 'Is it possible,' he asked, 'that someone could steal into the abbey precincts?'

'I asked Father Abbot that,' Coverdale replied. 'There are no secret passageways or galleries. You must remember, Brother

164

Athelstan, the Pyx chamber lies just before the chapter-house. Harnett, and the person who killed him, had to go – and his assassin return – through at least three lines of my guards.' He smiled thinly and shrugged. 'What more can I say? Knights from this shire or that were constantly going in and out. Some visited the shrine of St Faith, others the abbey itself. A few came back to collect possessions. You cannot blame my soldiers,' he continued defensively. 'They have their orders. Ask for the seal, ensure the person is carrying no weapons, and let them on their way.' Coverdale wiped his hand on the back of his mouth. 'There are so many representatives, and the abbey has a number of entrances.'

'And they must have one of these seals?' Athelstan asked.

'Yes,' Coverdale replied, 'or a special pass signed by one of the members. However, my men have strict orders to stop such a person and send for me.' He shrugged. 'But, since the beginning of this Parliament, no such letter has been offered, certainly not last night.'

'What happens if the killer was a monk?' Athelstan asked.

'Impossible,' Coverdale scoffed. 'The brothers are allowed to use the cloisters, but the vestibule and the chapter-house itself are strictly out of bounds. Moreover, my soldiers would remember a monk trying to enter and leave.'

'Which leaves us with one possibility.' Athelstan, rubbing the edge of his nose, took a step nearer to the captain of the guard. 'I don't want to give offence, sir, but what if Sir Francis Harnett's killer was a soldier?'

Coverdale's face reddened.

'I say this,' Athelstan continued remorselessly, 'merely

165

because a soldier is armed with sword and axe. He would also have every right to enter the vestibule leading to the chapter-house.'

'You mean someone like myself?'

'I did not say that, Sir Miles. I was only making an observation.'

Cranston, sitting on an overturned bucket, caught the drift of Athelstan's meaning, as did Banyard. The landlord stepped back, as if he wished to put himself beyond reach of Coverdale's anger. Sir Miles, however, despite the red blotches high in his cheeks, remained calm.

'You should continue your questions, Friar,' he snapped. 'Sir Francis Harnett's companions wait for us in the tavern. They will tell you that Sir Francis left them against my orders — and their advice — shortly before Vespers.'

'And, of course, you are going to tell us where you were?'

'Yes, Friar, I was at the Savoy Palace with others of the regent's commanders, preparing for the royal procession to Westminster this Saturday morning. My lord of Gaunt, not to mention a number of his knights, will swear solemn oaths that I was with them.'

'At the hour of Vespers?' Athelstan asked, noticing a shift in Coverdale's eyes.

'Well, shortly afterwards.'

Athelstan turned away. 'Master Banyard, how long will the corpse remain here?'

'Till this afternoon.'

'Was there any sign of robbery?' Cranston asked, getting to his feet, grunting and groaning.

'None whatsoever,' Coverdale hastily interrupted.

Athelstan went and looked down at the corpse and, as he did

166

so, noticed a trickle of blood, slow and sluggish, curl out from beneath the dirty sheet.

Coverdale saw it too and turned hastily away. 'The others are waiting,' he snapped.

Coverdale was about to walk away, but stopped just beside Athelstan: he pushed his face a few inches away from the friar's. 'Make your inquiries, Brother,' he whispered. 'I am no assassin.'

Athelstan was about to reply when there was shouting from the tavern followed by the patter of feet. Christina, her hair all flying, burst into the outhouse: she took one look at the corpse covered in the sheet and stepped back.

'What's the matter, girl? What's the matter?'

Athelstan and the rest followed her out.

'It's the knights,' she cried. 'Someone came to the tavern.' She shook her head. 'I don't know who. One of the potboys says he was dressed all in black. He gave him a pouch sealed at the top and a letter for Sir Edmund Malmesbury. The boy took it up to the knights. Sir Edmund opened it, now they are all shouting, "*It's been found! It's been found!*"'

'What's been found?' Cranston asked, pressing the girl's arm.

'I don't know,' she stammered. 'But they are all excited, arguing with each other about a cup which was stolen.'

Cranston strode back towards the tavern. Athelstan remained to ensure the corpse was decently covered. He closed the door and crossed the tavern yard. A cock, glorious in its plumage, crowed its heart out on top of a mound of rich, black earth. 'You have a fine voice, Brother cock,' Athelstan murmured, idly wishing he had such a bird and a collection of hens at St Erconwald's. Then he remembered Bonaventure and Ursula

167

the pig-woman's evil-looking sow and shook his head. 'You wouldn't sing there, Brother cock.'

He continued across the yard, glimpsing the river glinting in the distance and the long line of grain barges making their way up to Queenshithe or Dowgate. Athelstan put his hand into the pocket of his habit and touched the muzzle he had examined the night before. Amidst all this excitement, he had almost forgotten it; he must tell the worthy coroner to set a trap for that sinister thief of cats. He sighed and went into the tavern.

Cranston had cleared the taproom. All four knights were now seated round the table, faces flushed. They kept staring at a polished, cedarwood chalice which stood on the table before them. Every so often one of them would lean forward, eyes glittering, and stroke the chalice with the tips of their fingers. Coverdale lounged in a windowseat watching curiously. Cranston was over at the wine butts sampling, as he explained, mine host's best Gascony. Banyard was all excited: he kept staring at the cup and shaking his head.

'What is it?' Athelstan asked.

'What is it?' Sir Humphrey Aylebore rubbed his bald head with his hand and, like a child unable to restrain himself, leaned across and grasped the dark wood chalice. 'This is the Grail!' he explained.

Athelstan went over and took the wooden cup out of his hands. The bowl was shallow, the stem and base felt heavy in his hand. The wood was polished not only because of its texture, but also because of its great age. Athelstan recalled the legends of Arthur and wondered if this cup truly was the Grail; the very chalice Christ had used at the Last Supper to turn the wine into his blood for the world to drink.

The chalice bore no markings or etchings, and Athelstan hid his suspicions. He was growing increasingly wary of any relics. He had seen enough wood – supposedly belonging to the True Cross – to build a fleet of warships. Indeed, if he collected every scrap of cloth which was supposed to cover the Saviour's corpse, he was sure the roll would stretch from London to York. He glanced up. Malmesbury's eyes were glittering. Whatever I think, Athelstan reflected, these men really believe this is the Grail.

'Brother Athelstan, please?' Malmesbury stretched out his hands pleadingly.

Athelstan handed the cup to him. The knight took it tenderly, as a mother would her child.

'You say this once belonged to you?' Cranston asked, coming forward, a brimming wine cup in his hand. He winked at Athelstan and slurped quickly at the wine.

'It is ours,' Goldingham snapped. He plucked the chalice from Malmesbury's grasp, turned it over and pointed at the faint outline of a swan carved on the base. 'It disappeared,' he continued, 'one night, years ago, when we were at Lilleshall Abbey.' His eyes brimmed with tears, and his voice became choked. 'Since then, nothing has gone right for us.'

'What do you mean?' Athelstan asked.

Goldingham shook his head and, holding the chalice between his hands, rocked backwards and forwards, as if this relic would preserve him from all evil.

'And it was brought back now?' Cranston asked.

'Yes,' Malmesbury replied. 'A stranger brought it to the tavern door.' He picked up a leather bag which had been sealed at the neck. 'It was in this, with a scrap of parchment bearing my name.'

Athelstan took the bag and the parchment and examined them carefully.

'How?' Coverdale called out. 'How could anyone in London know that a cup stolen from a Shropshire abbey years ago belonged to you?'

'We don't know,' Sir Humphrey snarled over his shoulder. 'All we know is that the cup was stolen, and now it's back with its rightful owners.'

'Do you think it's connected with Sir Francis Harnett's death?' Athelstan asked.

Some of the excitement drained from the knights' faces.

'I mean,' Athelstan continued, 'is it possible that Sir Francis had the chalice all the time? And now he has been killed, the cup's been returned.'

'Explain yourself, Friar!' Goldingham interrupted.

Athelstan smiled and sat down on the stool opposite him. 'I can't. It just seems a coincidence that one of your companions died last night, and this morning a long-lost cup is returned.' Athelstan had his own suspicions, but he kept them hidden. 'Sir Francis is dead.' He emphasised his words. 'Do any of you know why he went to the Pyx chamber last night? Whom was he meeting? There's nothing down there,' he continued, 'so Sir Francis could only have gone there intending to meet someone. That person killed him.'

'We don't know,' Sir Thomas Elontius replied, running his hand through his bristling red hair. His popping eyes had a frightened, hunted look. 'We all stayed here at the Gargoyle.'

'None of you left?' Cranston asked, coming up beside Athelstan.

'Ask mine host,' Elontius replied.

'It's true,' Banyard declared, walking over to join them. 'All

170

five of the knights were here. I served them the speciality of the house: young goose, fresh and tender and served with a spicy sauce. My guests ate and drank their fill and went to their chambers. I did not even know Sir Francis had left.'

'And you all stayed here?' Cranston repeated.

'Yes,' the knights chorused.

'But it stands to reason,' Athelstan intervened, 'if Sir Francis Harnett left and no one saw him going, then any or all of you could have left unnoticed.'

Banyard looked surprised by Athelstan's remark: he sighed and scratched his cheek. 'The tavern has got at least three or four entrances,' he declared. 'And at night we become busy. Brother Athelstan, this is a tavern famous for its food, fine ales and strong wine. We have people coming and going. The Gargoyle is a hostelry, not a castle prison.'

'And on your oath,' Athelstan turned back to the knights, 'did any of you leave?' He stared at each of them in turn, but they all shook their heads.

'We were tired,' Sir Humphrey Aylebore declared. 'Yes, Brother, tried and frightened. We ate and drank our fill.' He forced a smile. 'I suppose my companions did what I did: I locked the doors and windows of my chamber and hid beneath the sheets. We have vowed not to go anywhere at Westminster without at least one other accompanying us.'

'Do you know why Sir Francis Harnett left?' Cranston slurped from the wine cup and smacked his lips noisily.

'No,' Malmesbury retorted, staring disdainfully at the coroner.

'Oh come, Sir Edmund.' Cranston beamed back at him. 'Sir Francis is now well known to us as a man constantly going in and out of the city, travelling hither and thither on secret errands.'

171

'Sir Francis was a fussy little man. God rest him,' Goldingham replied. 'Once we were a band of brothers, Sir John.' He pointed to the cup. 'But, when that was stolen . . .' He shrugged. 'Each of us went his own way, Sir Francis in particular. Oh, he whispered to himself and scurried about, but none of us knows why he left Dame Mathilda's, or why he should be so foolish as to go alone to the Pyx chamber.'

'Did he ever mention a young soldier called Perline Brasenose?'

'Not to my knowledge,' Sir Edmund replied. 'But Goldingham is correct: Harnett was his own man, with the carp ponds, books on beasteries and exotic animals. He never told us where he went or why. If he had, he'd be alive this morning.'

'You said Perline Brasenose,' Sir Thomas Elontius leaned forward. He turned and whispered in Sir Humphrey Aylebore's ear. The knight nodded. 'Perline's a soldier in the Tower garrison?' Elontius asked.

'Yes,' Athelstan replied.

'I remember him.' Elontius's fingers flew to his lips. 'Last Sunday we went to the Tower. As we left, I saw Sir Francis speaking to a young soldier just near the gatehouse.'

'What about?' Athelstan asked.

'I don't know,' Elontius replied. 'But Harnett came back here, rather excited.'

Cranston dug into his wallet and drew out the small wax candle, arrowhead and scrap of parchment.

'These were found beside Harnett's body, as they were with Swynford's and Bouchon's. Are you still going to maintain –' he looked at the knights in turn – 'that they mean nothing to you?'

'Well, they mean nothing to me,' Sir Thomas retorted, red

hair bristling, blue eyes popping. 'I don't give a shit, Sir John.' He jabbed a finger at the coroner. 'All I know is that some madcap is busy slaughtering members of our party and you have done nothing to stop it.'

'I can't be everywhere!' Cranston snapped back.

'It's a nightmare,' Elontius bellowed, snapping his fingers at Banyard. 'Serve us some drinks, man.' He smiled at the landlord. 'The only good thing about being in London is this tavern: the prices are reasonable, the food is delicious and the chambers are clean. Even Harnett, the miserly bastard, remarked on that.'

Athelstan waited until the landlord brought back a tray of cups and set them out before the knights. He leaned across with the jug.

'Do you want some, Brother?' Banyard asked.

Athelstan shook his head. For some strange reason his stomach felt a little queasy, and he still found it difficult to remove the image of that gruesome severed corpse from his mind. He remembered Banyard's description of the night Bouchon had died, and was tempted to ask what Sir Francis Harnett had meant by saying that 'the old ways were the best ways'. However, this would betray Banyard's eavesdropping, and in any case, these knights would just lie.

'Landlord!' Cranston called over his shoulder. 'Did Harnett send any messages into London, written or verbal?'

The landlord came back, scratching his head, a look of puzzlement on his swarthy face. 'No, he didn't.'

'I have been through his belongings,' Malmesbury intervened. 'Sir John, there's nothing there. A Book of Hours, an inkpot, cups, clothing, but nothing remarkable.'

'Do you know why Harnett wanted to meet a soldier from the

173

Tower garrison?' Athelstan asked.

'If I did, I would tell Sir John,' Malmesbury replied quickly.

Athelstan leaned across and picked up the chalice again. 'And you have no knowledge of where this came from or who returned it?'

'Now, that is a mystery,' Goldingham intervened, his cup half-way to his lips. 'The last time I saw that, Brother, was many years ago; now it reappears as if out of nowhere.'

'And you are not curious?' Cranston asked.

'Quite honestly, Sir John,' Aylebore retorted, 'I couldn't give a shit! All I wish is that we could put it in a box and go straight back to Shrewsbury with the corpses of our murdered comrades.'

'Why don't you?' Athelstan turned to Malmesbury. 'Surely the regent will excuse you?'

'That's impossible,' the knight growled. 'We represent the county and towns of Shropshire. What explanation can we give, Brother, for our sudden flight? And how do we know the assassin would not pursue us?' He ran his fingers round the brim of the wine goblet. 'Moreover, as Sir John Cranston said, in many people's eyes, flight might appear to be guilt.' He sipped at his wine. 'Finally, we have a task to do: the regent's demands for taxes have to be resisted.'

'And are you doing that?' Cranston asked.

'Aye,' Malmesbury replied.

'But if the young king comes down to the Commons and asks for your support?' Cranston continued.

Malmesbury shrugged. 'You know the old saying, Sir John: we'll cross that bridge when we come to it!'

'I'll go even further.' Sir Humphrey Aylebore pointed at the chalice Athelstan still held. 'Speaking for myself, Brother, I'd give that to you if you could unmask the assassin amongst us.'

'Amongst you?' Athelstan cocked his head to one side. 'Sir Humphrey, why do you think the killer is one of your company?'

'It stands to reason, doesn't it?' the knight blustered. 'Last night Sir Francis may have met this Perline, or maybe the fellow didn't turn up, but the assassin did.'

'And?'

'Oh, for God's sake, Brother, don't play games! The abbey is well guarded. Two or three lines of soldiers and archers. No one would be allowed into the vestibule leading to the Pyx chamber unless he carried a special seal . . . And don't say the seal can be forged. Green wax, not to mention the imprint of the Great Seal of the kingdom, are very difficult to obtain and impossible to forge!'

His words created a pool of silence in the taproom.

'I'm speaking the truth, aren't I?' Aylebore declared. 'The killer . . .' He jabbed the air with one stubby finger. '. . . The killer must have a seal. He must have known when Sir Francis left here; and he must be someone who could walk in and out of the abbey with the utmost impunity.'

'But what about the axe?' Malmesbury asked anxiously. 'The sword which took Harnett's head off? No representative is allowed to bear arms in the abbey precincts.' He looked over his shoulder at Coverdale slouched in the windowseat behind him.

'What are you saying, Sir Edmund?' Athelstan asked.

'What happens if the killer was sent into the abbey? Allowed to enter and leave at his own whim?'

'Be careful what you say,' Coverdale warned.

Athelstan rose, smiling, to his feet. He put the chalice back on the table. 'Whatever . . .' he said mildly. He could sense the atmosphere changing, and did not want to be drawn into a

175

fierce quarrel. 'Sir John, I think we should examine Sir Francis's possessions.' He pointed at the chalice and the leather bag in which it had been delivered. 'Gentlemen, may I borrow these for a while?'

Malmesbury looked doubtfully back. Goldingham shrugged but Sir Humphrey Aylebore rose to his feet and thrust the chalice and bag into Athelstan's hands.

'If it helps, Brother, keep them as long as you want.' He smiled. 'Just ensure our Grail doesn't disappear again.'

Cranston drained his cup and glared down at the knights. 'Gentlemen, I want your word. Stay together in this tavern. Do not go out at night, either as a group or individually. Tell each other where you are and what you are doing. Agreed?'

Each of the knights gave his word.

Cranston turned to Banyard. 'And mine host, you have chambers for my secretarius and myself?'

'You can have Swynford's or Bouchon's.' The landlord got to his feet and called for a potboy. 'Whilst you are visiting Sir Francis's chamber, I'll make sure the sheets are changed and fresh rushes are laid.'

Cranston thanked him. He followed Athelstan up the stairs. On the stairwell they met Christina, her arms full of sheaves of fresh rushes, the ends of which tickled her nose. Athelstan waited until she had finished her fit of sneezing.

'God bless you, girl!'

'Thank you, Father.'

'Sir Francis's room?'

'Go up another set of stairs. The door is open.'

Athelstan, followed by the coroner who was huffing and puffing, went up the stairs into Harnett's chamber. The room was pleasantly furnished with a four-poster bed, two large, metal-bound coffers, one narrow table and some stools. Braziers stood in the corner but these were unlit: the window was open, allowing the warm sunlight to bathe the room in a soft glow.

'They are still not telling the truth, are they?' Cranston asked, closing the door behind them.

'No, Sir John, they are not.'

'Do you think the murderer's one of them?'

'He must be, Sir John. There are more doors, passageways and galleries in this tavern than there are in a rabbit warren. Any one of them could have slipped out, followed Sir Francis into the Pyx chamber, and killed him.'

'And the weapon?' Cranston asked.

Athelstan sighed. 'Yes, yes, that is a mystery. But we must not forget Sir Miles Coverdale or His Grace the Regent's role in all this.'

'And the famous chalice?'

'Ah!' Athelstan lifted the lid of one of the heavy chests. 'Sir John, do me a favour please. Go down into the taproom, hire a boy to go to the abbey, and ask Father Benedict if he would be so good as to join us here. No, no, on second thoughts, Sir John, tell the boy we will meet him within the hour in St Faith's Chapel. I would also like to see the Pyx chamber where the murder was committed. Oh, and Sir John, what time does the Cheapside market close?'

'Just before sunset. It depends on the weather.'

'Well, whatever happens, Sir John, we must be back in Cheapside when it does.'

'Why?' Cranston asked.

But Athelstan, muttering to himself, was now rifling amongst the contents of the chest. Cranston stuck his tongue out at the friar's back and, going to the top of the stairs, shouted for

Banyard to send a boy up. When the coroner returned, Athelstan had laid the contents of the chest and Harnett's saddlebags on to the bed and was now sifting amongst these.

'Nothing remarkable,' Athelstan murmured. 'A cup with a swan on it. A collection of legends about King Arthur, clothing, belts and daggers, an inkpot and quills.' He straightened up, a Book of Hours clasped in his hand.

'Sir John.' He pointed to the chalice he had brought from the taproom. 'Let's leave this. Ask Banyard to seal the chamber.' He looked down at the embroidered belts, soft leather boots, hose, jerkins and shirts. 'There's something missing here,' he murmured, 'but I can't put my finger on it.' He scratched his cheek. 'Ah well.'

Athelstan picked up a coverlet and threw it over the contents of the bed; he was still distracted by what he had failed to see rather than what he had. The friar led a bemused coroner out of the chamber and down the stairs. Banyard, busy in the taproom, told him the knights had gone back to their own chambers.

'And Sir Miles Coverdale?'

'Oh, he started shouting at Sir Edmund Malmesbury, saying he didn't like his insinuations, and stalked off.'

'Master Banyard,' Athelstan said, 'would you lock Sir Francis's room? Please tell his companions that I have taken a Book of Hours but left the chalice there.'

The landlord agreed and Athelstan joined Cranston outside.

'Why bother taking his Book of Hours?' Cranston asked as they hurried up an alleyway towards the brooding mass of Westminster Abbey.

'Sir John, you have a Book of Hours at home?' Athelstan paused to open his writing-case and place the book inside.

'Yes, of course I do.'

178

'And you use it to pray?'

'Of course.'

'And what else?'

Cranston grinned and patted the friar on the shoulder. 'In the blank pages at the back and front I make my own notes, private prayers and devotions.' He gripped Athelstan's arm. 'Didn't you examine Harnett's before you left?'

'Very quickly,' Athelstan replied. 'I could see nothing. But come, Sir John, we have the Pyx chamber to investigate, as well as ask Father Benedict certain questions.'

Athelstan was relieved they had left in good time, as the soldiers guarding the abbey entrances were quite obdurate.

'I don't care if you're the Archangel Gabriel!' One of the archers snapped at Cranston, his nut-brown face fiercely determined. 'No one is allowed to pass here without a seal. You have not got one, so you can't go in!'

After a great deal of argument, the archer at least agreed to go and find Sir Miles Coverdale: when the captain arrived, he sullenly agreed to let them through, but insisted on escorting them himself through the Jericho parlour, around the cloisters and into the long vestibule leading to the chapter-house.

'The Commons are not meeting this morning?' Cranston asked as they hurried along.

'No, Sir John, that gaggle of geese have to rest their voices: their cackling begins late this afternoon. They are already complaining about Sir Francis Harnett's death,' Coverdale added morosely. 'Sending petitions to the regent for more soldiers and archers to be sent here.'

'Do you blame yourself?' Athelstan asked.

Coverdale stopped at the steps leading down to the Pyx chamber. 'Brother, there are over two hundred representatives

179

meeting in the chapter-house, and about a dozen clerks, not to mention the soldiers and archers on guard. Some of them are strangers to me, being drawn from garrisons as far afield as Dover and Hedingham Castle. If a man carries that seal, acts without suspicion and bears no arms, there is little we can do to stop him from entering here. But come, you want to see the Pyx chamber.'

He grasped a torch from a socket on the wall and led them down the steps. An archer at the bottom unlocked the door, and they entered the shadow-filled, eerie crypt. Coverdale lit more torches and pointed to a dark stain on the paved stone floor.

'We found the body there, bleeding like a stuck pig.' He moved his hand. 'Beside it the arrowhead, candle, and the scrap of parchment.' Coverdale pointed to one of the iron brackets. 'The head was tied to that by its hair.'

Athelstan followed Coverdale's direction. He recalled the care Harnett took with his hair; the memory only deepened his horror at the poor knight's death.

'And you found nothing else?' he asked.

'Nothing, Father.'

Athelstan walked round. He could not find anything amiss, except the dark bloodstains and a sense of malevolence, as if the assassin was in the shadows laughing at their blundering about. He recalled the exorcist's words and plucked at Cranston's sleeve.

'There may not be a demon in Southwark,' he whispered. 'But, before God, Sir John, one has been here!'

Cranston lifted his miraculous wineskin and took a deep draught. He replaced the stopper, stared round and shivered.

'Come on, Brother!' he snapped. 'Let's get out of here!'

CHAPTER 10

Cranston and Athelstan thanked Coverdale. They climbed the
steps, crossed the vestibule, and went up another flight of stairs
into St Faith's Chapel. They sat on a bench against the wall of
the narrow chapel. Cranston closed his eyes, half dozing.
Athelstan studied a painting: St Faith wearing a crown and
holding a grid-iron, the emblem of her martyrdom. Next to her
was a small, half-size figure of a praying Benedictine monk:
from his lips issued a scroll bearing the words:

'From the burden of my sin, Sweet Virgin, deliver me.
Make my peace with Christ and blot out my iniquities.'

'We could all say that prayer,' Athelstan murmured.
   'What's that?' Cranston stirred himself, smacking his lips.
'Beautiful chapel, Athelstan,' he murmured. 'Too much stacked
here, a little untidy. But what were you saying?'
   Athelstan pointed to the figure on the wall and the words, 'I
think that applies to our situation doesn't it, Sir John?'
   'I've done nothing wrong,' the coroner declared. He looked
sheepish. 'Well, I drink too much.' He nudged Athelstan. 'But
only occasionally.'
   Athelstan said thoughtfully, 'I wonder how that assassin

could enter the abbey cloisters, go down to the Pyx chamber, commit such a terrible act and walk away scot-free. Sir John, it must be a soldier or one of the knights?'

'But, surely, not a monk?'

Athelstan whirled round. Father Benedict stood in the doorway of the chapel. Athelstan and Cranston rose.

'Father, I thank you for coming.'

Cranston, embarrassed, tried to hide the wineskin peeping out from beneath his cloak.

'Sit down! Sit down!'

Cranston and Athelstan obeyed whilst Father Benedict went and pulled across a small box chair which stood in a corner of the chapel. The monk stared over his shoulder at the altar, where a candle burned beneath the pyx which contained the body of Christ.

'If you question me here, Brother,' Father Benedict said softly, 'I have little choice but to tell the truth.'

'About what?' Cranston asked curiously.

'Oh, not about the murders?' Athelstan intervened. 'Father Benedict is as innocent as a new-born babe. However, the chalice, the Holy Grail, the cedarwood cup which was sent to the Gargoyle tavern this morning. You sent that, didn't you, Father?'

The monk slid his hands up the voluminous sleeves of his black gown. He blinked and glanced away, as if fascinated by the tiled floor of the chapel.

'Your friend Father Antony gave it to you, didn't he?' Athelstan persisted.

Father Benedict nodded. 'Many years ago.' He began slowly. 'Father Antony arrived here from Lilleshall. We became firm friends. We had a great deal in common: a love of books and

182

manuscripts, nothing better than the smell of vellum, ink and chalk, burning wax and the study of the antiquities.' Father Benedict cleared his throat. 'After he had been here eighteen months, Antony invited me into his cell. He showed me the chalice you saw this morning. He confessed he'd stolen it from the Knights of the Swan. He described their junketings, tourneys and tournaments at Lilleshall, and how the cup might well have been the Grail.'

Father Benedict paused, rocking himself gently in the chair. He smiled. 'I examined the cup very carefully, I believe it's four to five hundred years old, probably from the treasure trove of Alfred King of Wessex, rather than from the court of the legendary Arthur.'

'And Father Antony?' Athelstan asked.

'He told me of its history and asked me what I should do. I declared the chalice must be returned to its rightful owners as, in my opinion, he had committed an act of sacrilege as well as theft.'

'But it wasn't?' Athelstan asked.

'No. Antony asked for absolution and entrusted the chalice to me. He insisted that, whatever the chalice's real origins were, it was still a sacred vessel and should not be returned to such wicked men. I asked him what he meant by that. Antony just shook his head and muttered that he did not want to add the sin of calumny to his other faults. I taxed him about why he had stolen the chalice in the first place.' The Benedictine smiled at Athelstan. 'Oh, don't worry, I am not breaking the seal of confession: Antony and I used to talk about this a great deal. The only thing he would say, and he kept repeating this time and time again, was that he believed it was blasphemy for the Knights of the Swan to pretend they were paladins of Arthur, to

183

meet on holy ground, never mind possess such a sacred relic.'

'So he claimed he had not really sinned,' Athelstan surmised, 'but had followed his conscience and removed something sacred from the hands of the wicked?'

'Yes, Athelstan, put most precisely: that's exactly what he said.'

'But this wickedness?' Cranston asked. 'Father, with all due respect, any wealthy landowner is hardly a St Francis of Assisi. Sir Henry Swynford and his companions are, like myself, men of the world.'

The monk's face broke into a genuine smile. 'I don't think so, Sir John. Antony mentioned murder, not just once, but on a number of occasions. And, before you ask, that's all he would say.' The monk looked towards the chapel door to ensure it was closed. 'Now, as you know, over the recent few years there have been a number of Parliaments at Westminster, and Sir Edmund Malmesbury, together with most of his companions, were always returned. Whenever they came, Antony declared himself ill and spent the entire time in the infirmary.' The Benedictine shrugged. 'Not that it mattered. The knights always stay at the Gargoyle or some other tavern and rarely frequent the abbey itself.'

'So, these knights have often been returned as members of the Commons?' Athelstan asked.

'Oh, of course, Brother. They swagger about as arrogantly as peacocks. They love London and its fleshpots. Moreover, Master Banyard is the most generous of hosts.'

'And nothing like this has ever occurred before?' Cranston asked.

'No, it hasn't. My friend Antony always stayed in the infirmary. Never once did these knights refer to him. I wager if they had met, they would not have recognised him. Now, a year ago,' the Benedictine continued, 'Antony died of the falling sickness. I heard his last confession and gave him Extreme Unction. He begged God for pardon and his dying wish was that, if I thought it right, the chalice should be given back to the Knights of the Swan.'

'And so you did?'

'No.' The Benedictine shook his head. 'Not immediately. I used the chalice at my own Masses because, the more I studied Sir Edmund Malmesbury and his coven, their love of harlotry and other fleshpots, the more I began to wonder. And then,' Father Benedict snapped his fingers, 'time passed; and I began to have scruples about keeping the chalice. So when Father Abbot asked one of us to volunteer as Chaplain to the Commons, I put my name forward.' He paused and drew his breath in sharply. 'But this time it all changed: Sir Henry Swynford sought me out, just after Sir Oliver Bouchon's corpse had been dragged from the Thames.

'Swynford was nervous and very agitated. He believed he was going to die. He asked if unforgiven sins pursue your soul? Or was it more the anger of God? I asked him what unforgiven sins? Swynford shook his head and said that if he returned to Shrewsbury, he intended to be shriven, confess all, and go on pilgrimage to Compostella.' The Benedictine drew his hands out from the sleeves of his gown. 'Well, he was killed, and then last night so was Sir Francis Harnett. The brothers are shocked, and Father Abbot is saying that the chapter-house and the vestibule will have to be reconsecrated because of blood being spilt on sacred ground.' Father Benedict sighed. 'I wondered if the knights were killing each other over the chalice.'

'So you sent it back?'

'Yes, I decided to wait no longer. This morning, after the dawn Mass, I cleaned the chalice and, choosing my moment carefully, brought it back to the Gargoyle.' He blinked. 'I heard you were there.' He looked full at Athelstan. 'You have keen eyes and a sharp mind, Brother. How did you know it was me?'

Athelstan pulled a face. 'When I first met you, Father, you were uneasy. Something in your demeanour: you were not comfortable being Chaplain to the Commons, yet you had volunteered for it. I wondered why. Moreover, your friendship with Antony and his connection with Shrewsbury were no mere coincidences.' Athelstan grinned self-consciously. 'To be truthful, Father, I don't want to appear cleverer than I really am. I examined the chalice carefully: it had been beautifully kept. When I held it in my hand this morning, I caught the faint fragrance of polish and wine. Finally, it was sent back in a leather pouch, specially made for sacred vessels. It had to be you.'

'Do you think I did right?' Father Benedict asked.

'I think so, Father.' Athelstan leaned over and clasped the monk's hand. 'You did right, but I tell you the truth: I do not think these terrible murders are connected with that chalice.' He stared across at Cranston. 'But some ancient sin. Time and again we come across this.' He released Father Benedict's hand. 'I believe Sir Edmund and his companions, either all or some of them, have committed horrible, dreadful murders, and now their guilt has caught up with them. Father, I ask you, on your immortal soul, do you know anything which might assist us?'

The Benedictine shook his head and got to his feet. 'On my soul, I do not.' He walked to the chapel door, opened it, but then turned. 'Oh, Athelstan!'

'Yes, Father.'

'This demon in Southwark?'

Athelstan pulled a face. 'That's as elusive as the truth behind this horrid business.'

'Then I shall pray for you.' The Benedictine left, quietly closing the door behind him.

'What do you think, Sir John?'

Cranston was now leaning forward, elbows on his knees.

'Sir John?'

'I can't understand, Brother, why these knights don't flee London. So, what I want you to do is stay here. Behind the abbey are the muniment rooms containing all the records of the itinerant justices, letters from sheriffs and royal bailiffs. I am going to go down there: onerous though it may be, I intend to obtain permission to go through every letter, memorandum, court case and petition from the king's county of Shropshire.' He clapped Athelstan on the shoulder. 'And you, Brother, are going to help me.'

And, before Athelstan could object, Cranston had risen, genuflected to the altar, and almost charged out of the chapel, slamming the door behind him. Athelstan sighed and leaned back against the wall. For a while he just closed his eyes and chanted psalms from the office of the day. He even tried to pray to St Faith, but stopped when he realised that his idea of the saint was very similar to that he had of Benedicta. He got up and walked towards the small altar and stood admiring the gold, jewel-encrusted pyx hanging on a silver chain.

'You should pray better, Athelstan,' he murmured to himself.

His hand brushed the small Book of Hours he had pushed into the pocket of his gown. He took this out, sat on a bench, and went through the blank pages at the front and back of the

187

prayer book, but there was nothing there. He turned to the beginning and read the first twelve verses of St John's Gospel but, even then, he was distracted, for the book was brilliantly illuminated. Harnett must have commissioned it specially for himself; the scribe had written the text in beautiful, broad black sweeps of the quill, and decorated the margins with miniature paintings of a variety of animals. A red-coated, black-eyed dragon thrust out its green flickering tongue; a wyvern of reddish-gold extended its great scaly wings; a silver greyhound pursued a hare, its coat a rich, deep brown.

'Harnett did love animals!' Athelstan exclaimed.

He particularly admired the phoenix at the top of a page. A mystical bird which consumed itself, and so was often used to represent Christ. Curious, Athelstan leafed over the pages. There were elephants, panthers, foxes, wolves of every hue, apes and peacocks. Then, at the beginning of the Office of Night, one picture caught Athelstan's attention. He sat, fascinated, before going across to sit under one of the windows so as to study the painting more carefully.

'It can't be!' he exclaimed. 'It can't be!'

Athelstan didn't know whether to laugh or cry. Suddenly the door swung open and Cranston swept in.

'Athelstan, we have got permission, we might as well start now.' He looked at the friar curiously. 'Brother, are you well?'

Athelstan recalled Benedicta's description of Simplicatas busy in the marketplace.

'Come on, Sir John.' Athelstan sprang to his feet. 'Never mind the archives! We are going to Southwark!'

'Oh, Brother, we can't!'

'Oh, Brother, we can!' Athelstan replied.

'Why?' Cranston hurried behind him as Athelstan left the

chapel, almost running down the steps to the vestibule. The soldiers on guard watched him curiously. At the bottom Cranston abruptly sat down and crossed his arms like a big baby.

'I'll stay here until you tell me,' he shouted.

Athelstan hid his impatience and came back.

'Sir John, I have just been through Harnett's Book of Hours: I know where Perline is and what he's been up to. Now, you can either sit and sulk until I come back–' he tweaked Sir John's bristling moustache – 'or you can come and help me.'

Within the hour, Athelstan and Cranston disembarked in Southwark just near London Bridge. By now Cranston was all agog, and kept crowing with delight as Athelstan, in hushed whispers, described a possible solution to the mystery. They strode through the alleyways and runnels of the stews. Cranston didn't know whether Athelstan was in a temper, or just eager to put his theories to the test. Half-way down one alleyway, Athelstan abruptly stopped before a house and knocked furiously on the door. A window opened, high above them, and Simplicatas poked her pretty blonde head out.

'Oh, good afternoon, Father.' She forced a smile. 'I can't come down,' she apologised, giggling behind her hand. 'I have to change my dress and—'

'*Simplicatas!*' Athelstan roared with a vigour which even surprised Cranston. 'You will come down and let me into this house. And you're not by yourself. You can tell that scapegrace husband of yours that I know he is hiding there.' Athelstan glowered up at the young woman. 'Now,' he threatened, 'are you going to open the door, or do I ask Sir John to remove it?'

The window closed hastily, there was a sound of running footsteps, the door opened, and a pale-faced Simplicatas invited them in. Athelstan brushed by her and walked down the

189

passageway. The house was small and dingy, with wooden stairs stretching up into the darkness.

'Perline Brasenose!' Athelstan shouted. 'I and others have had enough of your games to last a lifetime.' He looked at Simplicatas. 'And you, my good woman, must decide whether you are going to continue this mummery or go and fetch your scapegrace husband, whether he's hiding in the garret or the cellar.' Athelstan glowered at Cranston, who was standing behind Simplicatas. 'Sir Jack Cranston,' Athelstan continued, raising his voice so it rang through the house, 'is a terrible man with the devil's own temper. Perline, are you going to show yourself, or skulk like a coward for the rest of your days?'

A figure appeared in the shadows at the top of the stairs.

'I am sorry, Father. I didn't mean any harm,' a voice pleaded.

'People like you never do!' Athelstan shouted back. 'For heaven's sake, come downstairs! By St Erconwald's and all that is holy!' Athelstan pointed a finger at Simplicatas. 'You and your husband have made fools of my entire parish.'

Cranston opened his mouth to say that wouldn't be hard, but his little friar had, for one of those rare occasions, really lost his temper.

'You'd best come into the parlour,' Simplicatas whispered, tears rolling down her cheeks. 'I am sorry, Father, but Perline stole a Barbary ape.'

'Never mind,' Athelstan said softly. He glared over his shoulder at an unshaven Perline now squatting at the foot of the stairs. 'Just come in and tell me what happened.'

They all trooped into the sweet-scented parlour. Athelstan's anger began to cool. Simplicatas apparently was skilled in embroidery: some of her work, brightly coloured cloths, hung against the whitewashed walls. Fresh green rushes strewed the floor, and little pots of rosemary stood on the battered wooden table. Simplicatas waved them to the cushioned stools on either side of this. The friar glimpsed the small wooden cradle in the far corner, a sign that Simplicatas was invoking all the lore for, if a cradle was left standing in a parlour for a year, a bouncing child would fill it within six months.

'It's the baby, Father,' she murmured, catching his glance.

'What baby?' Cranston asked, staring around. 'Don't say you've sold that, Perline!'

The young soldier, his thin, narrow face even more pale and drawn, sat like a sleep-walker.

'No, we want a baby,' Simplicatas explained in a rush. 'Perline has fashioned the cradle. I have embroidered the cloths. We hope, Father, to have it baptised at St Erconwald's. We were thinking of calling it Athelstan if it's a boy – or John,' she added swiftly.

'And if it's a girl, I suppose Maude?' Athelstan asked archly.

Simplicatas sat down. She put her face in her hands and sobbed, though she left a gap between her fingers so she could study Athelstan and Cranston.

'Well, if you're expecting a child,' Cranston bellowed, 'all I can say is, bless your breeches and all that's within them!' He hit the table with his hand. 'But all this nonsense!'

'Tell him,' Simplicatas wailed.

Perline opened his mouth.

'From the beginning,' Athelstan added.

'I enjoy being at the Tower,' the young man began. 'Good food, good wages, free kindling, my own pot, plate and pewter spoon. A change of livery twice a year.' Perline smiled wryly. 'And not an enemy in sight. But it's boring,' he added, 'so I used to go down to the royal beastery.' He glanced at Athelstan. 'Father, something should be done about those animals. Since the old king died, no one gives a whit about them.'

'I intend to deal with that,' Cranston interrupted sharply.

'Well, there are some Barbary apes,' Perline continued hastily. 'I'd never seen one before: it wasn't like those little monkeys which sit and shit on pedlars' shoulders. Father, these are grand beasts. Anyway, I began to take them food, I'd just sit there and watch them. Now there's one, bigger than the rest, I became very friendly with him. He used to chatter through the cage but he always looked lonely. So, I says to myself, I'll have to help Cranston.'

Simplicatas's hands flew to her face whilst Perline's jaw dropped.

'What did you call him?' the coroner asked quietly.

Athelstan bit his lower lip, and just hoped he would not burst out laughing.

'What did you call him?' Sir John barked.

'No offence, Sir John, but I called him Cranston. You see, he was bigger and fatter than the rest and . . .'

'He was their leader, wasn't he?' Athelstan asked helpfully.

'Oh yes, Father.' Perline smiled gratefully. 'He always took the best food and there are two or three females there whom he er . . .'

'Paid court to?' Athelstan asked.

Perline's gratitude was more than obvious, but Cranston's face turned an even deeper red.

'Go on,' he growled. 'The more I listen to you, Master Brasenose, the more interested I am becoming.'

'Everything went well,' Perline continued. 'I used to take Cranston –'

Athelstan now put his head down, shoulders shaking.

'– anything I could find in the market; fruit, vegetables, whatever. Then the Commons met at Westminster. Some of the representatives came to visit the beastery and see round the Tower. I immediately noticed how Sir Francis Harnett from Shrewsbury was much taken by the Barbary apes, particularly Cranston.'

Sir John spluttered, but Perline blissfully continued. 'He noticed how friendly he was. Harnett said he had seen pictures of such an ape and how he had often wished to travel to Southern Spain to buy one.'

'I know,' Athelstan intervened. 'I have been through the poor man's Book of Hours. He has pictures of them.'

'Poor man?' Perline asked. 'He's rich, wealthy!'

'I'll come to that in a while,' Athelstan replied.

'Well, not to make a long tale of it,' Perline rubbed his mouth with the back of his hand, 'Sir Francis offered to buy Cranston and I agreed. Oh, it was simple enough. There were cages in the Tower. On Sunday afternoon, when the rest of the soldiers were sleeping or dicing, I put . . .' He look sleepily at the coroner. '. . . I put the ape in the cage. I loaded it on to a handcart and took it down to a postern gate overlooking the river. I then went back to see the constable,' Perline shrugged. 'I asked him for some leave and, well, you know how it is, he agreed. Now there was a skiff with a pole near the gate. Once dusk fell, I put the cage on the skiff and poled across the river to the Southwark side. I hired a cart from the market, covered the cage with an old cloth, and wondered where could I hide it until Harnett came to collect the beast.'

193

'And, of course, you remembered the death-house in St Erconwald's cemetery?'

'Well, it wasn't being used, Father. So off we goes. I still kept the cage sheeted, no one saw me. I was even able to go back and collect some scraps from the marketplace: apples, pears and a few bruised plums.'

'I know you did,' Athelstan remarked. 'Cecily the courtesan found them in the cemetery littering some of the graves. I wondered how they had got there.'

'Well, whatever,' Perline replied, sniffing. 'I opened the cage and gave some of the fruit to Cranston.'

'Stop calling that bloody ape by my name!' Sir John bellowed. And, taking his wineskin out, the coroner poured himself a generous draught into the pewter cup which Simplicatas had quickly brought across.

'I am sorry, Sir John,' Perline mumbled. 'Well, for a time, I just sat there and talked to Cranston,' he continued blithely. 'He seemed as happy as a pig in muck, chattering away. However, if he had eaten, well, he'd want to shit, wouldn't he? So I let him out. I thought he'd be safe in the death-house.'

'Which explains why the place stank like a midden,' Athelstan declared.

'I am sorry, Father,' Perline wailed. 'Well, I went out to get more of the fruit I'd left on the gravestone. When I came back, the ape had gone. You see, Father, I'd left the door off the latch.'

'Gone?' Sir John asked.

Perline snapped his fingers. 'Just like that, Sir John. One minute the ape was there chattering fit to burst, then he was off. I panicked. I took the cage out and hid it in an alleyway.'

Perline licked his lips. 'I didn't know where the ape had gone so I hid here.'

'And Sunday,' Athelstan pointed at Simplicatas, 'is when you appeared, claiming Perline was missing and had been for days.'

'We were frightened of Harnett,' Perline wailed. 'I didn't want him coming here.'

'But you met him on Monday evening?'

'I had to. I told him some lie but he became angry. I explained I couldn't speak to him in Southwark, people would become suspicious; Moleskin the boatman had already seen us. Harnett bundled me into a skiff and took me across to the steel yard.' Perline gulped. 'I told him the truth.'

'And he was furious?'

'He was more than that, Father; he accused me of being a thief. Harnett said that if I didn't produce Cranston . . .' Perline stopped, his fingers sliding to his mouth. 'I am sorry, Sir John . . . He said he'd have me put to the horn as an outlaw. He also gave me a letter, a pass to get into the abbey. He told me to tell him as soon as I found the ape.'

'Then you came back here,' Athelstan declared, 'and hid. Whilst you, Simplicatas, spread the lie as far as you could.'

'I am sorry, Father.' The young woman shook her head. 'But I was terribly a-feared.' Her voice trembled. 'Perline could hang; Sir Francis was a hard man.'

'Perline still might hang!' Cranston growled. 'And, if I had my way, that bloody ape next to him!'

Simplicatas threw her head back and wailed, whilst Perline began to shake. Athelstan caught Sir John's eye.

'Well, I don't really mean that,' the coroner muttered. He

patted Simplicatas gently on the shoulder. 'There, there, girl, don't weep!'

'I just thought I'd hide,' Perline confessed. 'Wait until Parliament was finished and Harnett had left.'

'Well, he has left,' Athelstan interrupted. 'Last night, someone invited Sir Francis Harnett down to the Pyx chamber at Westminster and took his head clean off his shoulders.'

'Oh, sweet Lord, mercy!' Simplicatas cried.

Perline leaned against the table, looking as if he had been hit by a rock.

'Here, you had best drink this.' Cranston pushed across his cup of wine.

Perline grasped it and raised it shakily to his lips.

'You know what they are going to say?' Athelstan declared. 'They might claim, Perline, that you double-crossed Sir Francis: that you not only stole one of the king's animals but, when it escaped and you were unable to keep your side of the bargain, you decided to kill Harnett.

'But how?' Perline screeched. He put the cup down on the table, his hands were trembling so much. 'How could I get into Westminster? It's closely guarded by soldiers.'

'You had a special letter,' Cranston declared.

'I tore it up and threw it away.'

'You are also a soldier. You wear the royal livery,' Athelstan warned. 'It would be easy to mingle with the rest. Moreover, you are able to carry arms, be it a sword or an axe.'

'But I never left here,' Perline groaned. 'Since Monday I have been hiding in the garret.'

'Though eating well!' Athelstan retorted. 'For a distraught woman, Simplicatas, you purchased a great deal in the marketplace.'

'I didn't kill him!' Perline declared. 'I never saw, met or heard from Sir Francis since that meeting near the steel yard.'

'You are sure of that?' Athelstan asked.

Perline sprang to his feet and walked across to where the cradle stood. He placed his hand on the wooden canopy. 'I swear,' he declared flatly. 'Father, I swear by all that is holy and by the life of my future child that I have spoken the truth!'

His voice trembled and he blinked furiously to keep back the tears. 'Father, you have got to help me. Sir John, I am sorry.'

'Please! Please!' Simplicatas grasped Athelstan's hand. 'We meant no harm.'

'Sit down,' Athelstan ordered.

Perline obeyed.

'How much did Sir Francis give you?'

'Ten pounds sterling, though I have spent one already.'

'Right.' Athelstan winked at Cranston. 'Perline, my boy, you are to take the money down to St Erconwald's church and seek out Benedicta. You know her?'

Perline nodded quickly.

'Benedicta will summon Watkin, Pike, Ranulf and Tab the tinker. You will offer each of them one pound for the ape to be recaptured. Now I suspect,' Athelstan continued, trying to keep his voice flat and avoid Cranston's eye, 'that the poor creature is terrified and has not wandered far from St Erconwald's cemetery: that's the last place it was fed properly and the last place it saw you. You are to put the cage in the death-house, keeping the door open, and spend another pound on fruit in the market. Nothing rotten, nothing that has been thrown away but good, ripe fruit.' He pointed a finger at Perline. 'Are you listening to me?'

The young soldier nodded.

'You are to sleep in that cemetery, day and night, until that poor creature returns . . . and it will!'

'How do you know, Father?' Cranston asked curiously.

'Because Bonaventure always comes back for his milk,' Athelstan replied. 'And, Sir John, though this may come as a surprise to you, certain human beings can also be found at certain eating or drinking places.'

Sir John made a rude sound with his lips.

'And you think I'll recapture it?' Perline asked hopefully.

'Oh yes. Tell Benedicta that the money is not to be paid to Watkins and the rest until that animal is safely caged.'

'And once it is?'

'Well, you had better take another pound down with you, hire Moleskin the boatman. Tell him you have spoken to me. He will take you and the animal back across the river to the Tower.'

Simplicatas was now smiling, drying her eyes quickly.

'And there's the constable?' Perline asked.

'Give him a pound,' Athelstan replied. 'Don't worry, he'll look the other way. Say you took the ape out to show it to other parishioners.'

'And what about the remaining money?' Perline asked hopefully.

'You may keep it,' Athelstan replied. 'Not for yourselves,' he added quickly, 'but for your child.' Athelstan shook his head. 'If you had only told me the truth, a great deal of confusion could have been avoided.'

'I know.' Perline glanced up from underneath his eyebrows.

'Simplicatas has told me about the rumours.'

Athelstan got to his feet. 'Yes, your fellow parishioners think that the ape is a demon. If they catch it, they would probably kill the poor creature. Now, you have your orders, Perline. You are not to come back to this house. You are not to see Simplicatas until that ape is back where it should be.' He glanced across at the wooden cradle. 'You'd make a fine carpenter, Perline.'

'I'll carve you a statue,' the soldier offered. 'A peace offering, Father.'

And, with the young couple's thanks ringing in their ears, and the coroner's parting shots of advice being bellowed through the doorway, Athelstan and Cranston went back along the alleyways of Southwark. For a while they walked in silence, then Cranston grasped Athelstan tightly by the arm.

'If I ever, Brother, hear the words "Barbary ape" and 'Cranston" in the same sentence again –' he shook a finger in the friar's laughing face – 'the devil really will come to Southwark!'

CHAPTER 11

They walked back towards the quayside, Cranston still loudly declaiming against an ape being named after the king's own coroner. Athelstan pulled the cowl over his face, nodded gravely, and hoped Sir John would not realise he was fighting hard not to laugh. Outside the priory of St Mary Overy, however, Cranston's mood suddenly changed. He turned to face his companion squarely.

'You don't really believe that scapegrace has anything to do with Harnett's death, do you?'

'No, Sir John, I don't.'

Athelstan glanced away; he studied an old beggar clad in tattered rags who stood at the mouth of an alleyway. The man's face was covered in bluish stains, as if he had been disfigured in some terrible fire.

'Well?' Cranston asked. 'Brother!' he exclaimed. 'What on earth are you staring at?'

Athelstan held a hand out. 'Stay there, Sir John.'

The friar marched towards the beggar, whose eyes widened in alarm as he recognised his parish priest.

'Mousehead!'

Athelstan seized the beggar by his stocky shoulder. The beggar flinched, but the friar held him fast as he scraped a finger down Mousehead's face, removing the dirty coating of powder and paint.

'Father!' The beggar began to hop from one foot to another.

'Mousehead!' Athelstan warned. 'If I have told you once, I have told you a thousand times! To beg if you are unable is acceptable to the Lord, but to beg when you are able and pretend you are the opposite, only makes the good Lord angry.'

Mousehead stared fearfully at the friar, his buck teeth even more protuberant, his nose twitching faster than usual. Athelstan pushed him away.

'Now go and see Widow Benedicta. You will find her at St Erconwald's. She'll have a task for you: tell her you can help Perline.'

'But Perline has gone missing, Father, and there's a demon near your church.'

'There's no demon, Mousehead, and Perline's not missing. You'll find him there.'

Mousehead scampered off. Athelstan walked back to where Cranston stood leaning against the wall, staring up at a cat which sat in an open window. Athelstan followed his gaze.

'Don't worry, Sir John, I think there's a solution to your missing cats.'

'And Perline and Harnett?' Cranston asked. 'You didn't answer my question.'

Athelstan sighed. 'I'd swear on the cross that Perline had nothing to do with Harnett's death. However, Harnett did go into the lonely Pyx chamber at a time when he and his companions were being stalked by a killer. Now, why should he do that? What would draw Harnett out away from the rest?'

'Some conspiracy perhaps?' Cranston replied. 'Or Perline Brasenose?'

'Or Perline Brasenose,' Athelstan repeated. 'No, no, Sir John, I am not talking in riddles. What I think happened is that someone knew about Harnett's secret negotiations with that young soldier. Somehow or other, the killer used Perline's name, and the prospect of buying a Barbary ape, to lure Harnett into the Pyx chamber where he was killed.'

'But, apart from Brasenose, the only people who would know that would be Harnett's companions, wouldn't it?'

'Not just them, Sir John.' Athelstan linked his arm through Cranston's as they walked down towards the quayside. 'You must never forget Sir Miles Coverdale, who hates the knights and also hails from Shropshire. Or, again, His Grace the Regent who, I believe is dabbling in this matter even though he acts the role of the aggrieved observer.'

Cranston stopped and took a swig from the wineskin. 'Riddle upon riddle . . . But come, Brother, these cats?'

Athelstan began to explain as Moleskin, sweating and cursing against the rising swell of the tide, took them across river to St Paul's Wharf. This time Athelstan totally ignored the boatman, but whispered his conclusions to an increasingly irascible Sir John. Only when they had disembarked, and Cranston had gone storming up the water-soaked steps, did Athelstan talk to the boatman.

'Moleskin.'

'Yes, Father?'

'Row back to the Southwark side, tie your boat up and go to St Erconwald's. Benedicta will tell you all about Perline and the demon you have been pestering me about.'

'Are you sure, Father?' Moleskin's face broke into a grin.

'You have just ignored me all the way across.' He pointed to Cranston striding up and down the quayside like Hector. 'Why do cats make Lord Horsecruncher so angry?'

'In time I'll tell you about that as well,' Athelstan replied and, leaving a mystified Moleskin, he hurried up the steps.

The coroner had now worked himself into a fine rage. He'd already hired a boy to take a message to his bailiffs, and would have gone storming into Cheapside but for Athelstan grasping his sleeve.

'Sir John, Sir John, the afternoon is growing on. The market will soon be finished and your bailiffs will be in place when that message is delivered.' Athelstan stopped speaking, his hand going to his mouth.

'What's the matter, monk?'

'Friar, Sir John, friar! I'm just wondering who could possibly have found out about Harnett's meeting with Perline Brasenose?' He steered Sir John towards a tavern. 'I mean, Harnett saw the Barbary ape on Sunday. On Monday he met Perline but, after that, our young soldier went into hiding. Now,' Athelstan scratched his chin, 'Perline can't write, so who told Harnett to go to the Pyx chamber?'

They entered the dingy tavern. Its walls were greasy and the ceiling beams blackened, but Athelstan knew the proprietor was one of the best cooks along the riverside, and might provide delicacies to distract Sir John's temper. They found an empty table well away from the sailors and fishermen who flocked there.

'You are forgetting one thing,' Cranston announced, leaning back and smacking his lips at the savoury fragrance coming from the buttery.

Athelstan raised his eyebrows.

'On Monday evening, Sir Francis left the brothel where the others were cavorting. They knew he'd gone.'

204

'Of course,' Athelstan murmured. 'And we know he went to Southwark, then on to the steel yard. Ergo . . .' Athelstan paused as the barrel-shaped landlord served Sir John his favourite fish pie and a cup of white Alsace.

'Anything for you, Father?'

'Oh, some ale, Bartholomew. Please.'

'Ergo,' Athelstan repeated, 'either Harnett was followed from that tavern –' he ticked the points off on his fingers – 'and his pursuer discovered what he was looking for; or, Harnett told one of his companions before he left, who later used that information to commit murder.'

'Coverdale could also have done that,' Cranston argued between mouthfuls of pie. 'Either he or some other of the regent's minions.' He sipped from his goblet. 'I am beginning to agree with you, Brother, the regent cannot be totally blameless in this matter. I am sure these worthy knights would flee back to Shrewsbury if it wasn't for him. But, there again,' Cranston slammed his cup down, 'Sir Edmund Malmesbury and the rest can hardly be described as John of Gaunt's most fervent supporters.'

Cranston ate on in silence. Athelstan could tell the coroner was becoming morose; even the pie and the wine didn't seem to cheer him. They left the tavern and went up an alleyway, along Thames Street, past run-down warehouses to a bare expanse of land where the Fleet river poured its filth into the Thames. Here all the great dung carts in London congregated to deposit the filth and muck cleaned from the streets into the Thames. Cranston, stamping his feet, glowered around, then caught sight of his bailiffs, two burly individuals who came striding towards him.

'You are here at last,' he growled.

'Sir John,' one of them replied, 'we came as fast as we could. The markets are closed.' He pointed to one of the dung carts. 'They are all empty, ready to go back to clean up during the night.'

'And our precious pair have flown,' Cranston grunted. 'Go back up Knightrider Street,' he ordered. 'When you catch sight of them, come back and tell me!'

The two bailiffs hurried off. For a while Athelstan and Cranston stood around, but the stench from the carts and the slime-coated Fleet grew so offensive that they, too, walked up Knightrider Street. The bell from St Paul's began to toll for evening Mass. Athelstan glimpsed the spires of Blackfriars and was wondering what Father Prior was doing when one of the bailiffs came running back.

'Sir John, Hengist and Horsa are here.'

'Good!'

With Athelstan hurrying behind him, Cranston strode up Knightrider Street, where Hengist and Horsa had been stopped by the bailiff. Both the dung-collectors protested loudly.

'This is against all the law and its usages, Sir John!' one of them squeaked. 'Any delay means longer working, so when the mayor and aldermen complain—'

'Shut up!' Cranston bellowed, grasping Hengist by the front of his dirty jerkin. 'You, my buckos, have been stealing cats!' Cranston snapped his fingers, and Athelstan handed over one of the small muzzles. The coroner shoved this in front of the man's face. Hengist spluttered and glanced fearfully at his companion. 'You mean-minded bastards!' Cranston roared.

Both men started to protest. Athelstan walked round, studying the cart carefully, noticing how its high sides were simply boards nailed across huge upright posts. At the back he saw

206

how one of these boards served as a small door or drawer, kept in place by newly attached bolts in their clasps. He summoned the bailiffs.

'Whilst Sir John argues,' he whispered, 'open that!'

The bailiff pressed his dagger between the boards, working the bolt free. Athelstan, pinching his nose at the fetid smell, crouched down and stared in. Five or six cats lay there, eyes glowing in the darkness. The poor creatures were bound hand and foot, and muzzles, similar to the one he had found, were tightly clasped round their jaws. One of the bailiffs gently took the cats out, cutting their thongs and muzzles free. The cats, backs arched, tails up, spitting furiously, danced round the carts and then fled away like arrows up Knightrider Street. The bailiff would have gone after them.

'Don't worry,' Athelstan called the man back. 'They'll all find their way home. I can personally vouch for that. It's Sir John I'm worried about.'

Cranston, who had witnessed all this, now had the two dung-collectors up against the wall, banging their heads slowly against it. At Athelstan's instruction, the two bailiffs gently squeezed their way between the irate coroner and his victims. Sir John, breathing heavily, stepped back glowering at the trembling cat thieves. He waved a finger at them.

'You heartless bastards!' he shouted. 'And don't lie that they were all strays. You pull that cart round the streets, and whenever you could you enticed some cat with a bit of meat or fish, covered with some sleeping potion. You then tied their feet together, muzzled them, and put them into that crevice beneath the cart. When you came down to the riverside to throw your refuse into the Fleet, you'd go along to the grain barges and offer the cats for sale. Isn't that right?'

Hengist nodded fearfully.

'A lucrative, profitable experience,' Athelstan spoke up. 'The barge-masters bring up grain and, where there's grain, rats and mice thrive. The barge-masters buy the cats, put two or three in each hold and the vermin are cleared.' He shook his head. 'Of course you couldn't care whether the poor cats were used to a ship or barge.' He took a step closer. 'And did you really care about the feelings of those who owned those animals? Did you ever think of the terror of those poor cats locked in the stinking black hold of some barge? Did it ever occur to you that some of them might even try and escape, being drowned in the river or ill-used by their new owners?'

Athelstan, catching some of Cranston's anger, thrust his hand under Hengist's chin and pushed his face up.

'What you did was wicked!' he whispered.

'No one cares.' Horsa sneered back; he wished he hadn't spoken as Athelstan seized his mouth between his fingers and squeezed it tightly.

'Haven't you read the scriptures?' Athelstan retorted. 'Not a sparrow falls from heaven that the Father doesn't know about.' He stepped back, wiping his hands, and stared at Horsa's leather apron. 'Do you know how we found out?' Athelstan taunted. 'Your own greed trapped you. You couldn't even be bothered to buy the leather to make the muzzles for the poor animals.' He poked Horsa's chest. 'You used the leather from your own apron to fashion those; the outside was black, but when I examined it more carefully, the inside matched the leather you wore.'

'Wilful destruction of city property will be added to the list of offences,' Cranston boomed.

'What will happen to us?' Horsa wailed.

208

Cranston scratched his head and smiled bleakly at them.

'Well, the silver you've collected will be seized. A fine will be levied. However, if you give us the names of the barge-masters to whom you sold the cats, mercy might be shown. Perhaps a period digging the city ditch to reflect on your crimes? And who knows? Unless we get all the cats back, a nice long sojourn in the stocks with a placard advertising your crimes.' Cranston snapped his fingers at the bailiffs. 'Put both of them in the cart. Take them to Newgate. Let them kick their heels there whilst I consider their punishment.'

Hengist fell to his knees. 'Sir John, we'll tell you everything.'

'Good.' Cranston patted the man heartily on the top of his balding head. 'That's my boys. I want to know where the silver is and I want to know the names of the barge-masters or else . . .'

And, leaving the dung-collectors to the mercy of the bailiffs, a more satisfied and harmonious Sir John, followed by Athelstan, made his way back towards the riverside.

'A good day's work!' Cranston growled as they climbed into the skiff to take them downriver to Westminster. He shaded his eyes against the glare of the setting sun. 'But not good enough, Brother.' He yawned. 'I feel sleepy, yet we have to examine those archives.' He turned suddenly as Athelstan's head came down on his shoulder; the friar, lulled by the rocking of the boat, was already fast asleep.

They disembarked at King's Steps, Westminster. The sun now hung like a blood-red ball in the west, turning the brickwork of the abbey to a soft, golden yellow. The day's business was drawing to a close; the king's justices, lawyers, serjeants, plaintiffs and defendants were streaming along the narrow alleyways, either up towards Fleet Street, or down to their waiting barges on the river. Convicted felons, all chained together, were carted off by drunken bailiffs towards the Fleet or Newgate Prisons. Tipstaffs and chamberlains, clerks and scribes now thronged into the taverns and drinking-houses. Quite a few stopped to chat with the young whores gathered round the gates and porticoes. For a while Cranston and Athelstan sat on a bench under the spreading branches of a great oak tree, intent on enjoying the coolness and beauty of the evening.

As Athelstan stared round, however, he felt a deep sense of despondency, of sin, of staring into the heart of human darkness. All these men in their silks, satins and samite robes, their fur-lined hats, leather, bejewelled gauntlets, gaudy baldrics, purses and dagger sheaths, their coiffed hair and the swagger in their walk. Athelstan experienced the wealth, power and the all-pervasive corruption of such men, who gathered to dispense justice but practised so little morality themselves. Cranston was dozing now, so the friar kept his thoughts to himself. Yet, not for the first time, Athelstan felt a deep empathy for men like Pike the ditcher. Perhaps the Lord, he thought, should come back to his temple and cleanse it of these money-changers, land-grabbing landlords, arrogant clerks, justices and lawyers puffed up like peacocks.

Suddenly the crowd streaming across the abbey grounds grew bigger as representatives of the Commons, their day's work done, returned to their taverns and hostelries. Although they must have talked all day, this had only whetted their appetite to hear further the sound of their own voices. Athelstan closed his eyes and half listened to the different accents; men from Yorkshire, Somerset, Norfolk, the Scottish and Welsh march. He heard their comments about the regent, and grumbled complaints about his wealth and ostentation.

"'He that is without sin among you,'" Athelstan murmured, quoting from the Gospels, "'let him first cast a stone.'"

He wiped the sweat from his brow and half smiled at the success of the day. But these murders at Westminster? He glanced quickly at Cranston, but the coroner had his head back and was snoring lightly. Now and again he'd smack his lips and mutter, 'Refreshments!' Athelstan recalled the corpses of Bouchon, Swynford and Harnett. What had he and Cranston learnt? He quietly ticked the points off in his mind.

Primo: Bouchon had left the tavern abruptly on Monday evening, therefore he was going to meet someone. The knight had already received the arrowhead and the other premonitions of his death. Where was he going? Whom was he meeting? Why hadn't he gone back to his chamber to collect his sword? Athelstan opened his eyes.

'We should check the river once more,' he murmured. 'Perhaps one of the boatmen can remember.' He closed his eyes.

Secundo: Bouchon had few marks on his corpse except that terrible bruise on the back of his head, the black marks under his fingernails and the crosses etched on his dead face.

Tertio: He had been found bobbing amongst the reeds near Tothill Fields, so he must have been killed in the early hours, just as the tide changed and the Thames ran swollen to the sea.

Well done, Friar, he thought. Was Bouchon's corpse ever meant to be discovered? If those reeds hadn't caught it, it might well have been taken down to the estuary and out into the sea.

Quarto: Swynford. He had gone to pray over Bouchon's corpse: the priest who had arrived and left so mysteriously had garrotted him. Swynford, too, had received warning of his

211

death. And why was it so important that the words of the *Dies Irae* be chanted by the killer? And why was that false priest so confident that Father Gregory would not arrive? And why, again, had those crosses been etched on Swynford's dead face?

Quinto: Who knew about Harnett's secret negotiations with Perline Brasenose? How had Sir Francis been lured to the Pyx chamber of Westminster Abbey? Surely the only person who could slip so easily out of the abbey was a soldier or another member of the Commons? Athelstan recalled Harnett's severed head; his features had not been disfigured. Why? Had the assassin been in a hurry?

Sexto: What was missing amongst Harnett's possessions? And, now he reflected on it, from the belongings of the other knights?

Septimo: Who had followed Bouchon and then Harnett? Pursuing them so easily, trapping and killing them?

Octavo: What had these knights done which was so terrible? And why didn't they just flee Westminster and go back to Shropshire?

Nono: What role did the regent play in all these deaths? How could he have influence over knights who, in the Commons, so bitterly opposed his demands?

'Wake up, monk!'

Athelstan opened his eyes. Cranston was grinning at him. Athelstan blinked.

'Sir John, I was not sleeping, just thinking.'

'As I was!' the coroner answered portentously. He stared across at the thinning crowds. 'Anything in particular, my learned friar?'

Athelstan heard the faint cries of a boatman shouting for custom.

212

'Well, Sir John, we know Sir Francis went to Southwark, but did any boatman take Sir Oliver Bouchon?'

Cranston took a swig from his miraculous wineskin and shook his head.

'My bailiffs have already made such inquiries,' he declared. 'So far as they can discover, no boatman took any member of the Commons either up- or downriver that evening.'

Athelstan rose to his feet and stretched. 'Is it possible, Sir John, that Bouchon didn't leave Westminster? That he was knocked unconscious here and thrown into the Thames?'

Sir John pulled a face. 'I hadn't thought of that, Friar.' He stared across the abbey gardens, narrowing his eyes against the dying sun. 'If this corpse had been thrown in, let's say near Dowgate, not far from London Bridge, from what I know of the Thames the body would have been taken out into mid-stream.' Cranston stretched his legs. 'However, at Westminster the tide loses some of its force: Bouchon's corpse would be taken rather sluggishly, which is why it was trapped in the reeds at Tothill. Where does that leave us?' He shrugged and sighed. 'Today is Thursday, let's be honest, Friar, we have made little progress this week.' He dabbed the sweat around the collar of his shirt. 'On Saturday the young king comes down to talk to his Commons; a few days later parliament is dissolved and Sir Edmund and his party will probably ride post-haste back to Shrewsbury.' Cranston stared up at the gables and gargoyles along the abbey walls. 'I wish I was home,' he murmured. 'A man should spend his nights sleeping with his wife. Ah well, Athelstan, one final call.'

They trudged round the abbey. Now and again some official tried to stop them to demand their business, but at Cranston's growl the official would hastily back away. At last they entered

213

a small courtyard and made their way across to a low-storeyed building. The coroner hammered at the door. An old, bleary-eyed monk, eyes screwed up against the light, ushered them into a low but very long chamber, full of manuscripts resting on shelves or spilling out of coffers and caskets. The old monk, his hand all a-tremble, stared up into Cranston's face, his eyes growing sharper.

'I know you!'

'Of course, you do, Brother Aelfric!' Cranston embraced the old monk, planting a juicy kiss on each of his dry, seamed cheeks.

'Why bless me, it's Jack Cranston! Good Lord, man, what are you doing here? And who is this?'

'Master Aelfric, Brother Athelstan, who, for his sins, is a Dominican and, for his love of drink and beautiful women, parish priest of St Erconwald's in Southwark.'

Aelfric peered at Athelstan. 'Don't worry, Brother,' he murmured. 'I know Jack Cranston's humour. I was one of his masters in the abbey school. If I had a pound for every time I switched his buttocks, I'd be richer than the Cardinal Archbishop of Spolero. Jack, do you remember the time you stole the ox from the crib?'

'Yes, yes.' Cranston put an arm round the old man's shoulders. 'But we are not here to reminisce, Master Aelfric. I have a task for your keen wits and sharp eyes.'

'Not so keen as they once were,' the old monk mumbled, ushering Cranston and Athelstan to stools next to his own high-backed chair.

Cranston stared round the chamber. 'Master Aelfric, this is the king's muniment room?'

'That's right, Jack. All the king's records are kept here.'

'What about Shropshire?'

'What about it, Jack?'

'Well, what records do you have from that county?'

The monk pulled a face and scratched his chin.

'Well, we have the sheriff's returns at Michaelmas, Christmas, Hilary and Midsummer. We have petitions to the king's council, bailiff's accounts.'

'What else?'

'Oh, yes, cases heard before the king's Justices in Eyre, gaol deliver, oyer and terminer.'

'Yes, yes.' Cranston held a hand up. 'Brother, you have heard about the murders at Westminster?'

Aelfric's eyes moved, for a few seconds Athelstan caught the cunning, shrewd nature of this old archivist.

'Who hasn't, Sir John?' he replied quietly.

'And do the names mean anything to you?' Cranston added. 'Sir Oliver Bouchon, Sir Henry Swynford, Sir Francis Harnett?'

The old monk shook his head. 'Until the brothers whispered their names in the refectory,' he answered, 'their names meant nothing to me.'

'You are lying!' The words were out of Athelstan's mouth before he could stop them.

Cranston turned in surprise. Old Aelfric's mouth opened and shut.

'You are lying,' Athelstan repeated, getting to his feet. 'I shall tell you what happened, Aelfric: no less a person than the Lord Regent has been here and asked you the same questions we have. He took certain records and examined them carefully. If he returned them, he told you to keep your mouth shut, should anyone else come here making similar inquiries.'

Aelfric blinked.

215

'Why do you lie?' Athelstan continued. 'Why do people like you, a priest and a monk, enter into complicity with those in power just because they tell you to? You called my colleague Jack; you hail him as a friend, you know what we are searching for. Indeed, you must have expected us.'

Aelfric half rose, then sat down again. 'You'd best leave,' he declared. 'Sir John, I do not like you, your companion even less.'

Cranston stretched out a hand towards his old teacher, but Aelfric didn't turn. Athelstan tugged at the coroner's cloak.

'Come on, Sir John. We are wasting our time.'

Cranston followed him out of the chamber; they were halfway across the courtyard when he stopped and grasped Athelstan's arm.

'You shouldn't have said that, Brother.'

'Why?'

Cranston flinched at the anger in Athelstan's eyes. The friar shook his arm free. 'Why, my lord Coroner, shouldn't I say that? Three men have been found slain and the regent sits all innocent and a-feared. Now, I can accept that. The psalmist says, "Put not your trust in princes". He also said, "All men are liars", but I didn't think that applied to friends and brother priests. A short while ago, Sir John, I sat under an oak tree and watched the power and the corruption seep like slime round this great abbey.' Athelstan glanced away. 'I just thought that an old monk would tell the truth.' He tapped Cranston's arm. 'You know he's lying, Sir John. Gaunt has been down here, that's how he could blackmail those knights, the representatives of the Commons. God knows what they have done,' he added fiercely, 'but the regent found out and Master Aelfric helped him!'

Cranston, surprised by the little friar's vehemence, walked on, then stopped. 'Come on, Brother,' he called. 'Don't be angry with old Jack!'

Athelstan joined him and they made their way out of the abbey grounds and back to the Gargoyle tavern.

The taproom was full of boatmen and fishermen: Athelstan glimpsed Sir Edmund Malmesbury and his company in the far corner, but whispered to Sir John to keep well away from them. Banyard came sweeping out of the kitchen, his sweaty face wreathed in smiles. He greeted Sir John and took them out into a small garden. Cranston, happy at the thought of veal in black pepper sauce and a deep bowl of claret, was his old self. Athelstan found it difficult to match his companion's humour, so they ate in silence until Athelstan apologised for his surliness.

'I'd best go back to my own chamber,' he concluded. 'Sir John, I shall see you in the morning.'

The friar went into the tavern and made his way up to his own chamber. He still felt restless and, for a while, lay on his narrow cot-bed. He tried to pray but, strangely enough, the only words he could summon up were those sombre sentences of the sequence from the Mass of the Dead, 'O day of wrath, O day of mourning. See fulfilled the prophet's warning!'

CHAPTER 12

Athelstan rose early the next morning and decided to say an early Mass in one of the chantry chapels of Westminster Abbey. He went down to the taproom. Scullions and maids were cleaning the fireplace. Cooks were firing the ovens in the kitchen and filling the air with the sweet smell of freshly baked bread.

'Good morning, Father!' Banyard, looking as fresh as a daisy, came up the stairs of the cellar, a small tun of wine on his shoulder.

'Good morning, mine host,' Athelstan replied. 'Is it too early to break fast?'

'It's never too early, Father.'

Banyard showed him to a table and personally served him small, freshly baked loaves, strips of salted pork and, at the friar's request, a stoup of watered ale. Athelstan ate slowly, conscious of the landlord hovering around him.

'Will you be glad when the Parliament is ended?' Athelstan asked. 'I mean, it will diminish your profits.'

The landlord pulled a face as he straightened some stools. He wiped his hands on a cloth and sat down opposite Athelstan, leaning his elbows on the table.

'It's as broad as it's long, Father. Once the representatives go, the lawyers and judges return.'

'And this tavern is always used by members of the Commons?' Athelstan asked.

Banyard spread his hands. 'This is the third Parliament in four years, Father. Yes, our rooms are always taken by visitors from the shire.'

'Including Sir Edmund and his party?'

Banyard smiled. 'Well, it's not always the same group but, yes, Sir Edmund stayed here last time.'

'And nothing untoward happened?'

'Well, not exactly, Father, but, in the Michaelmas Parliament of 1379 . . .'

'Last year?'

'Yes, Father, last year there was an altercation between Sir Edmund and my Lord Regent's bully boys.' Banyard raised a hand. 'Oh, no blood was spilt or daggers drawn. It occurred just as Sir Edmund was about to leave London for Shrewsbury. Whether by chance or accident, he met two of Gaunt's retainers in the courtyard.' Banyard finished wiping his hands and put the cloth under his apron. 'Nothing happened, but the air rang with threat and counter-threat.'

'About what?'

'Oh, the usual thing, Father. The regent's demands and the Commons' response.' He paused and looked over Athelstan's shoulder, his brown, sardonic face creased into a grin. 'And, speaking of the devil, it's best if I go about my business.'

Banyard scraped the stool back and returned to the kitchen as Sir Edmund Malmesbury swept into the taproom. He stopped opposite Athelstan.

'May I join you, Father?'

'Sir Edmund, be my guest.'

The knight sat down; Sir Edmund had apparently taken great care with his toilette, but Athelstan noticed his face was pallid, his eyes red-rimmed with dark circles beneath.

'You did not sleep well, did you, Sir Edmund?' Athelstan pushed his platter away.

The knight crossed himself and picked up a small loaf from the plate.

'These are worrying times, Father. The harvest has failed, the French attacks—'

Athelstan leaned across the table. 'Sir Edmund,' he interrupted, 'I do not insult you. Perhaps you can return the compliment. Your lack of sleep is not due to any French attack or the failure of any harvest. Three of your companions are murdered,' he continued, 'and yet you stay here, risking yourself and others?'

Malmesbury glanced nervously round. 'If I could tell you, Father, I would.'

'Then why not?'

Malmesbury stared at the piece of bread in his hand. 'It's too late,' he whispered. 'We are too far gone.'

'In what, Sir Edmund? For God's sweet sake!'

Sir Edmund lifted his head; a bitter, twisted smile on his face.

'I know you, Athelstan,' he murmured. 'You and your brother were archers, squires in Lord Fitzalan's retinue in France. At the village of Crotoy. Remember!'

Athelstan's heart skipped a beat. He glanced away. He recalled Lord Fitzalan's tent; he and Stephen were on guard inside when Fitzalan entertained certain knights. Yes, Malmesbury had been there.

'All things change!' Malmesbury muttered. 'Your brother?'

221

'Killed!' Athelstan replied, lifting his head. 'He was killed in an ambush.'

'So you became a friar: an act of reparation, so I'm told.'

'No.' Athelstan smiled bleakly. 'I became a priest because God wanted that. As, now, He wants the truth!'

'This morning,' Malmesbury replied, raising his voice and deliberately changing the subject, 'is important. We have finished the ordinary business and we'll have the final speeches about the taxes the Crown wishes to levy.'

'You mean the regent?'

'Yes, I mean the regent,' Malmesbury declared just as loudly.

Athelstan stared over his shoulder. Goldingham stood in the doorway, staring at them. Athelstan experienced the same depression and sense of hopelessness that he had the previous evening: these knights would tell him nothing.

'I must be going, Sir Edmund.'

Athelstan drained his tankard and left the tavern: he crossed the yard and went down a narrow alleyway to the riverside. He stood there for over an hour, watching the flow of the Thames, trying to calm his own mind and soul, as well as to observe the statutory fast before he began Mass. He walked slowly on to the abbey, its gardens and yards still silent. He entered the main door into the nave and went up the north aisle, where he found Father Benedict finishing Mass in a chantry chapel.

'Of course, Brother,' he replied when Athelstan made his request, 'by all means say Mass.'

He provided the Dominican with chasuble, alb and amice, and arranged for the bread and wine to be brought down to the small altar he had used. For a while Athelstan knelt, preparing himself, and then he celebrated the Mass of the day. He did his best to concentrate on the mysteries, forgetting the corruption; the lies, deceit and murder which confronted him.

Afterwards he disrobed and walked slowly back to the Gargoyle. As he made his way through the crowds now pouring up to and around Westminster Hall, Athelstan glimpsed Malmesbury and his party going towards the chapter-house for the first morning session of the Commons. When he reached the tavern, Sir John was already ensconced in the taproom, enjoying a breakfast of meat pie, a dish of vegetables and a pot of strong ale.

'You are in better fettle now, Friar.' He waved Athelstan to a stool. 'Rest your weary torso.' He beamed across the table. 'Slept like a little pig, I did: although the Lady Maude isn't here, this is the most comfortable of resting places.' He nodded towards the door. 'Our noble knights have gone to their important business, clucking like a collection of fowls. They're already thinking of home, mind you,' he added. 'Wondering how to explain to the good citizens of Shrewsbury why three of their number have not returned alive.' He was about to continue when he abruptly stopped eating.

'Sir John, what's the matter?'

Cranston took another bite out of the pie.

'What a vision of loveliness!' he exclaimed. 'Or, at least, one of them is.'

Athelstan whirled round on his stool as Benedicta, accompanied by a grinning Watkin, came into the tavern. Athelstan rose quickly; he called for more stools and asked Banyard to bring whatever his guests wanted.

'Good news?' he asked hopefully.

Benedicta, her face bright with excitement, nodded then blushed as Sir John leaned across the table and hugged her, planting a juicy kiss on her cheek. The coroner grinned at Watkin. 'I can't do the same for you, sir!'

Watkin grimaced gratefully.

'But, there again, you can be my guest.'

'What's the news?' Athelstan asked hastily.

'We have captured the ape,' Watkin declared proudly. The dung-collector shook his head. 'It came back just before dawn. Perline . . .' He sniffed. 'That rascal, well, he put fruit down. The ape was almost grateful to be back in its cage. Poor creature, he didn't look so fearsome.'

'And it's gone back?'

'Oh, yes,' Watkin said before he could stop himself. 'We lowered Cranston on to a boat and Moleskin and Perline took him back to the Tower.'

As Benedicta and Watkin described their achievements to Athelstan, the Commons assembled in the chapter-house, eagerly discussing once again the regent's demands for money. Father Benedict had begun the session by standing at the lectern and intoning the '*Veni Creator Spiritus*'. The Speaker had then gone through the day's business: he declared that they would meet for an hour and adjourn so that the representatives could break their fast either in the cloisters, where the good brothers would serve ale and bread, or in the cookshops and taverns around the abbey.

Sir Maurice Goldingham was very relieved when that hour finished: his stomach had been clenched in fear. Whilst speaker after speaker had gone to the lectern, Sir Maurice had been more concerned that he would not disgrace himself. At last the chapter-house bell had begun to ring and the Speaker had declared the session adjourned.

The representatives streamed out along the vestibule, past St Faith's Chapel and into the cloisters leading to the yards and gardens. Sir Maurice hurriedly made his excuses and went out through the east cloisters to where the latrines were. These were usually for the monks but, during their meeting of Parliament, they had been set aside for use by the Commons. A row of cubicles, each with its own door, built along an outside wall in one of the small gardens; these latrines were much admired, being washed clean by water taken through elm-wood pipes from the abbey kitchens. Sir Maurice smiled to himself as he lowered his breeches and eased his bowels. He sat there, eyes closed in relief. How luxurious these latrines were! The good lay brothers tended them every day; on the small stone plinth beside him was a clean supply of fine linen cloths. Sir Maurice rubbed his stomach.

'I'll be glad when it's all over,' he muttered to himself.

He doubted if these gripes were due to anything he had eaten either at the Gargoyle or the cookshops round the abbey. He was just feeling the strain of being forced to stay in Westminster, even though a killer was silently stalking himself and others. Sir Maurice closed his eyes. He recalled Shrewsbury, its guildhall, the marketplace; his own manor, fresh streams and fields and his mistress: a young, obliging widow who had become his heart's delight.

Sir Maurice tasted the dryness in his mouth. In Shrewsbury he would be able to order his own wines and foods and take his pleasure in a more leisurely way. He opened his eyes. Sir Edmund Malmesbury had warned them to stay close but, there again, he was not a child. He could hardly ask others to come whilst he squatted upon the latrine as if he was some little boy or frightened maid. Moreover, he could hear the doors further down opening and shutting; others were here. He'd perhaps take a little sugared mead to tighten his bowels and rejoin the rest.

Sir Maurice picked up a linen cloth. As he did so, he became aware of the growing silence outside. A spasm of fear jarred his stomach. Sir Maurice grimaced and decided to stay on the latrine. He heard a soft footfall outside and relaxed. Others were still around, the doors opened and shut. Sir Maurice straightened up. What was happening? Was someone checking to ensure each of the cubicles was empty?

Sir Maurice leaned forward and pushed on the door, suddenly deciding that flight was preferable to being attacked. He pushed the door but it wouldn't open. Sir Maurice sprang to his feet, pushing at the door with all his might, but someone outside had either jammed a log against it or were pressing their weight against it.

Goldingham hammered on the door. 'What's the matter?' he demanded. 'Is this a joke?'

He heard a sound and his stomach curdled so much he sat back on the latrine just as the candle, arrowhead and a scrap of parchment was pushed under the door.

'Oh day of wrath! Oh day of mourning!' the voice outside hissed. 'See fulfilled the prophet's warning! Heaven and earth in ashes burning!'

Sir Maurice opened his mouth to scream but his throat was dry. He stared at the door, recalling the corpses of Bouchon, Swynford, Harnett and, above all, those other dreadful cadavers hanging by their necks.

'Oh, help me!' Sir Maurice whispered. 'Oh, Lord God, help me!' He wetted his lips and opened his mouth to scream. The door of the latrine was abruptly flung open. Goldingham saw the shadowy figure standing there, glimpsed the arbalest and, even as he rose, the crossbow bolt took him straight beneath the heart.

Athelstan and Cranston were just about to return to their chambers after their guests had left, when the door to the tavern was flung open and Banyard rushed in.

'Sir John! Sir John!' he cried, wiping the sweat from his face. 'There's been another murder at the chapter-house.' The landlord sat on a stool. 'A messenger has just come, a boy!' he gasped. 'I sent him back and told him that you would be there in a while.'

'Who's been murdered?' Athelstan asked.

The landlord shook his head. 'I don't know. God have mercy on him, but I don't know.'

Athelstan and Cranston hurried out of the tavern and up into the grounds of the abbey. The news of the murder had already made itself felt. Men stood in groups gossiping. A royal messenger was running down towards the quayside, undoubtedly taking the news downriver to Gaunt's palace at the Savoy. Athelstan and Cranston hurried through the abbey. A captain of archers stopped them at the entrance to the cloisters, but Cranston barked at him furiously, threatening to report him directly to the regent. The man's face paled. He scratched his head and, muttering apologies, agreed to escort Sir John and Athelstan through the cloisters and into the yard where the latrines stood. Members of the Commons milled about there as Sir Miles Coverdale, helmet off, a drawn sword in his hand, tried to impose order. Athelstan glimpsed the door of a latrine flung open. Malmesbury, Aylebore and Elontius stood round a prostrate figure, faces fearful, as they

227

whispered to Sir Peter de la Mare, Speaker of the Commons. Athelstan followed Cranston as the coroner shouldered his way through. He ignored the knights and immediately crouched by the fallen man.

'God have mercy!' he breathed, staring at Goldingham's terror-stricken face, eyes staring sightlessly up; the trickle of blood seeping out of one corner of his mouth and the cruel crossbow bolt embedded deeply in the man's chest. Athelstan caught the foul smell from the privy and slammed the door shut. He, too, knelt down beside the cadaver.

'It happened so quickly,' Malmesbury explained. He pointed to Goldingham's hose, pulled only half-way up his thighs. 'We tried to make him decent but . . .'

'Coverdale!' Cranston roared.

Gaunt's captain came hurrying up. Athelstan studied his face closely. The soldier was pale, eyes frantic, but was he so upset, Athelstan wondered, by yet another killing?

'Sir John?'

'I want this yard cleared!' Cranston snapped, getting to his feet. 'Do you understand me?' He shouted. 'Apart from Sir Maurice's companions and Sir Miles Coverdale, I want everyone back in the cloisters.' Cranston held up his right hand with the huge signet ring bearing the arms of the city. He glared round at these arrogant men, so reluctant to move.

'I am Sir John Cranston, Coroner!' he bellowed. 'You must, and you will, move now!'

'If you are the coroner,' a voice shouted back, 'why don't you apprehend the person responsible?'

Cranston walked into the crowd, shoulders back, and bellowed; 'If the man who made that remark has the courage to step forward, then perhaps I can explain a few truths about the situation. If he doesn't, then I call him a caitiff, a coward and a knave!'

Cranston suddenly drew his sword with a speed which surprised even Athelstan. The coroner held it up, gripping the huge pommel, the long steel blade winking in the sunlight: a knight's gesture when challenging an opponent to combat. The anonymous detractor, however, and the other representatives, had the sense to keep silent. Cranston, legs apart, white hair bristling, eyes furious, was a fearsome figure, and even more so with that huge broadsword flashing in the sun. The crowd began to stream back towards the cloisters. Coverdale ordered the captain of archers to seal off all approaches, whilst Malmesbury and his companions stood in a little huddle by themselves.

Athelstan pulled up the dead man's hose. He grasped the cross which hung round his own neck and whispered the prayer for the dead. Once he had finished, he leaned down even closer: he recited an act of contrition on the dead man's behalf, and whispered the words of absolution into his ear. Cranston, his sword now sheathed, watched and waited until Athelstan made the final benediction.

'It's the least I could do,' Athelstan explained, getting to his feet. 'Sir Miles,' he called, 'where was the corpse found?'

Coverdale pointed to a latrine. Athelstan walked in, pinching his nose against the stench.

'He was found thrown against the wall,' Coverdale shouted. 'The crossbow bolt must have been fired at close range. He looked ridiculous,' the captain added, walking closer. 'Half sprawled on the latrine seat, his hose down about his ankles.'

'Who found him?' Cranston asked.

'I did.' Sir Humphrey Aylebore came forward, trying to hide

his fear beneath a show of defiance. 'When we were in the chapter-house, I saw Sir Maurice gripping his stomach,' he explained. 'When the session ended, he hurried off.'

'So, you knew he had gone to the latrines?' Athelstan asked.

Aylebore's lip curled. 'Don't insinuate, Father.'

'I am not!' Athelstan snapped back. 'I am merely trying to establish the truth. Sir Maurice apparently came here, as did others. They all left, and when the latrines were empty, the assassin struck.'

'And it was empty when I came here,' Aylebore answered. 'The first session lasts only an hour. Most men's bowels aren't as loose as Sir Maurice's.'

'Did he complain of any ailment before?' Cranston asked.

'Well,' Malmesbury came forward, 'Goldingham had a weak stomach. He contracted dysentery in France, as he constantly reminded us whenever he could.'

'Stomach, bowels!' Aylebore snarled, slamming shut the latrine door. 'What does it matter?' He glared at Coverdale. 'Who let the assassin through? How could a crossbow be brought to the cloisters?'

'Who said my soldiers let anyone through?' Coverdale retorted heatedly. 'The only people we let through were the representatives, the clerks: anyone who carried the lawful seal. I have already made inquiries amongst my men. Nothing untoward was noticed this morning. No arms were carried.' He advanced threateningly on Sir Humphrey, jabbing the air with a finger. 'Which means, sir, that the killer was already here. One of these good, gentle knights!'

'Peace, peace!' Athelstan came between Aylebore and Coverdale. 'Sir Maurice Goldingham is dead,' he continued quietly. 'Shouting abuse at each other will not bring him back, or trap his killer.'

'And when is he going to be trapped?' Malmesbury sneered. 'When we are all dead, bundled up in our winding sheets, thrown on a cart to be taken back to Shrewsbury?'

'If you had told the truth,' Athelstan replied. 'If Sir Edmund, you, or your companions had been honest with Sir John and myself, some of these deaths might not have happened. You could still prevent any more!'

'Oh, singing the same old song!' Aylebore sneered.

'Yes, I am singing the same old song!' Athelstan retorted. He went back to the latrine, pulled open the door and, bending down, picked up the small candle, arrowhead and scrap of parchment which he'd glimpsed lying there. Athelstan went and pressed these into Malmesbury's hand.

'"Remember" what, Sir Edmund?' he whispered hoarsely. Then, raising his voice, 'What are you all frightened of? What terrible crime haunts you from the past?' He stared round but the knights gazed blankly back. 'Let's leave, Sir John,' Athelstan said coldly. 'We'll find no truth here!'

They walked back through the cloisters and out in front of the abbey church. Sir John pointed to a bench beneath the tree where they had sat the previous day. Once they were settled, Athelstan glanced at the strangely silent, rather subdued coroner.

'What's the matter, Sir John?'

'I wish I hadn't lost my temper,' the coroner replied. 'I shouldn't have drawn my sword and challenged those men. They will not let such an insult pass.' He played with the ring on his finger. 'We have to trap this murderer, Athelstan,' he added. 'If we don't, I am sure that, before the Commons disperse, its Speaker will petition the king for my removal.'

231

'Nonsense!' Athelstan replied. 'How could we have prevented Goldingham's murder? He went to the latrines and the assassin struck. Oh, Malmesbury may splutter and protest, but his companions refuse to tell the truth. Come on, Sir John.' Athelstan patted the coroner's fat thigh. 'What you need is one of Master Banyard's pies and a blackjack of ale.'

Cranston rose mournfully to his feet and they made their way back to the Gargoyle. Athelstan took Sir John out to the small garden, but even the smell of a succulent beef pie and a frothing tankard of ale could not lighten the coroner's mood. He sat picking at his food, looking utterly woebegone.

They were almost finished when the potboy announced there was someone to see them. Athelstan followed him back into the tavern. He hoped it would be Sir Edmund or one of his companions, and was rather surprised to see the black cowled figure standing just within the doorway. A vein-streaked hand came out and pulled back the hood. Aelfric the archivist gazed shamefacedly at him.

'Brother, I am sorry about yesterday. As the psalmist says; "I am a worm and no man". The regent has already taken the evidence you seek,' he whispered hoarsely. Aelfric withdrew a roll of parchment tied with a scarlet ribbon from the voluminous sleeve of his gown and handed it to Athelstan. 'He forgot to take this,' Aelfric continued. 'I heard about the murder this morning. Ask Sir John to forgive his old master.'

And he left, like a shadow, through the doorway. Athelstan walked back into the garden, undoing the scroll even as he shouted at Banyard to fill their tankards.

'What was it?' Cranston asked nervously.

'Your old teacher,' Athelstan replied, unrolling the vellum. 'And he brought us something to study.'

Athelstan stared at the cramped writing, running his eye quickly down the roll which was made up of sheets of vellum stitched together. He put it down as Banyard brought the stoups of ale. Athelstan ignored the landlord's look of curiosity.

'What is it?' Cranston asked impatiently.

Athelstan just shook his head as he began to translate the Norman French and dog Latin of some obscure clerk.

'Oh, Athelstan, for the love of God!'

Cranston went to snatch the parchment, but the friar moved away.

'A door is beginning to open,' Athelstan declared. He tapped the parchment and stared across the garden.

'Well?' Cranston asked.

'These are petitions,' Athelstan replied slowly. 'They are divided into two, but all of them are about twenty years old. They come from the county of Shropshire. The first is a collection of petitions bearing the seals of men like Sir Edmund Malmesbury, Sir Francis Harnett and Sir Maurice Goldingham, vehemently protesting at the secret covens being organised in the shire by certain peasant leaders. Now, Sir John, you must remember that in 1359 and 1360, Edward III levied taxes to raise a great army to take to France.'

'Yes, that's true.' Cranston narrowed his eyes. 'There was a great deal of unrest, not only along the Welsh march but in Kent, Essex and elsewhere. Everyone complained, as they always do about taxes.'

'Ah!' Athelstan pointed to the parchment. 'Apparently the peasants in Shropshire did something about it. They actually organised themselves and resisted the tax-collectors. More importantly, they opposed the demands of their masters to work harder for less wages.'

233

Cranston sipped from the tankard. 'Ah!' he sighed, 'I understand. The burden of the tax levy would have fallen on the wealthy. They, in turn, would try to pass those demands on to their own tenants by making them produce more, or by cutting their wages. But what has that got to do with these murders?'

'Well listen, Sir John.' Athelstan glanced further down the parchment. 'About three years later, another set of petitions appeared; not from the knights or, indeed, from their peasant leaders, but from widows.' Athelstan pointed to one petition. 'Such as this from Isolda Massingham. She maintains that a gang of outlaws, cut-throats, wolfs-heads and felons were waging war on isolated farms. She talks of men masked, hooded and cowled, who burst into her house and dragged her husband Walter out. He was later found hanging from the branch of an oak tree some three miles outside the village.' He glanced up. 'They disfigured her husband's corpse by etching red crosses on his face.'

'So . . .' Cranston drank from his tankard. 'Two of our corpses were similarly disfigured but—'

'Ah!' Athelstan held his hand up. 'Now Isolda makes no allegations. She points no finger of accusation, but demands that the king's justices be sent into the shire to discover the perpetrators of this outrage. Isolda, I suspect, was no base-born peasant villein: her husband was of peasant stock but rather prosperous, hence the petition.'

'True, true,' Cranston interjected. 'After the Great Pestilence, labour was in short supply. Properties were left vacant, and the labourers and peasants, particularly the more prosperous, had more ground to till so could demand higher wages. They were also able to sell their own produce in the markets.' He shrugged. 'It's the same thing as today: the prosperous peasants want more freedom to work their own land and sell their produce, but the great lords are determined to keep them tied to the soil. But, Athelstan, what has this got to do with the murders at Westminster?'

'As I said,' Athelstan continued, 'Isolda was a fairly wealthy widow. She probably went to some clerk who drew up this petition and organised its despatch to the king's council at Westminster.'

'Yes, yes,' Cranston answered testily, 'I understand all that.'

'Well, I am going to make a leap in logic,' Athelstan went on. 'Massingham's killers were no band of outlaws.' The friar paused to choose his words carefully. 'I don't know whether widows like Isolda Massingham and others knew who was murdering their menfolk, but I suspect it was Sir Edmund Malmesbury and his knights.' Athelstan rolled up the parchment. 'Isolda's petition is important, and I'd love to know what the Crown did about it.'

CHAPTER 13

At first Cranston would not accept Athelstan's conclusions.

'You are saying,' he repeated, 'that Malmesbury and his companions, the so-called Knights of the Swan, carried out their own private war against these self-styled peasant leaders?'

'Yes, I am,' Athelstan replied. 'They are arrogant men, Sir John, fully aware of their rights and appurtenances. They grew up in a world where every man knew his place, particularly the peasants, but the Great Pestilence ended all that. Whole villages were wiped out. Labour became scarce and the peasants began to enrich themselves, not only through the acquisition of land, but also by selling their labour to the highest bidder.' Athelstan ran his finger round the rim of his tankard. 'And what could the Crown do? It needed those peasants for its wars in France, as well as the payment of its taxes, so the likes of Malmesbury took the law into their own hands.'

Athelstan paused and sipped at his ale, staring through the window of the tavern to ensure no one was eavesdropping. 'Imagine it, Sir John, these arrogant lords of the soil, cloaked and visaged, armed to the teeth. They would swoop on some poor peasant's house, drag him from his table, and hurry him off to execution whilst they chanted the sequence from the Mass of the Dead, the "*Dies Irae*".'

'And the arrowhead, candle and scrap of parchment?' Cranston asked.

'Oh, these knights always sent a warning. The candle is a symbol of their victim's impending funeral. The arrowhead a sign of a violent death, and the word "Remember" a barbed hint to reflect upon the other murders these men had already carried out.' He sighed. 'And the red crosses etched on the faces of their dead victims were a grisly warning to others.'

'Then what happened?' Cranston asked.

'I suppose Malmesbury and his gang had their way. After a number of these peasant leaders had been executed, others became more circumspect. But, of course,' Athelstan screwed his eyes up against the sunlight, 'the evil we do, Sir John, never dies. It dogs our footsteps and lurks in the corners of our souls. And so we come to the regent.' Athelstan lowered his voice. 'Gaunt holds lands along the Welsh march. He would make careful inquiries about these arrogant landowners. I am sure he discovered their secret sin. He organised their election to this Parliament and gave them a brutal warning: either they supported him or he might send the justices back into Shropshire to publicise their secrets.'

'But Malmesbury and the rest oppose the regent bitterly.'

Athelstan smiled bleakly. 'Oh, Sir John. How often have you played a game of chess? You watch your opponent's pieces being moved. Sometimes you believe his judgement is faulty, even foolish, but at the end, when he takes your queen and traps your king, you realise the subtlety of his design.'

'In other words, the game is not over yet?'

'No, no, Sir John, it certainly isn't.'

'But the murders?' Cranston asked. 'Surely Gaunt does not have a hand in these?'

'My lord Coroner.' Athelstan played with the tassel of the cord round his waist. 'He could do. He might even argue that he is carrying out lawful execution. But, *concedo*, I think there is little likelihood. No, someone else has entered this game. We have three possibilities. First, Sir Miles: we must remember that Coverdale also comes from Shropshire. Did one of his kinsmen die at Malmesbury's hands? Or, there again, Father Benedict. He seems very attached to the memory of his dead comrade Antony. Is he the sort of man to carry out God's judgement? Or . . .' Athelstan paused.

'Or what?' Cranston asked, intrigued.

'Well, I keep talking about the knights as a coven under the leadership of Sir Edmund Malmesbury and, Sir John, believe me, whatever is the truth, Malmesbury is their leader. However, there is one other consideration.' Athelstan leaned across the table. 'How do we know the others were involved? Aylebore or Elontius, or both, may be totally innocent of any crime, but might see themselves as angels of vengeance.'

'In other words, Aylebore or Elontius might have suffered because of those judicial murders in Shropshire so many years ago?'

'Possibly.' Athelstan stretched and turned his face to the sun. 'Come, Sir John.' He smiled at the coroner. 'St Dominic always said that, after a meal, a man should walk and talk with a friend in a beautiful garden.'

Cranston, his gloom now forgotten, got to his feet and joined Athelstan. They wound their way through the herb plots and flowerbeds. At the bottom of the garden they sat on a stone seat framed by a flower-covered arbour. Athelstan leaned back and listened to the lilting bird-song.

'It's at moments like these, Sir John, that I realise why

paradise was described as a garden.' Athelstan lifted his face to catch the sun.

'Aye,' Cranston retorted. 'And, as in Eden, Brother, there's always a serpent, a canker in the rose.'

Athelstan ran his thumb round his mouth. 'Let's summarise what we know so far.' He nudged the coroner. 'Come on, law officer, you've supped and dined well. Now use your razor-like mind.'

'Well, first, we know that Sir Edmund Malmesbury, and certainly those men who have been murdered, committed terrible crimes in Shropshire. Secondly, our noble regent is using that knowledge to blackmail them, though for what purpose we still have to discover. Thirdly, we know these good knights formed a fraternity or brotherhood of the Knights of the Swan. This broke up after their famous chalice was stolen, though this has now been returned.' Cranston paused. His hand fell to the wineskin nestling beneath his cloak, but Athelstan playfully knocked it away.

'My lord Coroner, we are not finished yet.'

'Well, we know these knights came here and the murders began.' At the time of their death, each knight received warning tokens. Sir Oliver Bouchon left this tavern and was knocked on the head. We suspect he probably did not leave Westminster; his body was dumped in the Thames and it floated down to the reeds near Tothill Fields. We do not know why he left, where he went or who followed him. Sir Henry Swynford was garrotted to death by a man pretending to be a priest.'

'And, in that, the assassin was most daring,' Athelstan interrupted. 'All we know is that he appeared in the tavern, executed Swynford and then disappeared. God knows what would have happened if the real chantry priest had arrived:

240

though, having met Father Gregory, I don't think he would be too difficult to fool.'

'And, finally, Harnett,' Cranston declared. 'We know he left that brothel on Monday evening and went upriver to Southwark looking for the rapscallion Brasenose. Someone used Harnett's desire to buy that bloody ape to lure him to the Pyx chamber at Westminster. But how the assassin could enter and leave the guarded cloisters, unnoticed, carrying a sword or an axe, is beyond our comprehension.'

'And then this morning,' he concluded, 'we have Sir Maurice Goldingham. He is taken short, hurries to the latrines and dies shitting himself. Again, how the assassin entered and left the cloisters carrying a crossbow remains a mystery.'

'Unless, of course; the assassin was already in the cloisters,' Athelstan added, 'being able to pass through the line of soldiers using his seal and, perhaps, smuggling the arbalest in.' Athelstan sighed in exasperation, 'Surely, Sir John, the assassin must have made some mistake? What was that black soil we found under Bouchon's fingernails?' He heard a snore and glanced sideways; Sir John, a beatific smile on his face, was now fast asleep.

Athelstan sat back, basking in the sunlight. I should go back to St Erconwald's, he reflected. He wished he could sit with Benedicta and gossip about the ordinary, humdrum things of everyday life. Athelstan moved on his seat. Yes, he'd like to be in his own house, or teaching the children, or even trying to arbitrate between Watkin and Pike in their interminable struggle for power on the parish council. And, of course, there were other matters. The bell rope needed replacing. He wanted to make sure that the statue of St Erconwald had been replaced correctly on its plinth, and Huddle had to be watched. If the painter had his way, he'd cover every inch of stone with paintings of his own choosing. Athelstan smiled as he recalled Perline Brasenose's escapade and hoped 'Cranston the ape' was safely back in the Tower. Some time in the near future he must have a talk with that young man and Simplicatas: the story must be all over Southwark by now. Athelstan closed his eyes and quietly prayed that none of his parishioners, particularly Crim, ever mentioned the Barbary ape and Cranston in the same breath again. Pike, too, could sometimes have the devil in him; he might even take Huddle for a pot of ale and encourage the painter to draw some picture depicting Perline's tomfoolery on the church wall.

Athelstan heard a sound. He opened his eyes, but it was only Banyard carrying two buckets of earth from the compost heap. He placed these down, smiled at Athelstan, and went into the tavern. Athelstan stood up, moving gently so as not to rouse Sir John. He breathed in the fragrance of the thyme, marjoram and rosemary planted in the herb garden.

'I'll go back to St Erconwald's,' he muttered, 'when all this is finished.'

A bee buzzed close to his face. He stepped back, wafting it away. What other mistakes, Athelstan wondered, had the assassin made? To be sure Swynford's murder was impudent, but those of Harnett and Goldingham? And what had been missing from Harnett's possessions strewn out on the bed? Athelstan yawned and turned back to the bower: he shook Cranston awake.

'Rouse yourself, Sir John.'

Cranston opened his eyes, smacking his lips. The coroner stretched. 'Where to now, my good friar?'

'The day is warm,' Athelstan replied. 'Let's return to our chambers, Sir John. Tomorrow we have to be up early when the king and the regent go down to Westminster. What o'clock will the procession start?'

Cranston lumbered to his feet. 'I don't know, but I'll send a messenger to the Savoy to ask.' And, grumbling about the regent's impositions, Cranston shuffled back into the tavern, making his way wearily upstairs.

Athelstan followed. He would have liked to have written down the conclusions he and Sir John had reached, but the sun and ale had made him drowsy. He lay down on his cot-bed; when he awoke later darkness was already beginning to fall. He roused Sir John and they spent the rest of the evening waiting in the taproom for Malmesbury, Elontius and Aylebore to return. It was fully dark when the three representatives came in, huddled together, each with their hands on the pommel of their daggers. They greeted Cranston and Athelstan with a cursory nod and sat at their own table. Their morose demeanour and air of despondency only lifted after Banyard had served them the best his kitchens could offer, placing an unstoppered flask of wine on the table before them.

'It's the best Gascony can produce,' the landlord declared. 'Come, sirs, fill your cups.'

He opened the flask and poured a generous measure into each of the knights' goblets. Frightened and anxious, all three drank quickly, refilling their cups, putting fire into their bellies and the arrogance back in their mouths. Cranston whispered that he could watch no longer, and stomped off to his room, but Athelstan, pretending to eat slowly, studied them carefully. As the evening drew on, all three knights returned to their pompous selves, braying like donkeys at what had happened during the afternoon and evening sessions of the Commons. Of course, their voices attracted the attention of everyone else in the

243

tavern: lawyers, clerks, officials from the courts or Exchequer. All congregated round the table, listening solemnly as these three representatives proclaimed what was wrong with the kingdom.

'Woe to the realm when the king is a child,' Malmesbury intoned. 'This –' he tapped the table, burping gently between his words – 'is the cause of all our ills!'

Athelstan, knowing what he did about these men, felt his stomach turn. He would have left them but, fascinated by their hypocrisy, watched and waited. Only now and again did their fear of the murder of their companions show. A clerk, with a snivelling face and lank greasy hair, asked who the murderer could be. Malmesbury glared at him like a frightened rabbit and dug his face into his cup, whilst Aylebore drew the conversation on to other matters. Every so often one of them would go out to the latrines. Athelstan noticed with some amusement how all three knights had hired burly servitors to guard them. As Aylebore returned, hastily fastening his points, Athelstan was waiting for him, just within the door.

'You have bought yourself protection, Sir Humphrey?'

The knight lifted his beery, slobbery face. 'Well, much good you are,' he sneered. He paused to loosen the belt round his girth. 'Can't even have a piss without someone watching your back.'

He would have moved on, but Athelstan blocked his way. The sneer died on Aylebore's face.

'If you are so frightened,' Athelstan whispered, 'why not go back to Shropshire?'

Sir Humphrey glanced away, his face sodden with drink.

'Or confess your secret sin,' Athelstan continued remorselessly.

Aylebore's head swung round, eyes stony.

'Confess to the murders of those men,' Athelstan whispered, his gaze not wavering. 'Do you remember, Sir Humphrey? The peasant leaders who wanted to better themselves, but whom you and your companions executed, or should I say murdered, in the pursuit of your own selfish interests!'

Aylebore's face turned ugly, yet Athelstan saw the fear in his eyes.

'Confess,' Athelstan repeated.

Aylebore pushed his face close to Athelstan, who did not flinch at the burst of fetid breath from the man's mouth.

'If I had to confess anything, Father,' Aylebore hissed, 'then it wouldn't be to you. And if I killed, then I did so in the name of a cause you wouldn't understand.'

Athelstan stepped back. 'Oh, I understand you completely, Sir Humphrey. It's a devil I meet every day. It goes under different names: jealousy, envy, anger, the lust for power.'

Aylebore was about to reply, but Malmesbury called him over. The knights shouldered roughly by, and Athelstan drew his breath in.

'I tried, Lord,' he whispered. 'There's little more I can do!'

He went across the taproom and up the stairs to his own chamber. Only then did he realise how frightening his confrontation with Aylebore had been. He found it difficult to pray, still repelled by the evil ugliness in the knight's face. Athelstan lay down on the bed and tried to control his breathing, diverting his mind by imagining he was in St Erconwald's, praying before the altar. At last he grew calm, his eyes heavy with sleep. As he began to doze, images floated through his mind, and Athelstan was almost off to sleep when he realised what was missing from Harnett's room. The friar sat up on the bed.

'It can't be! Surely?' He spoke into the darkness. 'Those two items were missing!'

He got to his feet, went across to the table and, lighting a candle, picked up his quill from the writing-tray. Athelstan worked till the early hours, listing everything that had happened since they had arrived at the Gargoyle and, on another sheet of vellum, the names of everyone he had met. Only as he lay down to snatch a little sleep did vague suspicions become much clearer.

The next morning Athelstan felt sluggish and heavy-eyed. He celebrated his daily Mass in one of the side chapels of the abbey, politely answering Father Benedict's inquiries. Afterwards, he hastened back to the Gargoyle, broke his fast, and went out to stand by the river where Cranston later found him.

'We have to go soon, Brother.' He clasped the friar's shoulder and turned him round. 'What is it, Athelstan? You look as if you have hardly slept.' He grasped the friar's hand and squeezed it. 'I know you,' Cranston continued excitedly, his face beaming with pleasure. 'You have begun to unravel this mystery, haven't you?'

'I am not sure, Sir John.' Athelstan looked towards the rising sun. 'But shouldn't we be away to join the regent's procession?'

'Pshaw!' Cranston made a movement with his hand. 'The good news, Brother, is that the regent does not expect us to be part of it. We are to await him in the cloisters after the king has addressed the Commons.'

They returned to the tavern, where Athelstan mysteriously wandered off, telling Sir John not to worry, that he wouldn't go

246

far. Cranston knew enough about his secretarius not to question him further. Athelstan would worry at something, closing his mind to everything, including Sir John's insistent questions.

An hour later Athelstan, washed, shaved and dressed in his best gown, knocked on Cranston's door. The coroner, who had been waiting impatiently, did not bother to ask any questions, but immediately hurried him down and out into the abbey grounds. Athelstan had never seen so many soldiers congregating in one place, not only guards and archers, but men-at-arms and knight bannerets from the royal household filled the cloisters and the gardens. Cranston had to exert all his authority, calling on Coverdale to help. At last they managed to fight their way through to the vestibule, which was thronged with courtiers, chamberlains, pages and squires, resplendent in Gaunt's livery, the blue, red and gold of the royal household. Coverdale who had led them there, pointed to the closed doors of the chapter-house.

'The regent is within,' he murmured, 'and has already spoken to the members. Now the young king has begun.' He paused as a great roar of approval, followed by cheering and clapping, came from the chapter-house.

'The young king has been well received,' Coverdale declared.

Athelstan recalled Richard's ivory face framed by that beautiful blond hair, those brilliant blue eyes, his ever-ready smile and innate tact and courtesy, Athelstan knew such acclaim would not be difficult for the young king.

'Just like his father, the Black Prince,' Cranston growled. 'Every man loved him, no man ever spoke ill about him.'

Athelstan nodded tactfully and stared up at the face of a gargoyle. He didn't wish to contradict Cranston, who had been the most fervent supporter of the young king's father.

Nevertheless, Athelstan had heard the stories about the Black Prince's cruelties in France, particularly at Limoges, where he had allowed women and children to starve in a freezing city ditch. Indeed, Athelstan had the same reservations about the young king. Too beautiful, he thought, too sweet to be wholesome. Athelstan had not been beguiled by those beautiful eyes and gracious smiles. Never before in one so young had Athelstan glimpsed such a darkness, which sprang from Richard's deep and lasting hatred for his uncle the regent.

Athelstan glanced back at the chapter-house as he heard the Commons give another roar of approval, followed by the stamping of feet and the clapping of hands. This went on for some time. A brief silence was broken by the shrill blast of trumpets. The doors to the chapter-house swung open. Two heralds in cloth of gold walked out, each carried a silver trumpet; after every few steps they stopped and blew a fanfare. Behind them came a knight banneret in shining Milanese armour. He carried his drawn sword up before his face, as a priest would a crucifix. Chamberlains began to clear the vestibule as the king, dressed in a brilliant silver gown decorated with golden fleur-de-lys, left the chapter-house, his hand clasping that of his uncle. Both princes were smiling at each other and at the crowd which thronged there. If he hadn't known better, Athelstan would have thought Gaunt and Richard were the mutually doting father and son. Behind the king came more knights and officials, then the mass of the Commons, some of them still shouting, '*Vivat! Vivat Rex!*'

'We'd best leave,' Cranston urged. 'Gaunt told us to meet him outside the doors of the abbey where the king has agreed to touch some poor men ill with the scofula.'

Athelstan followed him out of the cloisters and round to a

specially prepared area before the abbey's great doors. Here, workmen from the royal household had set up a dais covered in purple woollen rugs. In the centre were two chairs of state. On each corner of the dais stood a knight of the royal household holding banners depicting the royal arms, as well as the insignia of John of Gaunt. Archers wearing the livery of the white hart had now cordoned this place off. The crowds milled there, pressed against this wall of steel, eager to catch a glimpse of their king. Cranston had a word with the royal serjeant who led them into the royal enclosure. They had to wait a further half an hour before the king, still grasping his uncle's hand, finished his procession round the abbey and came out through the main doors to be greeted by a rapturous roar from the crowd. Once they were seated, flanked and surrounded by officials and knights of the royal household, Gaunt smiled and beckoned Cranston forward. Both Sir John and Athelstan knelt on cushions before the chairs of state, each kissing the ring of the king and the regent in turn. Richard, despite the majesty and solemnity of the occasion, did not stand on idle ceremony but clapped his hands boyishly.

'Oh, don't kneel, Sir John!' he exclaimed. 'You may stand – and you, Brother Athelstan.' He leaned forward and whispered, 'If I had my way you would sit beside me: one on my right and one on my left. Wouldn't that be appropriate, dearest Uncle?'

'Beloved Nephew,' Gaunt smiled back, 'Sir John and Brother Athelstan are two of your most loyal subjects.' He waved elegantly towards the crowd. 'But there are hundreds more waiting to greet you.'

The king refused to shift his gaze. 'They can wait. They can wait!' Richard snapped furiously.

For a few seconds the smile faded. Athelstan stared into

those blue eyes and knew that the young king would use this meeting to taunt and bait his uncle.

'My lord Regent, you told us to be here.' Cranston, eager not to be drawn into this deadly rivalry, declared.

'More deaths, Sir John,' Gaunt answered brusquely. 'More deaths amongst the Commons, which does not make our task easier.'

'What deaths are these?' the king interrupted.

'Beloved Nephew, I have told you already. Certain knights of the shire have been barbarously murdered. So far,' Gaunt murmured, glaring at Cranston, 'little has been done either to stop them or to unmask the assassin.'

The king, bored and resentful at being excluded from this conversation, sat back in his chair, apparently more interested in the tassels on the sleeves of his gown.

'Well?' Gaunt asked.

'My lord Regent,' Athelstan spoke up quickly, 'you said so far? But our business here is not finished yet.'

'Then, when it is, please tell me,' Gaunt snapped back.

The king suddenly leaned forward and grasped Athelstan's sleeve. 'I did very well in the chapter-house. I asked for the support and loyalty of my Commons.'

'We heard the cheers, your Grace,' Athelstan replied.

The king pulled him closer. 'It's Uncle they don't like,' he whispered loudly. 'I think if I had asked for the moon they would have given me it.'

'They may ask for the removal of the lord Coroner,' Gaunt taunted back. 'There were complaints, your Grace, at the terrible murders being committed here in the abbey.'

The king's mood abruptly changed. He made a cutting movement with his hand.

'Sir John Cranston is the king's coroner in London,' he snapped. 'And if the Commons try to remove him, I'll break their necks!' Richard sat forward. 'Brother Athelstan, Sir John, please stay with us. Uncle, if I am to touch the beggars, then let's have it done quickly!'

Gaunt snapped his fingers; Athelstan and Cranston stood back. There were more trumpet blasts, and royal heralds began to usher up towards the dais a line of ragged, poor men and women, eager for the king's touch on their heads. These were even more appreciative of the silver piece, bread and wine distributed by royal servitors from a table behind the dais. Cranston and Athelstan watched the beggars shuffle through. Some had made a pathetic attempt to wash or change, but they all looked unkempt and dirty with straggly, greasy hair and pinched narrow faces. Some of them had open sores on their hands and feet. Many didn't even wear shoes or sandals. Nevertheless, each came forward and knelt on the cushions before the king's chair. Athelstan had to admire how the young king hid his personal feelings behind a show of concern. The king would smile at each beggar, lean forward, and sketch a cross on their foreheads. Now and again he would clasp a hand or whisper a few words of encouragement. The beggar, his eyes shining with gratitude, would be led off around the dais for more practical help.

The line seemed endless. Athelstan, watching them intently, regretted that some of the beggars from his own parish were not there. He noticed two men edging their way forward. There was something familiar about them. They seemed more purposeful than those who had gone before. Athelstan watched the shorter one in particular and felt his stomach lurch: the man with his bloodless lips, ever-flickering eyes, broken nose and a scar just

251

under his left eye! Was he not one of those who, according to Joscelyn the taverner, met Pike the ditcher in the Piebald tavern? Athelstan turned to Cranston, but the coroner was now deep in conversation with one of the knights whom he had apparently known in former days. Athelstan tugged at his sleeve but Cranston just shook him off.

'Sir John, I think . . .' Athelstan now gripped the coroner's arm.

'For the love of God, Brother, what is it?'

Athelstan pointed to the man. 'Sir John, I do not think he is a beggar.'

Cranston caught the alarm in Athelstan's voice, as did his companion. However, as both men moved forward, the beggar, instead of kneeling on the cushion, suddenly drew a dagger, lunging in a cutting arc at the king's face. Richard fell back, but Gaunt was quick to react. Athelstan had never seen a knife drawn so fast. The beggar was bringing his hand back for a second blow when Gaunt sprang forward and, with two hands, drove his own dagger into the beggar's chest. The would-be assassin staggered back, blood spurting from his mouth and wound, even as squires and knights recovered from the shock of what was happening. The knifeman turned, mouth gaping, falling against his companion, who shook him off and tried to run back into the crowd.

Gaunt again responded rapidly. An archer had run forward, arrow to his bow string: Gaunt grabbed this, brought the bow up, the long, quilled shaft caught between his fingers. The beggar's companion was running back through the crowd which parted before him. The regent stood as if carved out of stone, the bow held firmly in his hand. There was a twang and the goose-feathered arrow caught the fugitive just beneath the neck, driving hard into his flesh. He staggered: took one, two more steps. He slumped to his knees then fell to one side.

Chaos and consternation broke out. Knights hurried up, forming a shield wall round the young king. Captains and serjeants barked out orders. Those beggars who had not yet reached the royal throne were brutally beaten off. Men-at-arms ran up, pikes lowered, archers took up positions behind them as Gaunt grabbed the young king who sat frozen in fear. The royal party, Cranston and Athelstan included, retreated back into the abbey, the great doors slamming shut behind them.

'So quickly!' Athelstan murmured. 'Sir John, so quickly! One minute all was calm, with the king delivering his touch. . .'

He'd have gone towards the king, around whom courtiers were thronging, but Cranston pulled him back. 'Leave it be, Brother,' he advised. 'They will allow no one near the king.'

Gaunt was now imposing order, shouting at captains, cursing their lack of vigilance, issuing instructions that the king should be taken immediately to the Tower. Heralds went outside to restore order and ask the crowd to wait. Athelstan heard the trumpet blasts and the shouts of the herald over the noise of the crowd. At last some sort of order was imposed, and Gaunt swept out of the abbey to address the crowd, proclaiming in sharp, quick sentences that, due to God's good grace, their young king was unscathed and his would-be murderers sent to hell. Even as he spoke, the regent's exploits in saving his young nephew appeared to be known by all. As Cranston and Athelstan slipped quietly up a transept, they could hear the roars of the crowd and their cheering at the speed and bravery of the regent.

'You said you recognised the would-be assassin?' Cranston asked.

'I have seen him in Southwark,' Athelstan replied defensively.

'He had a reputation as a trouble-maker.'

Cranston nodded. However, once they were outside the abbey, in a small alleyway leading down to the Gargoyle, he pulled the friar into the shadow of a doorway.

'He was one of those leaders of the Great Community of the Realm, wasn't he?' Cranston asked. 'One of those idiots with whom Pike the ditcher consorts.'

Athelstan caught Cranston's hand and squeezed it. 'Don't ever repeat what I say, Sir John,' he whispered hoarsely. 'Pike is a fool, a drunkard, a blabber, but he's no traitor or murderer. He had no hand in this.' He drew his breath in sharply. 'However, our regent did!'

'In God's name, Brother!'

Athelstan took a step back and stared down the alleyway.

'Sir John, think,' he said softly. 'How did those assassins get so close? And don't you think the regent acted quickly?' Athelstan smiled bleakly. 'Sir John, mark my words. Within the hour Gaunt will be the hero of London, and who will resist him then?'

CHAPTER 14

At the Gargoyle, Athelstan acted even more strangely. He made his excuses to Cranston and went up to his own chamber. This time Athelstan was determined not to tell his companion the conclusions he had reached. Instead he studied everything he had listed the night before. Certain facts he scored time and again with a quill: the black dirt under Bouchon's fingernails; the knight's abrupt departure; Harnett leaving the brothel; his journey down to the river; and, above all, what was missing from Harnett's room. Athelstan placed his quill down.

'Was it missing from the other two?' Athelstan whispered. He looked down at the parchment. 'Bow bells!' he murmured, 'Bow bells! How can I trap the assassin?'

Athelstan went and knelt beside his bed. He prayed for guidance but his soul was distracted, his mind wandering hither and thither. He stared across at the window: the sun was beginning to set. Athelstan knew he would have to act quickly or there would be more murders. He heard sounds, loud voices from downstairs, followed by Cranston's heavy footfall in the passageway and a pounding on the door. When Athelstan opened it, Sir John, grinning from ear to ear, seized the surprised friar by the shoulder and kissed him on either cheek.

'Oh, slyest of monks.'

'Friar, Sir John, I'm a friar!'

Cranston grinned. 'Well, whatever.' He nodded towards the stairs. 'You were correct. Malmesbury has just come back from the chapter-house. The news of Gaunt's protection of his nephew has swept the city. No less a person than Sir Edmund Malmesbury is loudly praising the regent. He has advised the Commons to grant all of Gaunt's demands.' Cranston studied the friar's anxious face. His smile faded. 'Brother, what have you found?'

Athelstan waved him into the chamber, closing the door behind him. He pointed to his bed. 'Sit down, Sir John. Most of the riddle is resolved.' Athelstan pulled a stool up opposite the coroner. 'First, we have a regent, John of Gaunt,' he began, 'who, for God knows what reason, needs more taxes. He is opposed, savagely disliked by the Commons, so he concentrates on his most vociferous opponents.'

'The representatives from Shropshire?' Cranston asked.

'Precisely. Sir Edmund Malmesbury and his companions, who once belonged to the fraternity of the Knights of the Swan. Gaunt is a ruthless and tenacious man. He discovers their secrets; how, many years ago, they took the law into their own hands and executed peasant leaders who tried to better themselves. Now Gaunt tells Malmesbury and his group just exactly what he knows and what they must do to obtain his forgiveness. The regent then secures their return to Parliament.' Athelstan pulled a face. 'That wouldn't be difficult. The official responsible for the returns is the sheriff, who is always a Crown nominee. Once they arrive in London,' Athelstan licked his dry lips, 'Gaunt tells Malmesbury and his group to continue their usual opposition, depicting the regent as an avaricious, arrogant and cunning prince.'

256

'Well, at least he was telling the truth,' Cranston interrupted. Athelstan smiled. 'The greatest lies, Sir John, always have a certain element of truth. At the same time -' Athelstan looked towards the door to make sure it was closed – 'Gaunt is busy with his spies amongst the Great Community of the Realm. I suspect some or many of its leaders are in his pay. Gaunt arranged that mummery this afternoon. The young king was never in any real danger; that would have been a perilous path to tread; Gaunt would always be blamed if anything happened to the young king. Instead, Gaunt acts the role of the saviour, the loving uncle, the powerful lord defending the golden child. For a while the Londoners, until they regain their wits, will hail him as a saint. Sir Edmund Malmesbury has also been given a sign; full of praise for the regent, he not only withdraws his opposition in the Commons, but actually insists that Gaunt's demands be approved.'

'But couldn't it have been done some other way?' Cranston asked, scratching his head.

'Oh, certainly. Gaunt could have demanded that Malmesbury and his group support him from the beginning, but that would have provoked suspicions. Indeed, the regent could have interfered with the election of all the representatives, but that would be a hollow victory; agreeing to the payment of taxes is one thing, collecting them is another.' Athelstan shook his head. 'Oh, it's true, Sir John, what the good Lord said: "The children of light." Just look at what Gaunt has achieved.' Athelstan ticked the points off on his fingers. 'Saviour of the King; the grant of taxes; and, because these representatives will go back to their counties and towns, the regent's great deeds will be proclaimed throughout the kingdom.'

257

'And these murders?' Cranston asked. 'Surely Gaunt didn't plan them?'

'No, I don't think he did, but he's wily enough to make use of them. True, there was a danger that the murders of the knights could be laid at his door, but he deftly avoided that problem by appointing a coroner, who dislikes him intensely, to investigate. Now, Sir John, if you succeed, Gaunt will again get the credit: a just prince who even pursues the assassins of his opponents.'

'And if I fail?'

Athelstan spread his hands. 'Gaunt won't care. All he'll see is that justice has been done in a strange form of way. Four of his opponents are dead, and Sir John Cranston gets the blame.'

'And will I succeed?' Cranston asked. He grasped Athelstan's arm. 'You know the murderer, don't you, Friar? Why don't you tell me?'

Athelstan leaned over and gently touched the coroner on his face. 'Because, Sir John, for all your buffoonery, drinking, swearing and belching, you are as honest as the day is long. You wouldn't be able to hide it and I wouldn't trap the assassin.'

Cranston blushed and shuffled his great boots. He glanced away, touched by the friar's compliments.

Athelstan continued. 'What I want you to do, Sir John, is be with me when I catch him.' He got to his feet. 'After I have left, go down to the taproom and make it known that I have trapped the murderer.'

'Where are you going?;' Cranston asked.

'To St Faith's Chapel,' Athelstan replied. 'But don't tell anyone that, promise?'

The coroner held a podgy hand up, then he took his knife

from his sheath. 'Take that, Brother.' He thrust the long Welsh dagger at the friar.

Athelstan balanced it in his hands and handed it back.

'"Put not your trust in chariots",' he replied, quoting the psalms, 'Or the strength of the bow; the Lord Himself will rescue you from the devil who prowls to your right and to your left!'

'Well, He'd bloody better!' Cranston muttered, resheathing the dagger. 'And, when you have gone, what shall I do?'

'Go outside, Sir John, wait and see who leaves the tavern. Stay awhile, then bring whoever remains with you.' Athelstan picked up his cloak and, going back, squeezed Sir John's hand. 'I'll be safe.' He smiled at the coroner.

'Is this really necessary?' Cranston insisted. 'Do you want to trap this assassin so much?'

'I don't want to trap him at all,' Athelstan retorted. 'God does!'

He left his chamber and went down the stairs. Cranston followed. He watched as the friar stopped to chat to the flaxen-haired Christina, and then to a potboy near the door. Once he was gone, drawing curious glances from those seated in the taproom, Cranston followed him down. Instead of going to a table, he deliberately marched into the centre of the room and beamed around.

'Why so pleased?' Sir Miles called from where he sat in a corner.

'Why, sir,' Cranston retorted, 'The king has been saved, the regent has his taxes, whilst Brother Athelstan, God knows where he has gone, believes he has unmasked an assassin!' Cranston was pleased at the surprise in the captain's face.

'Who is it?' the man spluttered harshly, shattering

259

the silence throughout the taproom.

The coroner slyly tapped his fleshy nose. 'A veritable ferret, our friar.' He beamed around. 'He knows the truth.' He shook his head. 'And the truth is never what you expect it to be.'

'This is preposterous!' Aylebore snarled, half rising to his feet from where he sat next to Elontius.

His sentiments were echoed by Malmesbury, whose face had gone deathly pale.

'Preposterous it may be,' the coroner replied, 'but my secretarius will only move in his own good time. Till then, you must wait.'

Cranston walked out into the darkness. He hid in a corner and watched the alleyway leading up to the abbey. He must have stood there for some time: he was about to wonder whether Athelstan was correct when a fleeting shadow caught his eye and a cloaked figure sped like the angel of death out of the tavern and up the alleyway.

The assassin, not realising he had been seen, sped on, determined to reach that inquisitive little friar and silence him once and for all. He recalled Cranston's statement in the taproom, and wondered if the coroner really knew the truth. Whatever, the assassin reasoned, he had to act; he had very little to lose and a great deal to gain.

He crossed the great deserted square before the abbey, and slowed down as he saw the line of archers around the entrance to the Jericho Parlour. Quickly wiping the sweat from his face, the assassin brought out the seal from his wallet; the guards, busily sharing a wineskin of wine, let him through without demur. At the entrance to the cloisters, the same thing happened. The assassin entered the vestibule leading to the chapter-house and breathed more easily. He went down, then paused: the door to the chapel was open and a faint glow of light peeped through. The assassin smiled. He went back to a long line of bushes which grew in a tangle of undergrowth just outside the east cloister. The assassin walked carefully. He stopped on the fourth paving stone and, crouching down, scrabbled about in the bushes till he caught the leather sack and drew it out. He undid the cord, grasped the small crossbow, and pushed two bolts into his wallet. He carefully hid the bag, slipped along the vestibule and up the steps to St Faith's. He pushed the door open. Only one candle was lit on the altar. He glimpsed the cowled figure kneeling at the prie-dieu. The assassin slipped through the door, inserted the crossbow bolt, and pulled back the winch. The chapel was deathly quiet. The assassin raised the crossbow, even as he began to chant those dreadful words, 'Dies irae, dies illa . . .'

He released the catch; even as he did so, he sensed something was wrong. The figure hadn't even flinched at his words. The assassin moved into the church; as he did so, the door behind him slammed shut. He whirled round. Athelstan was staring at him and, beside the friar, stood a young archer, an arrow notched to his bow.

'Good evening, Master Banyard. It is mine host from the Gargoyle?'

Banyard's hand fell to the second bolt in his pouch.

'Walk back!' Athelstan ordered. 'Simon here is an excellent archer. When I came through the cloisters, I asked him to accompany me. If you try to flee or draw the knife beneath your cloak, he will loose an arrow straight into your arm or your leg. You'll still have to listen, but in terrible agony.'

Banyard drew back the cowl of his cloak. His dark, thickset features betrayed no fear. His eyes flickered backwards and forwards, first to Athelstan then to the archer. He looked over his shoulder at the prie-dieu.

'Oh, don't worry about that,' Athelstan replied. 'Just a few sacks of grain; one of Simon's companions brought them in here for me. I put them on the prie-dieu and covered them with my cloak. In the poor light I thought it was rather lifelike – and so did you.'

Banyard took a step forward. The archer immediately loosed the arrow which sped a few inches past his face, making him swerve. By the time Banyard had steadied himself, a second arrow had been notched.

'I shall shoot again,' the bowman declared softly. 'This is God's house and Brother Athelstan is here on the orders of the regent.'

'Do what Simon says,' Athelstan said. 'It is useless to resist. Outside there are more archers. I have asked them to stop anyone who tries to leave.' Athelstan pointed to a bench next to the wall. 'Now, sit down there. Simon will look after you.'

Banyard obeyed. Athelstan went to the altar. He took the candle burning there and began to light more of the candles as well as two sconce torches. He then pulled across the sanctuary chair and sat opposite Banyard. The landlord just lounged back against the wall, staring at Athelstan from under heavy-lidded eyes.

'You are probably thinking about how you can explain the attack, aren't you?' Athelstan began. 'I wondered if you'd come. It's the only real mistake you've made, isn't it?'

Banyard just smirked.

'That's why I told Christina and the potboy before I left that I was going to St Faith's Chapel. When my lord Coroner made his announcement in the taproom, you panicked, made inquiries, and followed me here.'

Again Banyard just stared at him. Athelstan suddenly realised that the landlord probably didn't even suspect Athelstan knew about the terrible murders committed by Malmesbury and the rest so many years ago at Shropshire. Banyard was still confident: without any real evidence, he could worm his way out of this trap and scoff at any allegations laid against himself. Athelstan sat back, gazing at a point in the wall above the taverner's head.

'What are you waiting for, priest?' Banyard leaned forward, hands on his knees. 'So I came into St Faith's Chapel and shot an arrow into someone I thought was lurking here.' He pointed to the sacks still heaped on the prie-dieu. 'The church courts might fine me, but what else have I done?'

'You are a killer, Banyard,' Athelstan replied slowly. 'You murdered Bouchon, Swynford, Harnett and Goldingham!'

'And why should I do that?'

Athelstan heard footsteps outside. 'I shall tell you in a while, Master Banyard, but for the moment I think we have visitors.'

The door of the chapel swung open. Cranston came blustering in. He stared at the bowman, Athelstan, Banyard and then at the prie-dieu.

'Satan's tits!' he breathed.

Then he crossed himself: his surprise was echoed by Coverdale and the three knights who came in behind him. Athelstan sat further back in the sanctuary chair. He felt like a judge giving sentence. Cranston, Coverdale and the rest hurried to find seats. Banyard still remained calm, his eyes never leaving the friar.

'Bow bells,' Athelstan began, 'When I first met you, Banyard, you said you were born within the sound of Bow bells, a Londoner.' Athelstan leaned forward. 'In which Parish? Which street? Which ward? Tell me, and Sir John Cranston will check the records.'

Banyard stared back.

'You were born in Shropshire. Your father was a hard-working farmer,' Athelstan continued. 'He resented the taxes due to the seigneurs, and their demands for forced labour, when he preferred to sell his work to them for wages. He met with others who thought similarly, and they resisted the lords of the soil with their destriers, helmets, tournaments, tourneys, levies, taxes, exactions, bridge-tolls and constant streams of demands.' Athelstan shrugged. 'I don't know exactly what happened, but I think your father just ignored the likes of these three knights here, the so-called fraternity of the Knights of the Swan.'

'Brother Athelstan,' Malmesbury spluttered, 'I object.'

'Shut up!' Athelstan snapped. 'Now these seigneurs, led by Sir Edmund, petitioned the Crown, but to no avail; so they took the law into their own hands.'

'This is slanderous.' Aylebore half rose to his feet, his hand falling to his dagger.

Coverdale sprang to his feet; drawing his sword, he held the point only a few inches away from Aylebore's chest.

'Sit down!' Coverdale ordered. 'And if any of you move again, I'll strike and claim I was defending Brother Athelstan and the lord Coroner?'

Sir Humphrey slumped back on the bench. Coverdale, smiling from ear to ear, also took his seat, but he kept his sword before him, cradling the pommel in his hand.

'Continue, Brother Athelstan,' he said softly, 'because I

think you are going to tell a tale of which I know a little.' He tapped the point of the sword on the paving-stone. 'And no one will interrupt you again.'

'As I said,' Athelstan declared, 'Malmesbury, Aylebore, Goldingham, Harnett, Swynford and Bouchon and perhaps others . . .' Athelstan stared at the knights. 'I thought *one* of you might be innocent!'

Elontius put his face in his hands.

Athelstan sighed. 'But, no, you're all guilty.' He cleared his throat. 'Ah well, these seigneurs saw themselves as lords of the earth, the descendants of Arthur and his knights. They played at being paladins until they lost their cup whilst, outside their dreams, the world was changing. Men like your father, Master Banyard, caked in soil, were rising above themselves. These lords formed their coven; visored, hooded and cloaked they struck at individual peasant farmers. First they would warn them by sending a candle, an arrowhead and a scrap of parchment with the word "Remember" scrawled on it.' Athelstan saw the tears prick Banyard's eyes. Men such as your father must have wondered, "Remember what?"

'The threats soon became real enough, as individual farms were raided, the men dragged off and hanged, whilst these good knights sat on their horses and chanted the *"Dies Irae"*, their song of death.' Athelstan glanced at the three knights. They looked as if they had grown old in such a short space of time, faces crumpled, shoulders bowed. They didn't look up but just stared at the floor, lost in their own nightmares.

'Now, in God's eyes no sin goes unpunished,' Athelstan continued. 'These knights were probably successful, warnings were given, warnings received, but men like yourself, Master Banyard, never forget. You had nothing to do with Shropshire, but fled to London where, by hard work, you built up a tavern famous for its food and hospitality.' Athelstan cocked his head sideways. 'I wonder,' he said, 'did you always plot their deaths? Did you, over the years, nurse a terrible thirst for vengeance? Brood about the arrowhead symbolising violence, the candle for the funeral, and the terrible threat behind the word "Remember"!'

'They took him out,' Banyard began to speak. 'we were eating our supper round the table. My father, my mother and myself. The door was flung open. Armed men, masked and cowled, burst into the room. My father tried to resist but they knocked the knife from his hand. Laughing and jeering, they pulled him out into the darkness and bundled him on to a horse.' Banyard paused and put his face in his hands. 'My mother just screamed, like a whipped dog. She went into a corner, crouching there, stuffing the hem of her smock into her mouth.' Banyard, lost in the past, shook his head. 'We'd heard about the deaths, the other executions. My father had been sent the candle, the arrowhead and the note, "Remember", but he scoffed at them and threw them into the fire. Banyard glanced up with such a look of horror on his face that Athelstan felt a spurt of sorrow at how greed and power had destroyed this man's life.

'I ran after them.' Banyard declared. 'Fast as an arrow but it was too late. They took my father down to an oak tree at the bottom of a meadow just near a stream. I could see his body twirling and the bastards chanting. I hid there until I saw their faces, then I went back to our farm. Within a year Mother was dead. By then I had a list of my father's killers.' He rubbed his eyes. 'I sold our land and came to London.' Banyard stared down at his hands. 'I worked night and day. Brother Athelstan,

266

I have good cause to hate these men, but did I kill them?' His tone became more confident, a sly, secretive look on his face.

Athelstan realised how the pain and desire for revenge had, over the years, unhinged the taverner's mind.

'You killed them,' Athelstan remarked softly.

'But, Brother,' Coverdale interrupted, 'is it not the most remarkable of coincidences that these knights came to a tavern owned by the son of a man they had killed?'

'Oh, I think Banyard knew that these knights would come to London, Athelstan replied. Sooner or later every great lord must come to Westminster but, of course, Banyard helped matters along. Sir Edmund, you've stayed at the Gargoyle before?'

The knight seemed not to hear.

'Sir Edmund,' Cranston went over and shook Malmesbury's shoulder. 'Brother Athelstan asked you a question.'

'Yes.' Malmesbury raised his haggard face. 'Both I and my companions had stayed at the Gargoyle before. The hospitality, the food . . .'

'And the lowest rates?' Athelstan added. He glanced at the taverner. 'Only God knows,' he continued, 'what Master Banyard plotted. Did he hope to make enough money to go back to Shropshire and wreak his revenge on his father's assassins? However, as the Parliaments were called and Malmesbury and his companions began to attend, his murderous idea certainly took root. Over the years, Banyard would encourage, solicit their custom.'

'Why didn't he strike then?' Cranston asked.

'Oh, I am sure he was tempted to but, as I understand, not all the same knights attend every Parliament. What Banyard did was ensure that they always came to his tavern by charging them rates much lower than any other hostelry. Isn't that right, Sir Edmund?'

The knight just nodded.

'Oh course,' Coverdale intervened, 'Malmesbury and his companions always congratulated themselves on the tavern of their choice, on not being charged the exorbitant prices other representatives were.'

'That was the lure,' Athelstan remarked. 'Then someone else became involved in the game, no less a person than His Grace the Regent.' Athelstan held a hand up to still Coverdale's protests. 'No, don't object, Sir Miles. The regent knows I am telling the truth, as do these men here. Gaunt arranged for all the Knights of the Swan, all those involved in those dreadful murders at Shropshire, to be returned as representatives to the Commons. Of course, as usual, they sent a steward to London to look for lodgings, and mine host Banyard was ready and waiting.' He shook his head. 'It was no coincidence, Sir Miles, that all those knights found lodgings in the Gargoyle. I made inquiries amongst other representatives. I went into Westminster Yard yesterday. Oh yes, many of them had asked for lodgings at the Gargoyle, only to find the place was full. Mine host had arranged that. He was waiting for Malmesbury and the rest.'

'So, he turned others away?' Malmesbury asked. 'In order that we took lodgings with him?'

'Sir Edmund, whom did you send to London?'

'My steward, Eudo Faversham.'

'And he would tell Banyard who was journeying up to Westminster?'

'Of course!'

'And he found no difficulty in hiring rooms here?'

'No, no, as I have said, we have stayed here before. My

268

steward came back saying we had fair lodgings at reasonable prices.'

Banyard, who had been listening coolly to all this, uncrossed his arms. 'And, when they arrived, Friar,' he taunted, 'how did I kill them?'

'Oh, that you'd planned well,' Athelstan replied. 'Bouchon was easy. Remember the night he left the supper party at your tavern? He didn't say he was going anywhere. He simply went out. Now, if he was going to meet someone threatening, Bouchon would have taken a sword, but when his body was fished from the Thames, he wasn't even carrying his knife. No, what I suspect happened is that you, Master Banyard, lured Bouchon out into the tavern yard on some pretext. Perhaps he was wondering who had delivered the arrowhead and candle at the tavern. Anyway, you meet him near the compost heap, that mound of rich black soil. You felled him with a blow to the head. He falls on to the mound, which explains why we found the black soil under his fingernails.' Athelstan paused. 'You then slid back into the tavern, going about your duties. At the appropriate time you leave. You put Bouchon's body in a wheelbarrow, covered by a sheet of canvas, and trundle it down to the Thames, only a few yards away. The river was running at full tide; Bouchon's body, however, kept near the bank until it was caught amongst the reeds near Tothill Fields.'

'And Swynford?' Aylebore asked.

Athelstan noticed how all three knights now seemed frightened of Banyard. They hardly looked at him, as if he was the veritable incarnation of their terrible deeds and the vengeance they had provoked.

'Oh, that was not as difficult as it appeared,' Athelstan replied. 'Banyard himself sent for the chantry priest. He knew

Father Gregory would be away. Indeed, such a toper posed no real threat to his plan.'

'All that was seen of this strange priest was a cowled figure walking across the taproom and upstairs,' Cranston interrupted. 'However, nobody could remember seeing the priest leave.' Cranston beamed round, proud of his own conjectures.

'I was running a risk, wasn't I?' Banyard taunted. 'If anyone had stopped me . . .'

'Oh, you chose your time well,' Athelstan said. 'The tavern was very busy, more concerned with the living than the dead. Let us say someone had stopped or recognised you, then it would just be mine host returning to his chamber to doff his cloak and return to his duties. You were very clever. You can go missing from the tavern whenever you wish. No one asks questions. No one will object and, if inquiries are made – well, the Gargoyle is a spacious place. There are stores to be checked, cellars to be inspected, a whole range of outhouses where you could claim you had been busy. Oh, no, you were safe right up to the very moment you put that garrotte string round Sir Henry Swynford's throat. A powerful man like you, death would have occurred in seconds. Only once did you come near to being detected, when Christina heard that dreadful chant. After the deed was done –' Athelstan pulled a face – 'you slipped out of the chamber. You returned to your own room, the cloak was hidden and, once again, you became mine genial host.'

Banyard leaned forward, as if this was some game. 'And how do you explain, Brother, how I could go through so many guards, enter the Pyx chamber, and slay Sir Francis Harnett?'

'Harnett's death intrigued me,' Athelstan replied. 'A fussy little man, totally absorbed with buying that ape stolen from the Tower.'

'What was that?' Aylebore interrupted.

'It doesn't matter now,' Cranston replied. 'But your companion had bribed a guard at the Tower to steal an ape.'

Malmesbury sneered and shook his head. 'The man was always a fool,' he whispered. 'At his manor house in Stokesay, he was for ever trying to collect strange birds and animals.'

'Now Harnett went to the brothel with you,' Athelstan explained. 'But as Mistress Mathilda told us, no swords are allowed. You went unarmed?'

'Yes, that's true,' Malmesbury replied.

'However, later that evening, Harnett was seen along the riverside. He was carrying his sword.'

'So he must have gone back to the tavern to collect it?' Malmesbury asked.

'Precisely, Sir Edmund. Yet Master Banyard here never told us that. Now, when I was searching amongst Harnett's possessions, I noticed there were certain items missing. I couldn't decide what and then I suddenly realised: he had pen and ink but no parchment, no vellum; not a scrap to write upon.'

'What's the significance of that?' Coverdale asked.

'Well, first, I am sure all of Harnett's companions had similar writing implements: they would bring a roll of parchment for their own purposes, whether it be for private use or use in the Commons.'

'Yes, that's true,' Aylebore cried. 'Sir Francis was for ever scribbling.'

'But what's the significance?' Coverdale repeated.

'Sir Miles,' Athelstan asked, 'if you wished to steal an animal such as an ape from the Tower, what would you need? Remember, you have to keep it in London and then transport

271

it, somehow, back to Shrewsbury?'

The captain grinned and scratched his cheek.

'Well, the animal would have to eat. There'd have to be a cage.' His hands flew to his lips. 'And, of course, a place to hide it.' He pointed at Banyard. 'Sir Francis must have told you about his plot.'

'Of course he did,' Athelstan said. 'I suspect Sir Francis was very close to mine host. He not only went back to the Gargoyle to collect his sword. He must also have entered into negotiations with him about supplies, carts, a cage and, above all, a place around that spacious tavern to hide the animal he hoped to buy. Now, Sir Francis, as one of his companions has just described, was a constant scribbler. He must have listed all his requirements, yet I found not a scrap of parchment amongst his possessions. Of course, these would have been removed by Master Banyard after he had taken Sir Francis's head.'

'More importantly,' Cranston added, 'Sir Francis was lured to his death by Banyard who knew about his secret negotiations with the soldier from the Tower. In his haste and excitement, Sir Francis forgot about the killer stalking him: his mind was stuffed full of dreams about obtaining an exotic animal.'

'And how did I get into the Pyx chamber at Westminster Abbey?' Banyard taunted. 'How could I go through cordons of soldiers and archers? Whistling a tune, an axe over my shoulder?'

'Oh, no, there was something else missing from Harnett's possessions.' Athelstan retorted. 'His seal. And I wondered where the seals of the other two dead knights were as well.' Athelstan glanced at Coverdale. 'Did you ever find those?'

The knight shook his head. 'No, I . . .' His voice faltered. 'I never even thought about them.'

'Banyard did,' Athelstan retorted. 'He took the seals of the first three men he killed and used them to get into the abbey. After all, the soldiers on duty there can't be expected to recognise each of the two hundred different representatives who have come to this Parliament. People going to and fro. Typical soldiers, they had their orders: anyone carrying one of those seals bearing the chancellor's imprint were to be allowed through. Now, when Harnett was killed it was dusk. Members of the Commons were hurrying hither and thither. Banyard, probably wearing the cloak and hood he is now, slips in.'

'But the axe?' Aylebore asked.

Athelstan gestured round the church. 'Take a good look round here, Sir Humphrey. Look at the stacked stools and benches, the shadowy recesses, the small alcoves, the gap behind the altar.'

'You mean the axe is hidden here?'

'Probably,' Athelstan replied, 'or somewhere close to the Pyx chamber. I told the servants at the Gargoyle before I left that I was going to St Faith's Chapel to look for an axe. Banyard pursued me here, not only because I knew his true identity, but because I was searching for evidence. I am sure that, when we find the weapon, someone will recognise it as an axe used at the Gargoyle tavern.'

'But when did he put it here?' Coverdale asked.

'Long before the Commons ever assembled,' Athelstan replied. 'And the same goes for the crossbow he used to kill Goldingham. Remember that tangle of gorse bushes near the latrines off the east cloister?'

'Of course,' Coverdale replied. 'Before the Commons met here, Banyard could come and go as he pleased.'

Athelstan continued. 'Now, on the night he killed Sir Francis,

Banyard came into the vestibule, up into St Faith's Chapel, collected the axe, went down to the Pyx chamber and murdered Sir Francis Harnett.' He glanced at Banyard and saw the fear in the man's eyes. 'Poor old Harnett,' Athelstan declared. 'But he did not die in vain. Only when I reflected on what was missing from his possessions did the tangle begin to unravel: the lack of parchment, his personal seal, his desire to buy an ape stolen from the Tower. All this, together with the fact that he returned to collect his sword the night he left for Southwark, made me begin to suspect Master Banyard. I took what I'd learnt and applied it to the deaths of the other knights: Bouchon not wearing his sword; the dirt under his fingernails. The evidence still pointed to Banyard. The same is true of Swynford being garrotted in his chamber at the tavern.'

'And Goldingham?' Malmesbury asked.

'Well, once I knew how Banyard had passed through the guards, that was easy. Goldingham had a weak stomach. He was always talking about it . . .?'

Malmesbury nodded.

'And no doubt he approached mine host to ask for this or that special delicacy?'

'Yes, yes, he did,' Malmesbury replied. 'Sops soaked in milk. Goldingham always fussed about what he ate and drank.'

'And the morning he died?' Athelstan asked.

'He ate what we did. Porridge made of oatmeal, some bread.'

'Aye,' Athelstan nodded. 'He also ate something which was not in yours; a slight purgative, courtesy of mine host, to loosen the bowels and send him hurrying to the jakes. Banyard knew all about the Commons and its sessions, either by making inquiries or listening to your conversations. All he had to do was enter the cloisters and stand by those latrines, probably hiding in a cubicle holding the crossbow and bolt which he had taken from its hiding place. After that it was easy. He knew Goldingham would come, either during the session or after. It was just a matter of waiting. Once the latrines were empty he struck: a crossbow bolt into Goldingham's heart. The arbalest was hidden again and, in the confusion before anyone knew what had happened, Banyard was out of Westminster, hastening back towards his tavern.'

Athelstan spread his hands. 'We must also remember that, if anything went wrong, Banyard could easily explain his presence and wait for another opportunity either here or in Shrewsbury. Westminster, however, was an ideal place.'

'No one would miss him,' Cranston intervened. 'After all, mine host here owns the tavern. Where he goes and what he does is his own business. The Gargoyle is simply a walk away and, because he lives near the abbey buildings, no one would ever remark on his presence.' Cranston rose and stood over the taverner. 'Master Banyard.'

The taverner lifted his face, pallid and sweat-covered.

'Master Banyard, do you have anything to say?' Cranston asked. 'In answer to these accusations?'

Banyard half smiled, as if savouring a joke.

'The axe is behind the altar, Brother,' he declared, ignoring Cranston. 'You'll find it there.' He blinked and wetted his lips. 'I'd like a pot of ale,' he said quietly. 'The best my tavern can provide.' He laughed. 'But that's all over now, isn't it?' He sat up, breathing deeply. 'I was born Walter Polam in the parish of St Dunstan's, Oswestry, Shropshire. When I was fifteen these men killed my father, as they had murdered others. I left Shropshire and invested all I had in a tavern near Cripplegate.

275

I thought I would forget the past.'

He stared up at the ceiling. 'I changed my name. I married, but Edith died of the sweating sickness, so I sold the house and bought the Gargoyle tavern. Have you ever looked at the sign, Brother? It depicts a knight with a twisted, leering face.' He nodded, rocking himself backwards and forwards. 'Oh, of course, I dreamed of vengeance. After Edith's death these dreams began to plague me. I took a vow that I would return to Shropshire and seek vengeance on my father's assassins!' Banyard smirked at Malmesbury. 'And then you arrived at the Gargoyle, a knight of the shire, a representative of the Commons. Others came with you.

'I began to plan your deaths. I prayed that one day I would have all of you under my roof – and so it happened. That pompous steward of yours, Faversham, comes bustling along and, of course, I had rooms for you.' He glanced at Athelstan. 'Not all of them came, you know. There are at least another two in Shrewsbury with whom I have unfinished business. But,' he shrugged, 'what happened is as you described it. Bouchon, Swynford.' Banyard jabbed his finger towards Malmesbury. 'You I was leaving till last! I wanted to wait until you returned to Shropshire, so I could hang you from the same tree as you did my father—'

'Banyard,' Sir John broke in, 'I arrest you for the horrible crime of murder.'

'And what about these?' the taverner sneered back. 'Aren't they assassins as well?' He smiled. 'I'd like to hang from the same gibbet as they do.'

'You cannot touch us!' Malmesbury shouted back. 'The regent has offered us pardons for all crimes committed.'

He looked more fearful as Coverdale rose and unrolled a

piece of parchment from his wallet. The captain of guards tapped each of the three knights on their shoulders.

'Sir Edmund Malmesbury, Sir Humphrey Aylebore, Sir Thomas Elontius, I arrest you for murder.'

'This is hypocrisy!' Aylebore shouted, springing to his feet. 'The regent promised pardons. By what authority do you do this?'

Sir Miles lifted up the piece of parchment with Gaunt's seal affixed to it.

'All your names are written here, sir. The regent gave it to me this morning. I was not to execute it until after the king had visited his Commons.'

'But the regent offered us a pardon,' Malmesbury insisted, tears in his eyes.

Sir Miles smiled. 'Only His Grace the King can do that, sir.'

He deftly plucked the daggers from each of the three men's belts and, going to the door, shouted for the guards. For a while the chapel was plunged into chaos. Malmesbury and his companions shrieking their innocence, cursing the regent's treachery. Banyard laughed hysterically, shouting abuse, almost dancing with joy at what had happened. Eventually the chapel was cleared, the prisoners being led off, escorted by archers. Coverdale bowed mockingly at Cranston and Athelstan, then left them alone in the silent chapel.

The coroner sat down, mopping his brow. Athelstan went up behind the altar and, moving some benches, found a sharp-edged axe lying against the wall. He brought it back and sat where Banyard had, placing the axe gently on the floor beside him.

'At least he cleaned it,' he murmured. He glanced up as Cranston took a generous swig from the ever-present wineskin.

'We'll have to tell Father Abbot so this chapel can be blessed and reconsecrated.'

Cranston put the stopper back in the wineskin and gazed sadly at Athelstan.

'I can read your mind, Sir John,' Athelstan declared softly. 'Why didn't I tell you, eh?'

'You did it all yourself,' Cranston answered.

'No, I didn't, Sir John. You are as clear as the purest water on a summer's day. If I had told you it was Banyard, you would have betrayed it all with a look or a sign.' Athelstan jabbed a finger at the chapel floor. 'I needed to trap Banyard here. Now it's all finished.' Athelstan smiled bleakly. 'The regent is a cunning fox.' Athelstan stared up at the crucifix. For a few seconds he desperately wondered if the death of Christ, the love of God, or the service of religion had anything to do with a world where the likes of John of Gaunt ruled supreme.

'Gaunt was very clever,' Cranston declared. 'He forced those knights to come here. He blackmailed them, then turned his opponents into his most ardent supporters, only to close the trap and have them arrested for the secret crimes he had been threatening them with.' Cranston sighed noisily. 'How on earth will it end?'

'Oh, Gaunt will be merciful,' Athelstan retorted. 'Malmesbury and the likes will have to make a very full confession, pay a very heavy fine, and take a vow to go on pilgrimage. Oh yes, Gaunt will end up the richer. He'll hang them by the purse and have the likes of Malmesbury at his beck and call.'

'And Banyard?' Cranston asked.

'What do you think, Sir John?'

The coroner rubbed his chin. 'We can't hang one without the

278

other,' he replied slowly, 'so I don't think Banyard will hang at Tyburn or Smithfield. Gaunt will seize his chattels and goods and become the proud owner of a very prosperous tavern. Banyard will be forced to abjure the realm and wander Europe, a penniless beggar.' Cranston smiled grimly. 'Do you know, Brother, I glimpsed so much hate in that man. If I were Sir Edmund Malmesbury, I would not sleep easily in my bed.'

Cranston lumbered to his feet. 'Nothing really ends, does it, Brother? We are just like dung-collectors. We clean the refuse and take it away from the eyes and noses of those who live around us.' The coroner groaned loudly then nudged his companion. 'One thing you didn't explain. Why weren't the red crosses etched on Harnett's and Goldingham's faces?'

Athelstan shrugged. 'Banyard had made his mark in both senses of the word. He probably didn't have time.'

'Such dreadful acts,' Cranston declared mournfully.

Athelstan got to his feet. 'Sir John, you are becoming melancholic. Let us celebrate in the Holy Lamb of God. We have done what we can: that's all the Lord asks, and that's all the good Lord wants!' He thrust the axe he'd found into Cranston's hand. 'Now, come, let's be Jolly Jack again and, if you are,' Athelstan stepped back and held his hand up, 'I swear I'll never again mention a Barbary ape!'

John of Gaunt sat in his private chamber, high in the Savoy Palace. He stared out through the open window at the evening star, and secretly smiled at the success of his own subtlety. He played absentmindedly with the amethyst ring on his finger.

'Only one snag,' the regent murmured to himself. He glanced to where his cowled scrivener sat by a small writing desk. Gaunt had listened very carefully to Coverdale, secretly marvelling at Athelstan's sharp perception of the tangled web Gaunt had woven. The regent straightened in his chair. Cranston he could take care of, the coroner was a royal officer. But Athelstan? Gaunt glanced at his scrivener.

'Draft a letter,' he murmured, 'to Prior Anselm at Blackfriars. Tell him I am grateful for the good services of Brother Athelstan, yet now I do fear for him in the sea of troubles which now confronts us. Tell him . . .' Gaunt lifted up a finger. 'Tell him I would like to see Athelstan removed: his talents can be better used in the halls of Oxford.' Gaunt sat back in his chair and, closing his eyes, dreamed his dark dreams of power.